THE CLASS OF 1960

To Jonathan,
   With great respect,

   MIKE BAUM

19/11/2024

THE
CLASS
OF 1960

Michael Baum MD, ChM, FRCS, FRCR

Troubador Publlishing Ltd
Unit E2 Airfield Business Park,
Harrison Road, Market Harborough,
Leicestershire LE16 7UL
Tel: 0116 279 2299
Email: books@troubador.co.uk
Web: www.troubador.co.uk

ISBN 97 1 80514 190 7

British Library Cataloguing in Publication Data.
A catalogue record for this book is available from the British Library.

Printed and bound in the UK by TJ Books Limited, Padstow, Cornwall
Typeset in 11pt Aldine by Troubador Publishing Ltd, Leicester, UK

Matador is an imprint of Troubador Publishing Ltd

I dedicate this book to the memory of two of my brothers.
Dr Geoffrey Baum MB, ChB a general practitioner who died
during the Covid pandemic at the age of 92.
and
Professor David Baum MD, FRCP, who died in office as
President of the Royal College of Paediatrics and Child
Health at the age of 59.
They were the best of all physicians and my loadstars.

Contents

PART 1

Medical school 1955–1960

Chapter 1

The anatomy room
1955

The room was huge and very well lit, punctuated by dissection tables carrying sinister bundles, each covered by tarpaulin shrouds. It suggested the battlefield at the Somme in 1917 but it was the miasma of formaldehyde that had their eyes watering rather than mustard gas. They were all old enough to be called up for national service but would miss the next war because the country needed doctors more than cannon fodder.

Every four students, picked in alphabetical order, were allotted a cadaver to be dissected head to toe over the first three terms of medical school. It was considered a rite of passage. The subjects of this ritual had to stiffen their sinews, summon up the blood and tighten their esophagogastric junctions so as not to puke over your colleagues or the demonstrator who would guide your hand. The cadaver's sinews were already stiff.

Dylan Baddams, Alastair Bannerman, Peter Baring, and Mathew Barnet were allocated a desiccated grey/green male body on the fourth table. They were a mixed crew but, sharing this trauma together, would end up like a band of brothers in company C at Omaha Beach on D-Day. Their demonstrator was a friendly young doctor studying for part 1 of the FRCS called Geoffrey Oates, nicknamed Titus.

Dylan came from Caerphilly, a miner's town just north of Cardiff. His father was a coal miner but was ambitious for his son, who had performed well at the local grammar school.

3

Dylan was built like a neolithic henge and had played tight-head prop with the school's first XV. He also sang baritone in the Caerphilly district miners' male voice choir. He won a state scholarship and had the choice of almost any medical school, not just because his academic qualifications were excellent but also because of the competitive nature of the medical schools' rugby league. In the end he had chosen Birmingham because it was the nearest to home, having dismissed Cardiff because it was too close to home.

Alastair came from the Gorbals in Glasgow. They lived in a tenement on the south bank of the river Clyde. His father was unemployed, having lost a limb 10 years earlier in the last weeks of the war. He drank a lot, and his profanities were hard to translate because of his thick Glaswegian accent. His mother, who had married below her station, kept two jobs to make ends meet. She was ambitious for her son and recognised his intelligence at an early age. She taught him to read before he was six; he was a gifted artist and could draw recognisable portraits of his dad asleep with a lit pipe in his mouth. Like a stereotypical Scotsman he was ginger and freckled. He was nimble on his feet and always in demand to make up an 11 amongst the ragamuffins in the streets below. He passed his 11+ exam with such high grades that he was offered a place at the famous Hutchinson's Grammar School. At first the posh kids teased him for his thick accent but soon gave that up after the consequence of a bloody nose. Although prickly by nature, he soon gained popularity for his skills on the football ground. He worked on his anger management on the shins of the opposing side and helped the school to win the Scottish Under-18 Cup in 1954. Beneath his tough carapace beat a soft heart. He was appalled at the squalor of the Gorbals and the recognised fact that Glasgow had the lowest life expectancy in the country. He was determined to do something about it. He was successful in four applications to medical school but chose Birmingham because that was the furthest away from his alcoholic and violent father. Any Sassenach south of the border thought to give him the nickname Jock also got a bloody nose, so most of his friends called him Ginger, which he favoured.

Peter was six feet tall, with blond hair and the only one of the quartet to have gone to a public school. He claimed to be a Wykehamist, which was the posh way of saying he was a product of Winchester College. He was a fast bowler and batted as an opener in the school's first XI. The others were determined to hate him, but as well as his nonchalant demeanour he had such a natural charm and was such a good listener that they forgave him for the advantages of his upbringing. Mathew had a hunch about his surname that struck a bell. He looked up the name Baring in *Who's Who* and discovered that this was a famous banking family and that his father was a baronet. He had the choice of any medical school in the world where the dean might be fishing for a Baring Wing attached to the Department of Physiology. He chose Birmingham because it was the closest to where his girlfriend lived. His popularity increased when his new friends learnt that Peter had indulged in sexual intercourse and was surprised by the sceptical response around the dissection table. Mathew could have sworn that the corpus spongiosum of the cadaver responded to this incomparable news as well.

Mathew was five feet, seven inches and wore NHS frame glasses that made him look like Trotsky without the facial hair. His grandparents were all from Warsaw, then in the hands of the Russian Empire. Like all Jews they were blamed for the assassination of Czar Nicholas II and were escaping from the pogroms that included herding all the inhabitants into their synagogues before setting fire to the building. Mind you, the Bolsheviks weren't much better, once they found out Trotsky was a Jew. The level of orthodoxy diluted in the Barnet family along with the changing of their surname from Bialystok. Mathew claimed he was a secular Jew, but God forbid you suggest he was an atheist. He was not good at sports but was very talented at playing the violin klezmer style. His parents chose Birmingham Medical School because they lived in Birmingham and wanted to save money in paying for lodgings and because his big brother had qualified there three years earlier. All other students had to buy their skeletons for studying osteology, but Mathew was lucky to inherit his brother's bones in a long, sinister-looking brown box.

The first two years at medical school were spent studying the three gruelling subjects, anatomy, biochemistry, and physiology, with a tough exam at the end of two years to determine whether you could move on to the third year, where the fun stuff started being in the clinics and the wards. Word had it that these environments where heavily populated with very talented nurses. Apart from the dissecting room, there were lectures in theatres holding 300 students at a time and laboratories with long benches lined with Bunsen burners and glassware that could be "borrowed" to distil alcohol from mashed potatoes.

There were two types of lecturers – boring and very boring – and what made it worse was the wooden benches with narrow seats that made dozing off impossible.

The ambitious geeks took notes, but our four heroes developed alternative ways of passing the time. Peter wrote love letters, Dylan wrote poetry and Ginger and Mathew colluded on publishing a monthly magazine entitled *Woad*, based on the assumption that the medical school had been built on a Celtic burial ground. Ginger was responsible for the illustrations and cartoons, whilst Mathew wrote the text. The first edition developed a scale for the boredom of lectures with cartoons of sleeping students with the number of Zs coming out of their heads. The lecturers were thinly disguised. Other features pushed the boundaries too far until they were summoned to see the dean. They were terrified of being sent down, but the dean, a decent old bloke, explained they were wasting their talents and should join the staff of the official school magazine.

In their favour, most of the lectures were accessible in the textbooks that were on their reading list and, although all four played the roles of reprobates, they in fact studied very hard in the evenings and weekends except for Saturday night at the hop.

Now the Saturday night hop was something else. Students from all faculties, their girlfriends, or nurses from the nursing home nearby, pitched up the Guild of Students (club house by any other name) to dance and flirt and drink beer. There was live music from famous bands that often included Humphrey Lyttleton's ensemble, Chris Barber and his trumpet, or even Lonnie Donegan and his skiffle group playing "The Midnight Special". Peter and Ginger had no problem picking out the prettiest girls from amongst the wall flowers, but Dylan and Mathew preferred drinking beer with the rugger buggers. Dylan was there to meet his teammates, whilst Mathew was with him for fear of someone seeing him dance with a non-Jewish girl, not that he could work up the courage to invite any girl to dance. Nevertheless, once he'd drunk two pints of Ansell's best bitter beer, he enjoyed joining in singing the dirty songs, for example:

If I was the marrying kind, which thank the lord I'm not, sir,
If I was the marrying kind, I'd marry the hooker's daughter.
I'd push hard, and she'd push hard, we'd both push hard together
Etc, etc.

This made him feel manly but also made him vomit on the way home, held up by Dylan.

★★★

Towards the end of the third term, shortly before the long vacation enjoyed by the preclinical students, they were studying the anatomy and physiology of the central nervous system. It was quite interesting and challenging to trace the threads of the peripheral nerves from their roots at the

7

foramina at the junctions of the vertebrae, all the way to the gaps between the toes. But, when it came to the brain, they were in terra incognita.

They then learnt that there was a black market in pickled brains to dissect at home, organised by a one-eyed caretaker named Burke from the Department of Morbid Anatomy, where he looked after the autopsy room at the Queen Elizabeth Hospital. They later learnt that it wasn't his real name but chosen as a *nom de plume* out of respect for his forbears, Burke and Hare, the original "resurrection men". He wanted £5.00 but they negotiated a 20% discount and handed out £1.00 each. As Mathew was the only one living at home, he offered his partners in crime the use of one of his attic rooms, where he had a little workshop for carpentry and building model aeroplanes. He smuggled the pickled brain home in his sports bag from his school days that was never used for sport but useful for taking his violin to gigs at Jewish weddings.

After trotting up three flights of stairs in his old Victorian house just off the Hagley Road, he transferred the brain into a Victorian chamber pot full of carbolic acid, on the bench next to his skeleton box. Alongside he placed his volume of *Gray's Anatomy* open at the chapter "The Nervous System". This book, along with the box of bones, was also a bequest from his brother. He noted that the first illustration was the floor of the skull, illustrating the foramina for the spinal cord and the 12 cranial nerves: olfactory, optic, oculomotor, trochlear, trigeminal, abducens, facial, auditory, glossopharyngeal, vagus, accessary, and hypoglossal.

They were to remember their names, their surface anatomy, and their function. To help them on the way, previous students had taught them the mnemonic:

On old Olympus's towering top, a Finn and German viewed some hops.

Mathew couldn't even remember the mnemonic, never mind

what the letters stood for. So, this was a good place to start. He therefore took out the skull from the box, removed the cranial lid by lifting a cabin hook at each side and left everything in a tidy row: *Gray's Anatomy* pictures of the skull, the cranium of the skull, the rest of the skull, with its orbits, nasal bones, teeth, and mandible, looking like a pirate's flag. Last in the row was the brain, drying out on an old red rugby shirt.

He stood back to admire the set up when a deafening scream from behind made him jump out of his skin. It was Mary, the live-in Irish maid, who slept in the garret next door to the workshop.

Her screams followed her down two sets of stairs and into the street below. His mother, who had just come in from shopping, was pushed aside as the poor young girl kept running and was nearly run over by the number 11 bus on the Hagley Road.

The event was hushed up and Mary was dismissed with a month's wages and an excellent reference, but the brain dissection was cancelled. One morning, not long after, Mr Barnet discovered a red painted pentagram on the front gate. He reassured the family that a six-pointed star might be interpreted as anti-Semitism but a five-pointed sign is linked to mysticism and the occult. It implied: stay away from this house because they practise witchcraft. This way they might avoid beggars or Jehovah's Witnesses troubling them.

Chapter 2

On the wards
1957

All four friends passed their exams at the end of their two years of preclinical studies and, after the last of their long vacations, were looking forward to clinical training. Apart from lectures and seminars, the core of their teaching was membership of a "firm". It is critical to understand the structure of a firm in those days as it applied not only to their undergraduate but also their postgraduate training, having decided on one of three possible career paths: surgery, medicine, or – Jack of all trades – the general practitioner. From the standpoint of the students who at that point were pluripotential, there was a strict hierarchy. Without any say in the matter, the students in groups of eight were allocated to a surgical firm for six months and then a medical firm for six months or vice versa.

The students wore short white jackets like waiters at a posh restaurant. They all bought stethoscopes that were prominently bulging from their pockets long before they knew which end to put in their mouth and, if they were super cool, wrapped them round their necks. Their top pockets were full of pens and spatulas and, if they remembered, they changed their jackets for freshly washed and starched replacements every Monday morning. Blood stains or sinister yellow stains were perceived as badges of courage and undoubtedly vectors of cross infection. Every morning they gathered in the lab room of their ward to sterilise syringes and needles for venepuncture: disposable syringes and needles weren't invented until 1967.

They also had to test the urine of the patients on the ward for sugar long before dipsticks were invented; that involved test tubes, chemical reagents, and a Bunsen burner.

The urine tests and blood collection had to be complete before the consultant's round. Often it was impossible for the student to find a vein in the fat arm of a fat woman with a blunt needle. Often the poor patient was left with bruises over both arms before the ward sister came to the rescue. In addition, all the students were allocated patients to take a medical history and clinical examination to be fully prepared to present the case to the chief. God help them if they forgot to do a rectal examination even if the patient was complaining of a lump in the breast. "If you don't put your finger in it, you'll put your foot in it!" was the mantra they never forgot. To get all this done before the 09.00 ward round meant getting up at 07.00 instead of the "*lazy fair*" of the preclinical years.

If the students were the bottom feeders the housemen were one step up. Each of them might add MB, ChB, to their names but they couldn't be let loose on the public until they had completed six months on a surgical ward and six months on a medical ward before they could have that name registered by the General Medical Council (GMC). During those 12 months they lived "on the house", which in laymen's terms meant that, in return for free accommodation in a tiny bedroom shared with a colony of cockroaches, free meals, and free laundry, they were on call day and night for the year. The only compensation was the doctors' mess, just like fighter pilots enjoyed during the Battle of Britain. In practice it amounted to parties every night and a Christmas show where they were free to satirise their consultants. They elected a mess secretary and treasurer who collected subscriptions for the beer. They were paid below the official poverty level, but they had nothing else to spend their money on. Nurses were *absolutely* forbidden in the mess but somehow or other were often trafficked in clandestinely. One notorious house surgeon had a BSA air gun and a girlfriend in the nurses' home opposite mess. He knew precisely which room was hers and would rattle lead pellets on her window when the coast was clear.

Their duties were protean: first responders to cardiac arrest, bleeding from a major artery, or obstruction to the airways, as examples. In addition, they were responsible for the organisation of the waiting list for surgical procedures or running errands to the pathology or biochemical labs to collect urgent reports, catheterisation, venesection and setting up IV drips. In some cases, they were even expected to meet the consultant from his car on the steps of the hospital, carrying his coat and showing him the way to his ward. There were no bleepers in those days but sets of multi-coloured lights with an infinite sequence of patterns, on the ceiling of every corridor, that would alert all those on call to rush to the nearest phone to see where they were urgently needed.

The role of the senior house officer (SHO) was somewhat ambiguous. Their principal activity was dealing with minor trauma in Accident and Emergency (A&E) but they spent a good deal of time studying for part 1 of the Fellowship of the Royal College of Surgeons (FRCS). Once again, they were studying anatomy, physiology, and biochemistry, but at a much higher level and from their ranks were the demonstrators for the first-year undergraduates in the dissection room. They aimed to be one chapter of *Gray's Anatomy* ahead of the undergraduates.

The registrars were well on their way to a career in surgery. Most were already FRCS, and they were free to carry out simple operations towards the end of a list such as inguinal hernias, varicose veins, and haemorrhoids (piles). One of the vulgar Australian registrars at the Queen Elizabeth Hospital (QE) described "whinging poms" (English immigrants) as like haemorrhoids: "unwanted down south and a pain in the arse". There were usually two registrars on each firm, one homegrown and one from the colonies.

The senior registrar was the fulcrum of the firm, equivalent to the chief resident at an American teaching hospital. They were usually in their mid-30s and served on average for four years before ultimately winning a consultant slot: the peak of all ambitions. If they thought their chances were draining away, many of them ended up as whinging poms in the land of Oz or in Canada, where they were much more welcome. In practice, like the demi-god Hermes, he was the only one who could bridge the gap between the humble junior staff below and the gods on Mount Olympus, the consultants. He was left to do all the complex surgery and often substituted for the consultants in outpatients. He also ran the tutorials for the students and tended to be admired and popular amongst them all.

The collective noun for consultants in the NHS in those days was "an absence". And this can be explained as follows.

In 1948, at the time of the birth of the NHS, Bevan boasted that he was able to accomplish his goal "by stuffing the doctors' mouths with gold". What he meant by his famous and oft-quoted statement is that he allowed some British doctors, or consultants as they were called, to continue seeing private paying patients if they accepted NHS patients in addition to a "generous" salary for their NHS sessions. At that time many consultants had been worked pro bono in their local hospital for the poor of the parish and earning their living in the private sector. Furthermore, many of the surgeons had been seconded to the Royal Army Medical Corps (RAMC) in the years 1940–1945.

That generation who returned to their civilian status resented the words of Aneurin Bevan and only paid lip service to the NHS when they found that a consultant's part-time salary was derisorily, hardly a mouthful of gold. Furthermore, the private sector during the war years and post-war austerity had collapsed. Those consultants who might have been, say, 50 at the outbreak of war were close to retirement in 1957 the year that Dylan, Mathew, Peter, and Alastair were allocated to QE surgical wards West 2.

Before we follow the adventures of our protagonists, we

need to consider the non-commissioned officers: Matron, ward sister, and staff nurses. In practice they acted as sergeant-major, sergeant, and corporals. The probationers were ranked as privates. Everyone was terrified in case of an unannounced visit by Matron, so the ward sister was constantly getting the young nurses to make the bedclothes look perfect by tucking in blankets and allowing precisely 12 inches of white sheet running a precise parallel with the tucked-in foot of the bed. The uniforms they wore announced their rank but that was obvious in any case by the age and deportment of the woman. There were no male nurses in those days.

Matron wore blue/black and stormed into the ward like a ship in full sail including a complex bonnet acting as a spinnaker. Ward sister wore navy blue and a more modest cap with lace around the edges with a skirt below the knees. Staff nurses wore bright blue dresses with a tight waspy band around the midriff held in place with a silver buckle. In addition, they wore a white pinafore and a plain white cap with wings. The length of the skirt was variable according to the time of day and sister's time schedule. They wore black stockings and shiny black shoes. The overall effect was strangely sexy, and many nurses ended up marrying one of their patients or one of the doctors. The probationers wore unattractive yellow shapeless dresses yet, like all nurses of all ranks, had a small timepiece pinned to the top right-hand side of her uniform upside-down. That was so she could flip the watch up to count the seconds whilst taking a patient's pulse.

★ ★ ★

In the second week of September 1957 at 8.55am, Baddams, Bannerman, Baring, and Barnet (the consultants would only know them by their surnames) were waiting to join the tail of their first ward round. They were standing outside the glass panelled doors of the West 2 male ward. Looking into the ward, of Nightingale design, they saw 12 beds on each

14

side with curtains drawn back so they could see all the patients sitting or lying at attention. On the wall behind each bed was a painted number, 1–24, and a brass plaque hanging from a hook with the name of the consultant caring for the patient. Say the name of the consultant was Sir Ralph Bloomfield-Bonington; you could then precisely identify the coordinates of each patient. For example, "QE, W2, bed 12, BKA (below knee amputation), Bloomfield-Bonington". Just inside the door, arranged in a triangle, with Sister O'Connell at the head, were the guard of honour of the nurses in rank order.

Suddenly, in the distance of the west block corridor, a booming voice could be heard together with the sound of marching feet.

At the top of the pyramid of the W2 firm were the two consultant surgeons, Mr Alex McKenzie (Mac) and Mr Morgan Duffield (the title Mr in this context was shorthand for master, an example of English inverse snobbery and dated back to the reign of King Henry VIII, who awarded the royal charter to the Company of Barber-Surgeons).

It's worth describing these two consultant surgeons as their very different set of personality traits and skills had a very important impact on the direction of the careers of the undergraduates and their attitude to the care of patients.

Mac was a Scotsman who trained in Edinburgh. He was soft-spoken and had an elegant bedside manner, making him very popular with his patients. He was a handsome man with a ruddy complexion and was never happier than when on holiday, fishing for salmon in the Highlands of Scotland. His attitude toward surgery reflected his personality. He was very gentle in handling human tissue, although some formed the impression that, if anything, his surgical approach was too timid. His operations went on too long and the anaesthetists used to joke that they timed him by the calendar not the clock. He often appeared to find excuses to avoid surgery rather than proceed to what might have been a challenging or difficult case.

Mr Morgan Duffield, nicknamed Dudders, was almost Mac's opposite in character and behaviour. He was very large in all directions, probably six feet four and 18 stone. He had a booming voice and was "awfully well" married to a woman from the minor aristocracy – and he never let anyone forget it. As a student he used to play at number 8 in the pack for the Harlequins and of course captained the medical school first team. His self-confidence knew no bounds and he seemed to have an ego the size of the Isle of Wight. Of course, all of this made him a brilliant teacher at the bedside, and most of the students loved him as much as they feared him. Unlike Mac, Dudders was a gifted surgeon who loved nothing better than a complex surgical challenge, and his catchphrase was "when in doubt, cut it out". Despite having large hands, he operated rapidly and seemed to enjoy the challenge of difficult surgery. It was said that Mr Duffield recognised three indications for surgery. One: he'd seen it described and fancied having a go. Two: he'd done it before and rather enjoyed it. And three: the patient needed it!

The booming voice the young students heard on that morning in September 1957 was of course that of Mr Morgan Duffield, and the marching footsteps following him in the slipstream were the "firm". One senior registrar, two registrars, one SHO and two housemen on their way from the woman's ward on the rounds, which started at 08.00. (The poor students had been waiting at the wrong door and an hour too late: someone had played a dirty trick on them, and they were anticipating a right telling-off from the chief.) Yet Mr Duffield welcomed them with the wide smile of a cunning fox.

Having been greeted by Sister O'Connell, the firm were guided to bed 1, occupied by a male, aged 45, diagnosis left inguinal hernia. The undergraduates stood at the back, keeping their heads down and hoping they were not noticed. Sadly, for them Mr Duffield stood head and shoulders above his team and with an eagle eye scanned the students looking for the most vulnerable to eviscerate. His voice boomed out,

"You at the back with your NHS specs, what's your name?"

"Mathew, sir"

"Mathew! I'm not your bloody mummy. What's your surname?"

"Barnet, sir"

"Well nice to meet you, Barnet, welcome to my firm. Do step this way".

Mathew by this time had wet his pants and shuffled through the group around the bed, holding knees together, until he faced the consultant, who stood on the right-hand side.

This displeased Mr Duffield, who boomed out:

"What are you doing on that side of the bed, Barnet? Don't you know you always examine a patient from his right-hand side?"

Mathew didn't and for that matter had never yet examined a patient in real life. So, he shuffled through the crowd to the other side, sweating with fear.

"Now, Barnet, no need to be afraid of me; just tell me whether this man has an inguinal or a femoral hernia."

Mathew had no idea what he was supposed to do but he remembered from his first year of anatomy where the inguinal region was and that it had a canal, and that the testicular artery and vein, together with the spermatic cord ran, through that canal to the testes in the scrotum. In desperation he put his hand under the blanket and started to look for the man's scrotum. He knew he had found the right place when the man squealed at having his balls squeezed.

The whole firm burst out laughing, including their chief, who shoved Mathew aside and addressed Sister O'Connell.

"Sister please do the necessary"

She obeyed by pulling the blankets down to the patient's knees, followed by drawing his pyjama bottoms down as well. Unseen by the tyrant, she exchanged glances with one of the staff nurses, who nodded in agreement.

The tyrant then turned to one of his housemen, having

sufficiently humiliated a student as a warning to them all, and barked:

"OK, Caruthers, show him how it is done."

Caruthers, one of the housemen, with a smirk on his face, bent over the patient and asked him to cough. A bulge appeared just above the pubic symphysis. He then asked the patient to stand and cough, at which the bulge became more prominent. Caruthers then identified the pubic tubercle and confirmed that the hernia above and medial to that landmark, so had to be an inguinal hernia, rather than below and lateral if it were a femoral hernia. Leaving the man standing with his pyjama trousers round his ankles, looking like a victim in a concentration camp, he stood up to accept the chief's approval.

Instead of the accolade he had expected, Mr Duffield then turned to one of the registrars:

"Saunders, what has he forgotten?"

"The big X, sir."

"Correct. Please complete the demonstration."

Saunders then picked a felt nibbed pen from his coat pocket, indicted to the patient that he was to lie down again, and then marked the right groin with a big X.

"That, gentlemen, is so that Saunders won't operate on the wrong side when I leave him to do it at the end of the list." Throughout this whole circus act, Mr Duffield never once made eye contact with the patient. As he led his entourage away, one pretty probationer and Mathew Barnet stayed behind to comfort the patient on their own initiative. Mathew's humiliation at the hands of Mr Duffield and the sight of the patient's embarrassment standing in front of a crowd of strangers naked below the waist triggered a wave of hatred he had never experienced before. However, as a favourable consequence, he first set eyes on Mary O'Sullivan, with her freckles and emerald-green eyes, who gave him a warm smile.

Chapter 3

The first visit to the operating theatre

There were six operating theatres on floor minus-1 at the QE.
A floor below ground because daylight was not required in
this modernist hospital, unlike some of the operating theatres
at the old Victorian general hospital in the centre of town.
They still had skylights that predated electric lighting. It is
worth noting the use of the word "theatre", which dates back
to the 18th century, when students stood round in tiers along
with the curious bystander to watch the performance. Such
a theatre is still to be seen at St Bartholomew's in the City of
London.

The "operating room" (OR) is an American abomination
that was first popularised in the early 1960s by the TV series
Dr Kildare. Other outrages, including appendectomy instead
of appendicectomy, were imported at the same time.

Each operating theatre included a suite of rooms, the
anaesthetic room, the theatre itself with an alcove of taps and
basins for scrubbing up and finally the recovery room, where
the patient was monitored until judged fit to return to the
ward.

Everyone shared the changing rooms, one for the men and
one for the women. In theory everyone was allocated a locker
with a key, but in practice, apart from the consultants who
had their names on printed cards, it was a free-for-all. Freshly
laundered pyjamas that started up as an orderly layered pile on
shelves ended up as the day went on as a pile on the floor as
the bins for the blood-stained used articles spilled over.

Then there was the farce of the footwear. Conventionally

everyone wore ankle-length rubber boots that for some reason were sized in the European scale 30–40 instead of the British size 7–12. The consultants had their own pairs with their names clearly written across the toes.

God help any student who made the mistake of slipping on one of those bootees.

For everyone it was a free-for-all, whilst the students, new to the game, were left with the boat-size 42s.

There were six surgical firms each with two consultants and each designated an operating suite. Mr Duffield and Mr McKenzie were allocated theatre 1, in recognition of their seniority. They had operating lists Monday to Thursday, leaving Friday for a private hospital beyond bounds to the students, but illegally manned from time to time by a NHS SHO or registrar, to hold a retractor. When Dudders operated it was *sturm und drang*, in contrast to when Mac operated, which more like *l'après-midi d'un faun*.

★ ★ ★

The week after their first ward round experience, Peter, Dylan, Ginger, and Mathew experienced a baptism of fire in their first visit to the operating theatre.

On a Monday, Mr Duffield operated in the morning between 08.30 and 12.30, whilst Mr McKenzie operated between 14.30 and 17.30, in theory. In practice they always overran because Mr Duffield was too ambitious and Mr McKenzie too slow.

Mr Duffield believed it should be knife to skin at 08.30 and if the students were late he would welcome them with a tirade. They were only late once during their tenure.

Mr McKenzie also believed in punctuality and was always scrubbed up to start at precisely 13.30, assuming the morning list hadn't overrun. If the students were late and saw their chief ready to go, they felt ashamed. Dudders ruled by fear whereas Mac ruled by example.

On the morning in question the four students arrived in good time as observers as they had not yet learnt to scrub up, gown, and glove. The theatre manager, a very senior nurse, was scheduled to teach them these rituals later in the week.

The students arrived at 08.00 and were shown where to change and warned about choice of footwear. They then had a look at the schedule of cases in theatre 1 posted on a pinboard by the entrance. There were three cases listed – partial gastrectomy, breast frozen section query proceed, and right inguinal hernia. They recognised the name of the third case, the subject of their first ward round, who had been cancelled last week as the list overran. They had no idea what frozen section with a question mark meant but were too inhibited to enquire.

As predetermined, Mr Duffield's knife cut skin at precisely 08.30. The slice was a straight line from xiphisternum to umbilicus, so fast you would have missed it if you blinked. Unfortunately, Mathew blinked and the first sign that the procedure had begun was the sight of the blood bubbling up from the wound. He came over faint but was held upright by Dylan on his right and Ginger on his left, just like a hooker in the scrum. The wound was opened down to the peritoneum and the abdominal wall was pulled apart by retractors held by the houseman and registrar, Caruthers and Saunders. This was made possible because the anaesthetist had injected the patient with a muscle relaxant, curare, a poison popular amongst the natives in the Amazon basin for pasting on the arrow heads in their blow pipes. What happened next was impossible to witness by the students as Mr Duffield's size 8 hands filled the abdominal cavity. Scissors, forceps, and sutures were passed back and forward every time his right hand was offered to the scrub nurse without raising his head. The scrub nurse slapped the instruments into his palm, knowing precisely what was needed at every stage of the procedure. If she made a mistake the surgeon simply threw the offering over his left shoulder, where it clattered on the floor below the sinks, and proffered his hand again to the white-faced, sweating nurse. They were only allowed one mistake before being replaced by another victim. After about 40 minutes, two-thirds of the stomach connected to the first part of the duodenum were pulled out and dumped in a kidney dish that was sent off to the pathology department. Curved needles with silk thread or catgut were offered to the maestro and the gastric remnant was attached to the divided end of the duodenum. Once that was complete, Mr Duffield stepped back, threw his glove and gown on the floor and left Mr Saunders to close the wound. Whilst this was going on he sat on one of the stools in the anaesthetic room to entertain himself with the *Times* crossword.

In the interim, Peter picked up the courage to ask the senior nurse what "Frozen section query proceed" meant. She was happy to enlighten him, "This woman has a lump in the breast that is suspicious of cancer; the frozen section will confirm the diagnosis and if positive Mr Duffield will proceed to a radical mastectomy." Peter thanked the nurse but still had no idea what a frozen section was. He didn't have to wait long to find out.

The next patient was wheeled into the anaesthetic room and put to sleep. Mr Duffield popped in and palpated her left breast to satisfy his clinical diagnosis and marked the suspicious area with a cross with purple ink. He then re-entered the operating theatre to wash his hands and slip on his gown and to hold out his hands to be gloved by a nurse. The skin under the cross on the breast was sterilised with an iodine solution and framed by four sterile drapes.

With a flash of his scalpel the surgeon cut the skin transversely where the mark had been made and winkled out a lump of flesh packing the cavity with swabs to thwart the haemorrhage. He tossed it into a porcelain dish and shouted at the theatre porter to take the specimen for frozen section in the pathology department and to complete the proforma with patient's details and add "LILB? Ca FS". As he was shouting through a facemask something was lost in translation. (Of course, LILB was shorthand for lump in left breast, Ca short for cancer and FS short for frozen section.)

He pulled off his gown and gloves and gestured to the students to join him in the anaesthetic room for a short seminar, leaving the anaesthetist and the nurses to await the results from the path lab. He seated himself on a chromium plated round stool with the students in a semicircle in front of him and embarked on a well-rehearsed monologue.

"That woman presented with a hard lump and a dimple in the skin in the upper-outer quadrant of the left breast. My clinical diagnosis was that was a cancer. I told her it was a *lesion* as I didn't want to alarm her with the word cancer. I didn't allow anyone else to palpate the lump for fear of spreading the cancer cells along the lymphatic channels and the same concern excluded a conventional biopsy as that would certainly spread cancer cells in the wound cavity so that is why we are doing a frozen section. Instead of fixing the tissue in wax and waiting for two days for a result we get the pathologist to freeze the specimen and then cut very thin slices to be viewed under a microscope almost immediately so I can get the result in 20 minutes, during which time I take my coffee and do a bit of teaching." He paused as a young nurse handed him a mug of steaming coffee. "If the result comes back benign, she goes straight back to the ward, but if, as I suspect, it comes back positive, I'll sterilise her breast, chest, and axilla and proceed to a Halsted radical mastectomy. Do any of you know what that is?" His little audience shook their heads in unison. "I wonder if you lot ever open a textbook of surgery. Well, William Halsted was a great surgeon who worked at the Johns Hopkins Hospital in Baltimore in the late 19th century. In 1895 he described this procedure for the cure of breast cancer. The trick was not to cut across any lymphatic channels that might spill cancer cells into the wound. To avoid that he stipulated that all breast tissue and overlying skin be excised and removed *en bloc*, along with the fatty tissue all the way up the axilla up to the axillary vein.

This fatty tissue encompasses all the lymphatic channels and all the lymph glands. But to gain access all the way up to the apex of the axilla it is essential to cut away the major and minor pectoral muscles. Now, who can tell me what the first step of the operation might be?" None of the students had a clue but in fact the question was rhetorical.

"No ideas? The first step is to take a skin graft from the right thigh in anticipation of not being able to close the wound at the end of the op. If you can close the wound, then you have compromised the outcome by leaving subcutaneous micro-lymphatics carrying cancer cells that will announce themselves as chest wall recurrences within the first five years post-op."

What with drinking his coffee and delivering his drone, 20 minutes had passed.

He looked at the wall clock and then shouted to the scrub nurse, "When's that bloody frozen section report to be ready?" The scrub nurse then asked a junior nurse to phone the pathology department. This call went on for an awful long time until the junior nurse put down the receiver and whispered into the scrub nurse's ear. The senior nurse's face went white as she walked to the entrance of the antiaesthetic room and declaimed, "The pathology department have no record of receiving a frozen section specimen this morning."

Then hell broke out!

We will skip the profanities and the shaming and blaming but the net result was one porter being sacked, one nurse running out of the theatre in tears and the students trembling in fear, after discovering that the specimen had already been fixed in wax for a more leisurely approach to a histopathological diagnosis. The explanation for this cockup was the porter misunderstanding the chief and thought that his masked muffled words, "LILBCaFS" was the patient's name, Lily B. Caffs.

Once calm was restored thanks to the diplomacy of the anaesthetist, Mr Duffield decided to procced to a radical mastectomy because the lump looked and felt like a cancer, and he had a lot of experience in this game. Having restored his dignity, he embarked on his leadership role and started up barking his orders. "Nurse, paint the chest, left axilla, and upper arm with iodine, Saunders, put on the drapes as you have been taught and start work on a split-thickness graft, measuring about 5cm×7cm, from the right thigh and pop it in a screw cap jar of saline and, Barnet, pop up to the men's ward and tell *whatsisname* with the hernia that his op has been postponed until next week due to unforeseen circumstances."

An hour after the radical mastectomy was completed, the mutilated woman, known to her family and friends as Sandra, was wheeled back to the ward after a short sojourn in the recovery room. She woke up about 20 minutes later and her first reaction was relief that she had survived the procedure. Her second thought was of concern to find her chest so tightly bound with bandages wrapped all round her chest wall that it made it difficult to breath. She tried to take a deep breath but experienced agony from the long diagonal wound across her chest, together with sharp dagger-like pains from two rubber tubes draining blood from under the skin flaps and the eviscerated arm pit. Sandra then deduced that she must have breast cancer and had a mastectomy notwithstanding the sensation of a "phantom breast" that would haunt for at least seven days. With that realisation she started to sob and was unreconcilable despite the best efforts of one of the staff nurses. The pain got worse and worse to the point she was frightened to breathe and kept pressing the bell to attract a nurse to give her something for the pain. She was ignored for an hour as the nurses were at a meeting in sister's office at the changing of the shift. Eventually a junior nurse appeared and looked at the notes on a clipboard hanging on the foot of the bed. The nurse shook her head and explained she was written up for six-hourly 50mg of pethidine and her last dose was only four hours ago. Sandra, by this time going out of her head, lost her temper and screamed, "I don't care what's written on your bloody clipboard I'm in fucking agony!"

Sister heard that and came running out of her office to remonstrate with this intractable patient. "Sandra, we have to be guided by the rules. If we give you too much morphia you can become addicted and furthermore morphine can suppress your breathing; you must have a very low pain threshold."

Sandra wasn't standing for that; as the landlord of the Rose and Crown in the seedy side of Spark Hill, she was not going to put up with this any further. "Low pain threshold, eh? I wonder what your pain threshold is when my old man comes to visit. He 'appens to be a welterweight boxing champ."

As chance would have it, Mr Alex McKenzie was doing a teaching round at the other side of the ward and picked up on the ugly drama that was playing out in front of all staff and patients. He strolled across and asked sister what was the problem. Having looked at the clipboard his face turned red as he tried to control his temper. "Sister, the patient has not been prescribed an opiate but pethidine 50mg six-hourly. That is not sufficient for a mouse. Who was responsible for prescribing this?"

"Mr Duffield delegates that to the houseman," replied sister.

"Well, allow me to correct that." He crossed out the initial prescription and wrote morphine sulphate 20mg IM prn. (prn stands for *pro re nata*, Latin for on request) He then turned to the patient's nurse and insisted that the first dose be delivered at once. The nurse rushed off to the locked medicine chest and sister walked off in a huff, muttering that she would report this to Mr Duffield. Of course, she never dared to.

Mr McKenzie then walked to the head of the bed, having made a mental note of the patient's name on the drug list, and took her right hand. "Mrs Templeton, I'm sorry for your suffering. For the next two days, if you are in pain, just ask for an injection. I can assure you that this will not make you a drug addict. That's an old wives' tale."

Sandra nodded with a smile between her sobs and Mac went back to his students.

Forty-eight hours later, to everyone's peace of mind, the final pathology reported that the lump was indeed a 3cm cancer, grade III, with four out of 12 lymph glands involved. Sadly for Sandra, those pathological details were an indication for six weeks of radiotherapy aimed at her chest wall and axilla to reduce the risk of a "local" recurrence. This would almost guarantee swelling of the left arm through lymphoedema, adding insult to injury.

Chapter 4

A teaching ward round

Because of the debacle in theatre 1, Mr McKenzie's list was delayed by an hour for the theatre staff to break for lunch. As this was often the case, he had got into the habit of taking his students on a teaching round. Once the altercation over pain control for Mrs Templeton was over, he returned to his students and guided them away from the beds into his office to explain what had upset him so much and to teach a lesson of lasting value. His preamble was quite unexpected.

"During the war, I served in the Royal Air Force Medical Service under the command of a great surgeon, Sir Geoffrey Keynes. In the last few months of the war, long after the Battle of Britain and at the end of the destruction of German cities by Bomber Command, I was seconded to work with the RAMC in the 11th armoured division. On 15 April 1945, in woodland not far from Bremen, we encountered the Bergen–Belsen concentration camp. What we encountered I have difficulty putting into words; because we doubted anyone would believe what we saw, many of us took photographs." He then pulled out an envelope full of photographs from his desktop, having warned us to turn their heads away if we had a queasy stomach. There were pictures of the pits filled with naked bodies piled one on top of each other and looking like ragdolls, pyramids of rotting corpses, and horse-drawn carts with corpses spilling over their sides. The survivors in their striped pyjamas were skeletally thin and staring towards the camera with sunken, vacant eyes. He quickly put the pictures away and then continued. "We then organised a triage plus

28

one. Those who had a chance of survival for active treatment, those who were dying beyond help and those who were dead. Sometimes it was difficult to be sure. The fourth group behind the wire of the camp were the German guards and officers. They were stripped of their uniforms and forced to wear rags and were organised into gangs to give the dead a decent burial in mass graves. To aid them, we rounded up the residents of the nearby villages, Bergen and Belsen, to join the work gang in spite of them claiming they had no idea what was going on. On my tour around the camp, I came across a large hut labelled in German *Krankenhaus*. The interior was filled with the dead and dying on each side with a surgical table and instruments at the far end. In addition to those dead and dying were those with rotting surgical incisions, undoubtedly human experimentation, and vivisection. You will be aware of the Nuremberg trials. Well, only a few of the medical perpetrators were captured and paid the final penalty; many, I suspect, are practising to this day.

"As you can imagine, that experience has haunted me to this day and has had a major impact on the way I practise my trade. First, I hate the tradition of bringing men into the hospital 24 hours before their surgery and then insist they wear pyjamas. It's only for the convenience of the nurses to make sure they are ready for the consultants' round the next morning. It always triggers memories of the victims of Belsen clutching the wire fence, wearing striped prison garb, watching us suspiciously to judge whether we were liberators or persecutors.

"Next and more important is my intolerance of post-operative pain as if it was normative and blaming the patients if they complained. I pledged an oath to myself, after witnessing the evidence of torture by the Nazi war criminal doctors, that I would do my best to free my patients of pain instead of inflicting pain.

"After the war I returned to this hospital to pick up where I left off but the first thing I did was to embark on a study of analgesia after surgery. I carried out an audit of the prescribing and dispensing adequate doses of opiates for pain relief. As a base line I used the textbook recommendation of intramuscular 20mg morphine sulphate every six hours. To my dismay I discovered that only half our patients were offered that standard of care. To make it worse I learnt that the nurses only dispensed the drugs in half of those who had the correct prescription. For a surgeon not to know the correct dose of analgesics after major surgery is either ignorance or idleness. The problem with the nurses is that they are taught obsolete beliefs that therapeutic doses of opiates can supress respiration. The opposite is true in that the pain impairs deep breaths and contributes to post-operative pneumonia. The other myth is that treating post-operative pain with opiates can make the patient a drug addict. This is simply not true. I'm not complacent on this subject and doing some research on providing analgesia at the patient's request rather than by the clock.

"So, my message to you is: learn all about pain relief and be prepared to have a question on that topic in your final exam."

★ ★ ★

Later that day the students had an appointment with the head nurse in the operating theatres.

She was a jolly fat woman with a thick Liverpudlian accent who was close to retirement and loved teaching the medical students. Within an hour they had learnt to scrub their hands with a sharp bristle brush that drew blood from the soft skin of their hands. Along the way they learnt to open and close the taps with their elbows, shrug on a gown to be tied at the back and slip on powdered gloves without allowing naked fingers touching the outer surface of the glove. The most difficult lesson was remembering not to scratch an itchy nose under the face mask once you were gowned and gloved.

The following Monday morning they were to be initiated

into the entry level of a budding surgeon: the second assistant. For a start, Ginger Bannerman and Mathew Barnet had already decided to be any kind of doctor apart from a surgeon. Dylan Baddams had postponed any decision until he had tasted more that was on offer, but Peter Baring had already become a zealot for the art of curing patients at a stroke. He had become a favourite of Mr Duffield because the great man was a snob and liked the posh accent of this tall, blond young man. He himself was a public-school boy and boasted Harrow School and Christ Church, Oxford, in his CV. So it was Peter who was first to be offered up as a sacrifice to play the role of second assistant. The first case on the list was a cholecystectomy for gall stones in a fat man whose abdominal wall measured 10cm in depth. Peter had two roles in the procedure: to retract the abdominal wall incision along with the lower reaches of the thoracic cage to allow the surgeon a clear view, and to cut the sutures after every knot was tied. In return Peter would get a good view of the operation but at a cost. The retractor was made of stainless steel, with a sharp-edged handle attached to a wide blade with a curved lip. At first glance it looked like something used at a BBQ. Standing on the right side of the anaesthetised man, holding the handle with sharp edges in his left hand and pulling the chest wall upwards and outwards, was exhausting and painful. Every time he let the burden down a little, he was rewarded with a sharp knock on his knuckles from the large dissecting scissors held in the surgeon's hand. His other task, the cutting of the knots with scissors in his right hand. This was more difficult than he had predicted because he had to bend over the abdominal cavity whilst lifting the chest wall towards the ceiling. Inevitably the suture was cut too long or too short. Too long could be corrected but to short might allow the knot to be compromised. This happened towards the end of the operation when Peter cut the knot and arterial blood spurted out into Mr Duffield's right eye. His first assistant quickly picked up a small "mosquito" forceps and clipped the little artery and then with dexterity tied another silk suture around the stump of the blood vessel.

Mr Duffield, blind in one eye, cursed everyone in the room, stood back from the table, threw his gloves and gown on the floor, allowed a terrified nurse to wipe his eye with a wet swab and strode out of the theatre, leaving the first assistant to clean up and close the abdomen.

The watching students had difficulty supressing their laughter, whilst poor Peter assumed that his ambitions to be a surgeon were over before he'd even started.

Chapter 5

Christmas to the New Year
1957–1958

For the students the last two weeks of the year were bacchanalian. Every night someone would organise a drink party. There was a competition between the firms to decorate the wards as anything from Santa Claus's grotto to the set for *Scheherazade*. There was the Christmas show written and acted by the undergraduates. Then the Christmas Day tradition for the visit of Father Christmas, the carving of the turkey and handing out gifts to the patients. Later in the afternoon the nurses and students would finish off the turkey with its stuffing, the sausage rolls and plum pudding. As most of the patients left behind at Christmas were "nil by mouth", on drips or unconscious, the leftovers were a feast for the staff and students. Furthermore, the traditional brandy and sherry provided for the patients without much thought was also left unopened for the debauchery that followed.

Ward W2 was dressed up with an underwater theme, with green streamers hanging from the roof looking like seaweed, the plain off-white walls painted in water colours with serpents, starfish, dolphins, and barracuda, with a large placard bearing the image of Poseidon with his trident, surrounded with mermaids with fishtails and large err, mammary glands, outside sister's office. That painting was completed by Ginger Bannerman, a very talented artist.

The students' Christmas show was a hoot. It was performed on three nights the week before Christmas Day, in the main lecture hall that could hold 300. The title of that year's show was *The Comedy of Errors*. It was performed like a pantomime, with the principal boy played by the girl with the best legs and the pantomime dame played by the largest of the boys as a caricature of Mr Morgan Duffield. The dancing chorus line were played by the eight-member scrum of the first XV wearing tutus, high-kicking and waggling their buttocks to the audience. But the funniest entr'acte was the four members of the National Elf Service, dreamt up by Mathew Barnet. Mathew, Dylan, Ginger, and Peter created huge green felt elf hats that covered their heads and shoulders. They stitched little arms and hands also of felt, to hang down from each side of the cap. They then decorated their naked bodies in a way that their nipples looked like eyes with long lashes and their umbilici were encircled with red lipstick to appear as pouting whistling lips. They finally attached a beard from the belt that hung down to their knees and then danced with their arms behind their backs to a recording of a whistling song. The net effect was hilarious, and they were called back for an encore. As an encore, Mathew disrobed, picked up his violin and played Liszt's *Hungarian Rhapsody* at top speed, leaving the other three to dance like lunatics whilst the audience clapped to the frenetic rhythm.

★ ★ ★

A few days before Christmas, Peter invited his three best friends to spend the holiday with him at his girlfriend's home in Berkeley. Ginger and Dylan had to turn down the offer as they were expected back at home. Mathew was keen to accept the invitation as Christmas was not a festival they celebrated. "Have you got enough room for me?" he naively asked.

"Not to worry old chap; they're going to open up the west wing for the holidays because my family are going to join us," he replied.

Whilst digesting the significance of a house with wings,

Mathew responded, "Very decent of you to ask. I'd love to, but I better check if my folks have anything planned first. By the way, you've never told me your girlfriend's name"

"Sorry, how delinquent of me. I call her Fifi, but her real name is Fiona Berkeley."

At this Mathew burst out laughing. "Funny, all this time I assumed Berkeley was a place, not a lady friend."

"Berkeley is a place but also the surname of Fifi and what's more their ancestral home is Berkeley Castle." Responded Peter.

Blindsided and bewildered, all Mathew had to say was, "Of course, how silly of me, I'll let you know tomorrow." Leaving Peter to chuckle interiorly.

At the first opportunity, Mathew went to the library and checked out the Berkeley family in *Burke's Peerage*, and this is what he found.

> The **Berkeley family** is an ancient English noble family.
> It is one of only four families in England that can trace its
> patrilineal descent back to Anglo-Saxon times. The Berkeley
> family retains possession of much of the lands it held from
> the 11th and 12th centuries, centred on Berkeley Castle in
> Gloucestershire, which still belongs to the family. The current
> head of the family, Earl Maurice Berkeley (b. 1901), served
> as Lieutenant-Colonel in the service of the Royal Artillery.

Armed with this knowledge, he approached his father, explaining that he had been invited to a country house estate for the winter vac with his student friends to study together for the next set of exams. Surprisingly, his parents, who were a little bit snobbish, rather liked the idea of him mixing with the gentry providing he promised not to eat *traif*.

He couldn't wait to tell Peter that he was free to accept his kind invitation.

Early on a freezing Christmas Eve the two of them huddled in the tiny MG roadster with its top down. Their suitcases were tied to the pannier frame covering the spare tyre. On arrival at Berkeley Castle, they could barely stand up straight and made for a sorry sight as they walked bow-legged and cyanosed towards a welcoming party. Standing at the main entrance with its Norman arch and portcullis were the butler and the angelic Fiona, the spitting image of Grace Kelly. Peter introduced Mathew, whose facial colour turned from blue to beetroot red on shaking her hand. In that instant he was smitten. She was the most desirable yet the most unattainable specimen of young womanhood he'd ever encountered. In 1945 Evelyn Waugh published *Brideshead Revisited* and Mathew had got round to reading it the previous year. At once he saw himself cast into the role of Charles Ryder, but at least Charles was a tall English middle-class boy of the Anglican confession, whilst Mathew was a short Jewish boy of humble origins.

The medieval remains of the castle were in ruins, and little was left of the Tudor structures, but the family lived in a perfectly symmetrical Palladian mansion hidden behind the battlements that supported the Norman arch and its portcullis. Facing them at the end of a long gravel lane running through a deer park was a three-storey block centred on a clock tower rising two stories higher. The octagonal superstructure bearing the clock face was crowned with a cupola bearing a gilt weathervane. At ground level an imposing flight of steps flanked by heraldic beasts, lead up to an arched doorway with intricately carved panels evoking folded linen. Above the arch was a coat of arms almost weathered away by the 250 years of conflict between English climate and Cotswold sandstone. On either side were symmetrical lines of windows obeying the architectural code of the golden ratio. At each flank, the east and west wings completed an open rectangle so that the living rooms at the rear enjoyed unimpeded views of the rolling hills that led down to the valley of the River Severn. The interior although grand in scale, including a staircase with one flight going up and another coming down, was sadly shabby and the furniture looked frankly hand-me-down. The newcomers were bustled into a drawing room with a roaring wood fire in the grate and offered hot punch that restored their circulation. Drinks were served from a silver tureen and a ladle. Other drinks were displayed in crystal decanters with silver engraved name plates, whisky, brandy, port sitting on an antique console table at the back of an old leather settee with its stuffing peeping out of cracks. Early 19th-century occasional tables were scattered round the room, carrying back copies of *Country Life*, *Punch* and *The Tatler*, whilst stacked on the floor by the battered club armchairs on either side the fire were recent copies of the *Daily Telegraph*. Next to capture Mathew's attention were the paintings, covering so much of the wall that the faded and peeling wallpaper was barely visible. Most of these were old family portraits of little distinction but he could have sworn that the marble-floored entrance hall sported two Gainsborough ladies on either side of the grand staircase.

Whilst Peter was distracted greeting his parents, who had just arrived, and introducing them to Fiona, Mathew, hot punch in hand, made a tour of the room to study the paintings in greater detail when a pretty young lady with black curly locks, materialised at his side. She introduced herself as Minxy, a close friend of Fiona who had recently enrolled at the Courtauld in Bloomsbury, to study the history of art. She went on to explain that the painting he was looking at was by Joshua Reynolds of the 18th Earl Berkeley. He took a liking to her immediately; she had a twinkle in her eyes, a sign of intelligence, and was only about five feet, two inches tall, a comfortable height when compared with the aristocratic ladies sashaying round the room. They were interrupted before Mathew could properly introduce himself when they were called by the butler to be shown to their rooms.

Mathew's room was on the third floor of the central block close to the clock tower. It had a polished wooden floor with a threadbare mat, the walls were covered with faded blue damask with little pink flowers, the window looked out over the front drive, and the furniture was old mahogany. The bed was high with a thin mattress covered with a patchwork quilt and the nightstand carried an antique stoneware washbasin and pitcher with an elaborate black and red floral pattern. The Victorian look was completed with a candlestick furnished with a box of matches. Later he was to learn that this was intended to light the way to the nearest lavatory, three floors below. Opposite the bed was a little fire grate with coke and kindling and alongside that was a Shaker-style rocking chair carrying a rag doll with a malicious grin. Mathew washed his hands a face in cold water from the pitcher, changed into a fresh shirt, put on his best suit, in fact his only suit, and composed himself or the ordeal to follow. He discovered the library by following the sound of voices, before shyly entering the room where he was to meet the remainder of the family and guests.

The first new face was Fiona's young brother, Anthony, a delightful self-confident young man of 18. He was the only one present dressed informally, sporting a vee-necked, cable-stitched cricket sweater with his public-school colours framing the neckline. Although the cricket season was five months off, he carried it off nonchalantly so that Mathew felt overdressed. He was then reintroduced to a close friend of Fiona, one from her old school at Roedean, the pretty brunette he had already met on the stairs, but Mathew never really caught her full name. On closer examination, as well as already been classified in his mind as petite, she was also vivacious, with an attractive olive complexion, and dark, long-lashed, luminous eyes, so far scoring nine out of 10 in his schoolboy classification of female pulchritude. The next member of the female persuasion he was introduced to was at the opposite end of his ranking system: an elderly and slightly batty Aunt Jocasta, who had lost her husband at the Battle of the Somme. She asked Mathew if he was one of the Devonshire Barnetts, and, although tempted, he denied membership of that clan and by way of a half-truth explained that he was one of the Edgbaston Barnett families. That seemed to satisfy her.

The party was completed as Lord and Lady Berkeley entered

the room. Fiona's mum looked wonderful in a slinky number cut on the bias looked as you might imagine Fiona would look like 25 years later. Lord Berkeley looked dapper in blazer, grey flannels, and regimental tie. He walked with a slight limp because of shrapnel in his left thigh, a permanent record of his gallantry at the fateful Battle of the Somme. He spent the last year of the war as a prisoner of war. It was rumoured that the king recognised his gallantry, but it was considered bad form to enquire further. Mathew then noticed something odd as Peter introduced his parents to the Berkeleys. He had assumed they were all old friends, but this was obviously their first visit.

At the table Mathew found himself flanked by Aunt Jocasta on his left and on his right was the girl on the stairs whose name on the place setting card was simply Minxy. As the old aunt was deaf in her right ear, he spent most of the evening talking and flirting with the young lady on his right. The next cultural clash that he experienced concerned the drinking and appreciation of fine wines. The Berkeley cellar was spoken of reverentially as a place where wine had been laid down for generations. Each wine was discussed with unaffected connoisseurship. The fish course was accompanied by an amusing young Sauvignon Blanc from the Rhone valley, the shoulder of lamb heralded in a rather good claret, a pre-war Chateau Lafite, actually, decanted earlier in the evening, and the dessert wine was a legendary Chateau D'Yquem 1937. Mathew felt happy and eloquent and regaled Minxy with his wisdom and delighted when she laughed at his jokes. At 9.00pm the ladies retired to the drawing room; a discrete tap on the shoulder by Peter cautioned Mathew to stay put and the men gathered around the master of the house for a goblet of Napoleon brandy and a smoke, so he lay back in his chair, stretched out his legs and enjoyed the masculine camaraderie of the moment. After a short interlude Lord Berkeley tapped his goblet with a spoon to catch their attention. "Gentlemen, I have an important announcement to make. Peter Baring has asked my permission to take my daughter Fiona's hand in marriage and I am very happy to offer my consent. Now let's join the ladies and share the good news."

On the short stroll to the sitting room, Peter pinched Mathew's elbow and whispered, "I say, old boy, would you do me an honour and act as my best man?"

Christmas Day dinner was a large and elaborate affair finished in time to catch the queen, Elizabeth II, deliver her Christmas Day address to her subjects. After that most fell asleep in their chairs as a physiological response to the heavy meal, plum pudding, and vintage port. The next day, Boxing Day, was fun. The morning was crisp and cold, with a clear eggshell blue sky and two inches of snow crunching underfoot. They enjoyed a long walk through the village and round the deer park, with Minxy holding Mathew's elbow to help herself over the icy stretches. The afternoon was spent playing traditional party games and they all had to do their party pieces. Fiona turned out to be a gifted pianist whilst her fiancée, Peter, sang along with a beautiful baritone voice. His Lordship did magic tricks and Anthony had them all in fits with his hopeless attempt as a ventriloquist using the ragdoll as a dummy. Mathew's party piece was playing on his violin a suite of lively Gypsy dances, ending with the traditional Jewish dance theme *Hava na'gilah*, which he played at increasing tempo until one of his strings broke. This was received with thunderous applause. At 6.00pm the serious drinking began. A toast to the queen, followed by a toast to their hosts, involved getting through a couple of bottles of Dom Perignon and then everyone took it in turns to fill their glasses from a well-stocked bar. Come 9.00pm, someone suggested rolling up the carpets in the great entrance hall so that they could dance "The Twist" with Chubby Checker, the "Loco-Motion" by Little Eva, and "Stranger on the Shore" by Acker Bilk, ending up with "I Can't Stop Loving You" by Ray Charles. Mathew ended the evening dancing cheek to cheek with Minxy and gave her a lingering kiss as they all turned in at midnight. Thirty minutes later he lost his virginity as Minxy found her way to his room. Full of languor, he rapidly fell into a deep sleep and awoke refreshed, unsure to this day whether or not he had dreamt the whole episode. At breakfast the party then broke up to go their separate ways and Minxy and Mathew exchanged telephone numbers. Mathew then jumped into the passenger seat of Peter's MG, steeling themselves for a freezing drive back to London. On the drive back home, Mathew asked Peter why he had been chosen as best man. Peter's surprising response bonded them for the rest of their lives: "Mathew, you are the most self-effacing man I know. We share values of scientific and moral integrity that I believe all aspiring doctors must share. I have started life with all the advantages in the world, a long line of scholars and bankers, a public-school education and soon to be married into the nobility. Your grandparents had nothing when they migrated to this country, and you are of the first generation to go to university. Many of your relatives were murdered by the Nazis and in spite of that we still witness anti-Semitism by right-wing politicians in our green and pleasant land. Whenever you ask questions in tutorials I listen carefully, because they are always formulated by an intelligence you are unaware of. Best of all was the act of the National Elf Service, which was a work of genius. I admire you and value your friendship." On New Year's Eve, Peter demonstrated that his words were not empty, when he endangered his whole career in support of his best man.

* * *

The occasion was the New Year's Eve firm party hosted by Mr Morgan Duffield in his magnificent home in Solihull, Old Warwick Road, 10 miles south-east of Birmingham. Those 10 miles were why he always resented being called out at night or the weekends. Just to cover their backs if there was a serious risk of losing a surgical emergency when Mr Morgan was notionally on call, the duty senior registrar would telephone him to describe the case. The standard response was always,

"You're the man on the spot, you decide, call me if you get into trouble." On those rare occasions when the man on the spot was in deep trouble, his chief would appear in black tie eveningwear and with the smell of alcohol on his breath.

The junior medical staff and students on the firm were invited to the party together with their wives or girlfriends. Peter brought his fiancée, Fiona, Dylan brought his girlfriend, Bronwen, all the way from Caerphilly, and Mathew brought nurse Mary O'Sullivan because Minxy was out of the country. Ginger Bannerman dropped out as he preferred to celebrate Hogmanay in Scotland.

They were invited for drinks and canapés at 6.00pm followed by a buffet feast. All the girls looking gorgeous in the very fashionable wide taffeta skirts with frothy white petticoats and brightly coloured tight leather belts that accentuated their wasp waists. Bronwen notably had difficulty in breathing so, later on, discreetly abandoned her waspy. They were rather overwhelmed when a liveried footman opened the door and called out their names before passing their heavy coats to another lower-ranking footman. Mr Duffield's rather timid and mousy wife, the honourable Daphne Duffield, welcomed them into the marble-floored colonnaded entrance hall and instructed prim waitresses in black uniforms with white aprons to provide their guests with sparkling wine. Mr Duffield was loud, red-faced and clearly drunk on our arrival. He enjoyed being the centre of attention whilst all his acolytes guffawed at his jokes and anecdotes. He started to annoy Peter and Mathew when in conversation with his senior registrar, in a thundering voice, he dismissed Mr McKenzie as a lily-livered surgeon who couldn't cut his way out of a paper bag. He further rankled them when he turned the conversation to making fun of the Irish, when Mathew felt Mary stiffen on his arm. "Have you heard the one about Paddy and Donal, who missed the last bus home after the pub closed? Well, they decided to break into the bus station and couldn't find the number 11, so they decided to steal the number 39 and walk home from the stop at Cambridge Circus." Haw, haw, haw. Some of his adoring audience laughed along with him but as he started the next joke the room went silent. "What do you call a bunch of Jewish shyster lawyers at the bottom of the ocean? A bloody good start!"

The silence deepened and the atmosphere froze. At this point Peter Baring broke the silence and saved the day. Using his poshest public-school accent, he began a speech in order to offer a toast to their hosts. "Mr Duffield and honourable Daphne Duffield, speaking on behalf of all the students here, I thank you for your generous hospitality. Mr Duffield, again on behalf of your students, I want to thank you for all we have learnt over the last four months on the firm." At this point Morgan Duffield, beetroot in colour, broke into a delighted smile. Peter continued. "In addition, we have learnt something else of value about how accomplished a man you are. It is commonplace for someone telling jokes at a party to refer to one racist stereotype but two without taking a breath is some achievement. I'm sure that our Irish and Jewish friends in this room can take a joke as best as anyone. I'm sure my good friend Dylan wouldn't mind me teasing him by describing Wales, where men are men and sheep are nervous. My friend Alastair Bannerman, who can't be with us this evening, wouldn't mind if I told the story about the time I was in Glasgow last year. Unfortunately, when the bill came, I found I only had the money to pay the bill but there was nothing left for a tip. The waiter responded by saying, 'No problem, sir, let me add up the bill again.' I could even tell jokes about public-school boys like you and me, but they might embarrass the young ladies in this room. So, ladies and gentlemen, let us raise our glasses to toast our host and hostess." There was thunderous applause and laughter, leaving Mr Morgan Duffield so drunk and confused that he joined in the ovation whilst vaguely thinking he might have missed the point. The students then excused themselves as they had a long way to drive back to Birmingham before supper was served, leaving the honourable Daphne mortified.

Chapter 6

Graduation
1960

The three years 1957–1960 flew by as our protagonists worked harder and harder, leaving less and less time for play. They spent time learning the basics in all the 'ologies from anaesthesiology to zoology although, in fairness, their interest in animals' health was limited to experimentation in the pathology department. Whilst on that topic as well as spending hours looking down a microscope to learn the distinction between lung cancer and a hair follicle, they were also introduced to "morbid anatomy", learning how to carry out an autopsy. In those days, all deaths in hospital were sent first for a post-mortem before freed to the undertakers. Having tasted all the specialities and sub-specialities whilst leading up to finals, the undergraduates how to consider the initial three paths they might follow: general surgery, general medicine, or general practice. Peter had already decided on surgery and Dylan and Ginger were motivated to return to their hometowns and look after their kinfolk in general practice, whilst Mathew could not yet make up his mind. However, this decision was resolved when Mathew won the prize for psychiatry for coming top in the examination at the end of that teaching module. From there on in he was mentored by Professor Gunter Hoffbrand, who had studied under Sigmund Freud in Vienna and had followed his master to London in June 1938.

On the domestic front, they had each experienced a life-changing event. Sadly, in 1958, Alastair lost his father, who died from a haemorrhage from oesophageal varices, a consequence of cirrhosis of the liver that in turn was the consequence of alcoholism.

On the happy side, Dylan and Bronwen got engaged on the understanding he would return to the green valleys of South Wales.

In the spring of 1959 Peter and Fiona got married in the little chapel attached to Berkeley Castle. Mathew was the best man, whilst Dylan and Ginger were ushers. They all looked splendid in their morning suits with grey striped trousers, black tailcoats, dove-grey waistcoats, striped silk ties, shiny black shoes, and shiny black top hats. The groom wore a similar outfit but had a white carnation in his buttonhole. The bride looked divine in a sleek figure-hugging cream satin dress, designed by Pierre Balmain. The wedding breakfast was in the great hall of the castle bedecked with flowers of the season. Before the guests sat down to eat, they were served perfectly chilled Dom Perignon by perfectly dressed servants. When ultimately called upon to deliver the best man's speech, Mathew was well prepared, with his bloodstream bearing an ideal 40 milligrams of alcohol per 100 millilitres of blood. His speech did not descend into the conventional vulgarity expected of the best man but was more a sincere plaudit of the beauty of the bride and the wisdom of the groom and the honour to have been chosen. However, he lightened the tone describing how Peter's speech at Mr Duffield's New Year's Eve party had saved the day and bonded their relationship. Finally, he ended with an old Jewish joke that has them all in tears.

"Shoshanna has just got married to a much older man with a limp. A woman she has not met before comes over and says, 'My, that's a beautiful diamond you're wearing. In fact, I think it's the most beautiful diamond I have ever seen!' 'Thank you,' replies Shoshanna. 'This is the Plotnick Diamond.' 'The Plotnick Diamond? Is there a story to it?' 'Oh yes, the diamond comes with a curse.' 'A curse?' asks the lady. 'What curse?' 'Plotnick.'"

Mathew then sat down, relaxing now his ordeal was over and allowing himself to drink more champagne. As the groom responded with equal fluency and spontaneous humour, Mathew looked round the room and noticed that one of the bridesmaids was smiling and waving her hand at him. She looked familiar but at that distance he couldn't quite place her. However, once the meal was over and the bride and groom had started the dance with a waltz played by Joe Loss and his big band, the bridesmaid came running over, grabbed his hand and dragged him onto the dance floor. Of course, it was the petite pretty girl with black curly hair, Minxy. He was delighted to see her again and to have a willing dancing partner. After the first set from the band, they sat in a cosy corner by one of the tall neo-Gothic windows and started chattering away like old friends.

"Minxy, if you will stop talking for a second, I never got your real name when we first met, please enlighten me."

"My name is Shoshanna Plotkin."

"No, it's not, please don't keep it a secret, what is your real name?"

"My real name is Rebecca KaMinxy, but don't you dare call me Becky!"

"Minxy is fine by me. Dare I assume that like me you are one of the chosen?"

"Well, I'm certainly not one of those six-foot Aryan blonds like the bride and other bridesmaids," she responded with a big smile and a twinkle in her eye.

The band the struck up again with a South American beat and Mathew there and then decided he had met his future bride.

★ ★ ★

The final exams went on for six weeks in May and involved three-hour written papers in all the main subjects, followed by viva voce tests where the student faced two examiners, one from their school and one a visiting examiner. The pathology exam involved diagnosing something down a microscope or identifying some grotesque specimen in a jar. The clinical "practicals" involved taking a patient's history and then examining them all in 20 minutes.

As well as taking the exams the students revised every night the subject for the following day. At the end of the six weeks, they were exhausted and needed sleep more than a booze-up that could wait until they learnt whether had had passed or failed.

They didn't have long to wait. "The famous four", as they liked to call themselves, all passed comfortably; furthermore, Mathew was awarded a distinction, whilst Peter won the Aston Webb Prize for Surgery in addition to a distinction.

Everything after that was an anti-climax in spite of the ritualistic debauch fuelled by cheap ale, and the famous four didn't reconvene until the degree congregation in July.

The campus of Birmingham University in Edgbaston, established in 1900, features a magnificent semicircle of red-brick domed blocks. The Aston Webb building is central to the design and houses the great hall with its impressive glass dome. Adjacent to that complex is the tallest freestanding clock tower in Europe, designed to mimic the town hall tower in Sienna. The clock at the summit of the tower is named "Old Joe" in memory of the Right Honourable Joseph Chamberlain, the founder of the university.

That day the medical and dental students together with the life scientists were to get their certificate confirming their graduation. They sat in rows according to their faculty and in alphabetical order. Their proud parents were allowed one guest, and all sat on the elevated rows of seats at the back of the hall.

All the students had hired a black cap and gown, with their faculty identified by the colour of the silk band that ran round the edge of the hood of the gown. The "cap" for bachelors was a mortar board, and was worn by medical students who graduated MB, ChB (Bachelor of Medicine and bachelor of surgery). More elaborate headgear was the sign of those postgraduates who would be called up first to receive their doctorates.

The event was well rehearsed, and each student was to walk up smartly when their name was called by the dean of their faculty, doff their cap to the chancellor and receive their parchment scroll bound with a red ribbon. The chancellor was an honorary appointment that had been held for many years by Sir Anthony Eden. This year Sir Anthony performed his duty sitting in a grand neo-Gothic cathedra. Many of the new medical graduates, fresh from their studies, couldn't help noticing that Sir Anthony was jaundiced. In truth he was still recovering from surgery to the bile ducts that had gone wrong.

Peter Baring turned his head around and just caught sight of his parents together with Fiona. Sitting next to them were the proud parents of Mathew along with Rebecca KaMinxy, Mathew's fiancée. Somewhere in the crowd would be the parents of Dylan with his fiancée, Bronwen, who had been primed to look after Alastair's mother, who was reluctantly attending the congregation on her own.

As each student walked off the stage with scroll in hand, they were navigated to a dark room just off the corridor to have their picture taken. The assumption was that all parents would want a framed photograph of their child to stand on the mantelpiece to show off to their friends. Once the individual pictures were taken and the medical school class of 1960 were all gathered together, the photographer took a group photograph and then a cliché picture for the local newspapers showing the graduates throwing their mortar boards in the air.

Formalities complete, the famous four made their way to one of the marquees to meet up with their families who were already tucking into cucumber sandwiches, cupcakes, and tea. The parents greeted each other with awkward kisses on cheeks. The foreign habit of cheek kissing was just taking root thanks to package tours to Europe. When Peter was introduced to Ginger's mother, Lily Bannerman, he was charming as ever without a hint of patronisation. Whilst telling her how proud she should be of her son, he was subtly summing her up. Alastair had already confided that he was born "out of wedlock" when his mother was only 18; that meant she was now 41. She looked about 10 years older, scrawny and underfed, worry lines wrinkling what would have been a pretty face, dry hair simply tied back in a ponytail, but still attractive because of her wide dark eyes and the spark of intelligence dancing in the sunlight.

Lily was flattered by the interest of this handsome young man and started to enjoy the event. In fact, she realised she had never felt so happy since her old man had died. Ginger stood back and was delighted to note his mother melting thanks to the charm of his good friend.

★ ★ ★

Come 1 August, the new graduates became housemen. Patients should do their best not to be in hospital on 1 August when the junior staff change over and as a result mistakes are made. Things were made worse by the fact the consultants were on holiday either in the Caribbean or their second home in Cornwall. Peter was offered the prize posting as house officer to the academic unit headed by Professor Iain McGregor. It is to be noted that most professors of surgery in England were of Scottish extraction. The reason was that professors in England, paid by the university, were not allowed to supplement their income with private practice. Furthermore, there had been little private practice in Scotland since the NHS was introduced.

Mathew, Dylan, and Alastair all got jobs in one of the two teaching hospitals, the QE in Edgbaston or the General on Steelhouse Lane in the city. They all switched round from surgery to medicine or medicine to surgery after six months. For the best of that time, they never saw anything of the outside world, working day and night, always on call and living in the austere doctors' quarters. At least they had free meals and lodgings but were only paid £700 a year. Peter was denied a double bed and only got to see his wife one Saturday a month.

The only thing that saved their sanity was the camaraderie, a bit like the spirit of the Blitz as they were all in it together. The doctor's mess at the QE had a bar and Dr Ginger Bannerman painted a perfect reproduction of a hanging pub sign with a coat of arms. It was called "The Nurses Arms". At the general hospital in the city there was nowhere comfortable for the housemen to relax, so they made use of the White Swan on the corner of Steelhouse Lane. There were 18 wards in the hospital and, just like the golf links, the pub was known as the 19th ward. The hospital telephonists were in on the game and understood when any of the young doctors alerted them that they would be on ward 19 if needed for an emergency.

The year flew by, learning on the job, skilled at taking blood and setting up drips. Competent at inserting urethral catheters and removing drains from the chest. All these minor procedures were mostly taught by the ward sister. The most important learnt skill, was, to put it simply, learning to judge whether a patient was ill enough to call for help. This judgement was made by the colour of the skin, the patient's cognitive functions, the elasticity of the skin, the capillary response below the fingernail, and the chart that recorded pulse, blood pressure, temperature, and respiratory rate. This was complemented, if the patient had a catheter, by urinary output each hour. At the other extreme, when the patient was recovering, they enjoyed sitting down for a chat and learning of the lives of those who put their trust in the NHS. If they had done a good job above and beyond expectations, the best reward was an excellent reference from the consultant that would help them on their way.

Chapter 7

The parting of the way
1961

There was no postgraduate dean to advise and guide newly registered doctors on their future career, so it was left to their own resourcefulness to make decisions with informal advice from any consultant they found approachable during their undergraduate years or the paternalism of the consultants they served as housemen.

Alastair Bannerman had no doubts. His priority was to get his mother away from her frugal life in the squalor of the tenements of the Gorbals to a healthier environment where he could serve the local community as a general practitioner. So, he started his searches on the back pages of the *British Medical Journal* (BMJ), where the small adverts were to be found for employment in all the branches and seniority of the profession.

Dylan Baddams had no choice as Bronwen issued an ultimatum that if he didn't return to South Wales she would give back her engagement ring. What he would do in the land of his fathers was left to his imagination, so he kept his options open with the caveat that whatever he did there must be a first-class rugby football club as he fancied his chances of playing for Wales one day. He also kept his eyes on the small ads at the back of the BMJ.

Mathew Barnet was unsure what career he wanted to pursue: certainly not surgery but something like general medicine or psychiatry. He therefore applied for an SHO appointment in general medicine at the city general hospital, keeping his options open.

Peter Baring had no doubts. He wanted to be a professor of surgery. He was not concerned about private practice as he and his wife would in due course benefit from their inheritances. Moreover, Peter had a genuine enquiring mind and had little respect for relying on *authority* to determine decision-making after his experience with Mr Morgan Duffield. In this way it was easy to share the mindset of Professor Iain McGregor. The good professor was flattered to be asked for advice and happy to plan the route to augment the chance of Peter fulfilling his laudable ambition. The milestones were laid down:

- Study for part 1 of the FRCS whilst acting as a demonstrator in the Anatomy Department.
- Spend a year as an SHO in the A&E department at the General.
- Work as a junior registrar in one of the respected surgical units in the West Midlands whilst studying for his final FRCS.
- Work towards a doctorate, MD or PhD would do, whilst taking a furlough from clinical work that might also be a good time to get your BTA (Been To America) award.
- Then take a lectureship in an academic unit for two years after which he would be a perfect candidate for a senior lectureship and only then start applying for a chair in surgery. With any luck he would fulfil his ambition by the time he was 40.

But then, as Robert Burns would say, "The best laid schemes of mice and men go oft awry."

PART 2

Alastair Bannerman's story 1961–1965

Chapter 8

From Glasgow to Campbeltown

Alastair stepped down from the bus at the end of Battlefield Road, named after a battle where Mary, Queen of Scots, was defeated by James VI. He had just arrived off the train at Glasgow Central, having left Birmingham three hours earlier. He carried all his worldly possessions in one battered suitcase. He paused to look up to the darkening sky where he could make out the smoke-stained Victoria Infirmary, which carried awful memories of having his tonsils and adenoids removed as a child. He imagined the wards tightly packed in Nightingale fashion on both sides with barely room enough for a nurse to squeeze between them. These beds would surely be full of middle-aged men and women suffering from chronic bronchitis, lung cancer, premature heart attacks, and the ravages of late-stage cirrhosis of the liver. He turned north on Cumberland Street to catch the bus to the Gorbals to meet up with his mother. The Gorbals were bordered by black rat-ridden banks of the Clyde to the north. South was the railway jungle that spread out from the big Goods and Mineral Depot on Pollokshaws Road. The western end of the ward had the handsome classical terraces of Abbotsford Place and Warwick Street, the eastern end bounded by the lowering mid-Victorian tenements. Within these bounds lived some 40,000 shockingly housed people. He got off the bus at Caledonia Road and walked the last half mile up hill to the humble third-floor apartment where he had grown up, in Lawmoor Street. To say the Gorbals was a slum was an understatement; to add insult to injury, the shanty town looked more like a bomb site. The year 1961 was when the city council decided to pull down the Victorian tenements and rehouse the residents. Glasgow Corporation's replacement of old, outdated, and crowded housing with new high-rise towers of social housing in the 1960s greatly improved living conditions. Sadly this had unintended social consequences, as friendly neighbours were separated from each other in giant silos. Alastair was determined to save his mother from the current squalor and spare the isolation living on the 20th floor of a tower block where the lifts would give up under the effort of weightlifting 40,000 people a day.

Alastair was in town not only to see his mother to discuss his future but also en route for an interview for the position as a trainee in a general practice on the west coast of Scotland and with a healthier environment than the Gorbals. A recent news story that he had read in *The Guardian* reported that Glaswegians had a 30% higher risk of dying before they were 65 than people in comparable deindustrialised cities such as Liverpool and Manchester. They died from the big killers: cancer, heart disease, and strokes, as well as the "despair diseases" of drugs, alcohol, and suicide, all exacerbated by overcrowding. Medical care was just sticking a plaster over the wounds; the real problem was political, with inadequate housing and poorly funded social services.

★ ★ ★

In his youth he had been motivated to become a doctor by the writings of AJ Cronin, especially *The Citadel*, which described how poverty denied most patients adequate care and was considered an important stimulus for the post-war Labour Party to plan the NHS. For something more entertaining, Alastair chose to reread one of the other books by Cronin, *Dr Finlay's Case Book*. This was published in 1935 and he thought it might be fun to compare medical practice with a GP's experience in rural Scotland 25 years earlier. Dr Finlay was a young doctor who trained in the Glasgow and worked in a fictious small town, Tannochbrae, on the west coast of Scotland. The first and obvious difference were the anecdotes about Finlay and his senior partner, Cameron, getting paid by the tight-fisted local population. Many were dirt poor, and the good doctors either asked for a nominal sum of a penny or two, but some of the relatively wealthy on their list tried every trick of the trade in forgetting to pay their medical fees. The first comical story was about a fat and lazy lout who claimed he was paralysed below the waist following a bicycle accident and demanded compensation and a wheelchair. Dr Finlay discovered he was a fraud whilst Alastair recognised this as Munchausen syndrome, which had been described in the BMJ 10 years earlier.

The next story was tragic and described an elderly opera singer dying of pulmonary tuberculosis. This would not happen today 20 years after the first trial of streptomycin.

Then there was a story of a rancorous spinster suffering from influenza followed by pneumonia. The good Dr Finlay looked after her by daily visits and holding her hand at night until the fever broke. This reminded Alastair of his favourite painting that he once saw on a visit to the Tate Gallery in London. It was painted by Luke Fildes in 1901 and entitled *The Doctor*. It looks like a theatre scene, showing a kindly bearded doctor in his frock coat, leaning over a sick child asleep on a chair, holding her hand in the midnight hour whilst the poor humble parents look on in despair in the background. Although Alastair couldn't help himself loving this mawkish Edwardian painting, he confessed to himself that this doctor, for all his gravitas, was a charlatan with nothing but false reassurance for the parents. Assuming the child had pneumonia, we now had penicillin to offer, apart from the fact that the child might have avoided her near fatal condition by vaccination and a warm dry house.

The most remarkable case report was the story of Dr Finlay doing his first appendicectomy at the local cottage hospital, at a time when there was still a debate whether there was such a thing as "appendicitis". And so it carried on, with Alastair feeling more and more smug, until he came to a case of ocular melanoma and conceded there had been little progress since 1935 in looking for a cure for cancer. Dr Bannerman was determined to keep his own casebook, not as a collection of stories but as a scientific effort to embark on his interest in epidemiology.

★ ★ ★

Alastair knocked on the door of the humble home and his mother, on opening it, squealed with delight. She had not seen him since graduation day, although he phoned her once a week. During his year as a houseman, he had little chance of visiting Glasgow let alone sufficient money to pay for the train. He wanted his visit to be a surprise so as not to pre-empt her response to his exciting news. Sitting down to a cup of tea and shortcake biscuits, Alastair explained the reason for his unexpected visit. He had been browsing the small ads in the back pages of the BMJ and came across a vacancy that intrigued him. A GP practice was looking for a trainee in Campbeltown on the southern tip of the Kintyre peninsula. On the map this looks like a flaccid phallus hanging down from the west coast of Scotland, but he didn't share that observation with his mother. The salary offered was only £750 a year, but the job came with a flat over the shop and the cost of living in this remote area was much less than Glasgow.

He was on his way for an interview and was thinking she might be interested in joining him there for a better quality of life. Lily Bannerman's eyes lit up and she smiled in a way to expose the latent prettiness of her face. "Oh, my darlin' bairn, how could I refuse that offer? I could start life afresh. Since your father died, despite his drinking and temper tantrums, I miss his company. To confess the truth, I'm lonely. With the tearing down of the Gorbals I'm losing many of my friends who don't want to live in high-rise flats. I hear that the folk in Argyll and Bute are warm at heart and I might find work to add to your income and we might be able to live in comfort without constant fear of visits by the bailiffs."

That settled it for Alastair, assuming he got the job, but he felt confident that an invitation for an interview all this way from the Midlands was an encouraging omen. The next day he busied himself making preparations. He opened a bank account at the nearby branch of the Bank of Scotland and at the same time they agreed for him to take out a loan as he needed to buy a car. His certification as a medical man served as a recommendation and he gave the names of his best friends to act as guarantors. He then went round to a garage owned by the father of his best friend at school, who found him a Hillman Husky shooting brake in good condition that had, honestly, been driven by an old lady with only 15,000 miles on the clock. That cost him almost as much as his first year's salary but would be paid off to the bank in instalments, plus interest, over the next five years.

To his surprise his mother begged to join him on this adventure, as she hadn't had a holiday in years, so they set out with overnight bags after the rush hour with the idea of spending the night before his interview at a B&B in Campbeltown.

The first leg of the journey was uneventful: the sun was shining, and they shared beautiful views of the bonnie, bonnie banks of Loch Lomond on the eastern side of the A82, driving due north. Towards the north tip of Loch Lomond, they turned west on the A83, crossing Loch Long and entering the Trossachs craggy hills and distant views of mountains. Then their troubles started. The Hillman Husky was acting like a breathless old man, struggling to cope with the uphill sections of the road whilst the temperature of the radiator was starting to climb. They just made it to Inveraray as the A83 turned south at the tip of the long finger of the Firth of Clyde. They were in no mood to appreciate the beauty of this little town with a pretty shopping main street flanked by white shop fronts twinkling in the afternoon sun. Fortunately, they found a garage at the junction of the A83 and the road leading to the little harbour. The garage man, who introduced himself as Donald, was a jovial, bald, and obese old guy who spoke with a soft highland accent. As he lifted the hood of this sad old car, a cloud of steam shot up and Alastair assumed that this was a symptom of a mortal sickness. Donald quickly looked inside the engine once the cloud had drifted away and then, on lifting his head, noticed the signs of dismay on the face of his client. "Dinnae worry, laddie, who stole yer scone? It'll be a skoosh to fixit." He then pointed at the fan belt that wasn't there. His response, once translated by his mother, explained the problem was easy to fix: the car would need a new fan belt and then, once the engine had cooled down, he would refill the radiator and then he would be safe to continue his drive to the bonnie little town at the tip of the Mull of Kintyre. It took an hour to fix during which time mother and son found a charming little tea house to enjoy a pot of strong tea and excellent shortcake fingers.

During that time indoors they had not noticed the sky darkening as cumulonimbus clouds drifted in on a westerly wind. It was nearly 5.00pm before they were on their way again, driving downhill at the western edge of a long finger of water running down to the sea about 100km to the mouth of the Firth of the Clyde. Then the storm broke and blinding rods of rain hurtled down on the Hillman Husky. In a short space of time, it was almost impossible to see the road and a skid to the east lane would have them tumbling into deep water. Alastair slowed down and then searched for the switch to turn on the window wipers. To his horror, nothing happened after several attempts. Fortunately, in a classic car of this vintage there was a back-up device of two knobs that could be turned back and forth to move the wipers manually. Driving at only 20mph, with his mother working the window wipers, they limped into Campbeltown at 9.00pm and considered themselves lucky to find a pub overlooking the harbour that had two vacant rooms and a hot dinner.

★ ★ ★

The following morning Alastair was woken by the rising sun shining through the gap in the inadequate curtains over the dormer window in the attic of the Crown and Anchor. On drawing the blinds, the view was spectacular. From his high lookout he could see the hills of the Isle of Arran and the early-morning ferry leaving the dockyard just across the street. The storm had long past and the puddles on the pavement were sparkling as they reflected the low-level sunshine from the east. Fishermen's boats were returning with their early-morning catch and others leaving for a deeper dredge. The fishermen's boats had red painted hulls that shone brightly against the backdrop of an ultramarine sea and a cobalt sky. There and then the young doctor determined to pick up his paintbrushes again, having given up painting since starting his third year at medical school. He suddenly felt ravenously hungry, having caught the smell of frying kippers. When he was washed and dressed in the suit he bought for the interview, he jumped down the stairs two at a time nearly knocked over the landlord's daughter, who was acting as a waitress. He found that his mother had pre-empted him and was already tucking into a steaming bowl of porridge. Taking the empty chair next to her at the little wooden table, he had a quick look at the menu and without looking up ordered porridge and a pair of grilled kippers. His mother looked happier and more animated than he could remember and agreed that the view was bonnie and that her son also looked bonnie in his brand-new suit. After a hearty breakfast Alastair and his mother were energised enough to explore Campbeltown, so he summoned the waitress over to pay the bill. This time he looked up and was stricken with a bolt of lightning or a hot tipped arrow from the bow of Cupid.

The landlord's daughter was stunningly beautiful, about 18 years old, with wide eyes the colour of the morning sky, shaded by long thick eyelashes, white flawless skin and lustrous black hair flowing down over her long neck. He was struck dumb and handed over his cash together with a generous tip. This provoked a smile that displayed a perfect set of iridescent white teeth that melted his heart. He staggered backwards out of the breakfast room, knocking chairs over on his way and provoking laughter from the young bonnie lassie.

Once they were outside his mother expressed concern at his panic-stricken behaviour. That he explained away as nervousness before his interview later that morning. Left with an hour to play with, they decided to explore the little town.

Nothing could take away the beauty of the seascape or the emerald-green rolling hills that surrounded them, but they couldn't ignore the down at heel appearance of the buildings lining the port and the shops along the main street, some of which were boarded up. Originally the town had been prosperous, with shipbuilding, fishing, dairy farming and, most of all, its fame as a centre of whisky distilleries. Campbeltown was the centre of whisky smuggling in the early 17th century but started legally making whisky in the early 19th century. By 1890 it had a bustling legal industry, with nearly 30 distilleries and a population of about 2,000. It was reputed to be the richest town in Britain per capita. Sadly, with the recession and the prohibition of alcohol in the USA in the 1920s, most of the distilleries had closed down, leaving only two, Springbank and Glen Scotia, active in the 1960s. The shipbuilding industry had failed, but there was still a lively fishing industry and the dairy farming up in the surrounding hills was still providing milk and cream to most of south-west Scotland. Despite this, there were still landmarks from the good old days. There was the hideous black Lorne and Lowland Church with its disproportionate tall tower, a beautiful white town hall looking like a church with a spire built to mimic St Martin's in the Field in Trafalgar Square, and, curiously, a well-preserved art deco "Wee Picture House" cinema built in 1913.

Mother and son reached their destination on Main Street with 10 minutes to spare. The only way of identifying the surgery amongst the row of flat-fronted brick-and-granite building was the brass plate on the wall by the door.

Dr Walter Campbell MB, BS Cantab
Dr Colin Campbell MB, ChB Edinburgh

Their names were very appropriate, and Alastair had already discovered they were father and son. He rang the bell and a large man about the age of 50, wearing a three-piece tweed suit, opened the door instantly. Alastair was taken by surprise, having expected the door to be opened by a receptionist, and this bear of a man must be Dr Campbell junior. With a booming voice the ursine character said, "Dr Bannerman, I presume, but who is this charming young woman standing by your side?" Alastair's mother blushed with pleasure not just at the compliment but simply by being noticed as a woman.

"This is my mother, Dr Campbell, who has accompanied me all the way from Glasgow. May she sit in the waiting room during my interview?"

"With pleasure laddie. Would you like a cup of tea and a shortbread biscuit, Mrs Bannerman?" Without waiting for a reply, he led them into a mahogany-walled room with the floor covered with copies of hunting and fishing journals and a random collection of antique and overstuffed armchairs, more like a gentleman's club than a medical establishment.

Facing them there was a counter for the receptionist and a stack of NHS note folders in disarray but no sign of a receptionist. To the left side of the counter were two doors with brass plaques reading "Dr Walter Campbell" and "Dr Colin Campbell". On the other side was the entrance to a corridor. "Just wait here for a wee moment until my father arrives and we can begin the interview." With that Dr Colin disappeared down the corridor. Ten minutes later he returned with a tray bearing a pot of tea, four cups, a jug of milk, and a plate of biscuits, followed by an elderly man, with grey hair and ruddy cheeks, somewhat bent over, looking as if in his late 70s and also wearing a tweed three-piece suit. Without doubt this had to be Dr Walter Campbell. After introductions all round they settled down for tea and biscuits.

Once tea was drunk and shortbread consumed, very much to the bewilderment of Alastair, the interview began in the presence of his mother. It was conducted by Campbell junior, with nods and grunts from Campbell senior.

"Doctor Bannerman, I'll come straight to the point and be perfectly honest with you. You are the only candidate and, after you hear what I have to say, you might decide to return to Glasgow, and I would fully understand. GPs in the NHS receive a capitation fee for each patient who registers with them, and they have to meet the costs of running the practice out of those fees. The population of this town is shrinking and many of our young folk can't find jobs and are leaving us for the big cities. As our list of patients shrinks, so does our income shrink. My father is close to retirement and our last junior partner left a year ago because we couldn't increase his salary. The same happened to our receptionist, who recently got married and she and her new husband went to Edinburgh for better-paid jobs. All we can afford is a very modest bursary of £750.00 a year plus free lodgings upstairs above this room. Of course, if you do well and our list grows, then my father can retire, and you could become a salaried partner. There is talk of opening a new distillery and the Scottish touring board have started featuring the Kintyre as a perfect holiday venue for those who like boating, fishing, grouse shooting, and golf. A new golf link has just been opened on the west coast only 20 minutes away. What do you have to say?"

Before Alastair had thought it through and was ready to respond, he was alarmed when his mother intervened. "Dr Campbell, I worked as a receptionist at an optician in Glasgow and I can take dictation and type. I'd be happy to work for you for as little as £350.00 a year but first I would have to approve the living conditions."

The two Doctors Campbell fell about with laughter at her effrontery and Alastair didn't know whether to laugh or cry. "Mrs Bannerman, that is a very generous offer that we will consider seriously but first we need to know whether your son will take the doctor's job," responded Dr Walter Campbell turning his gaze on Alastair, who instantly replied with a big smile on his face, "Yes please sir." The two Doctors Campbell nodded at each other and led the way along the corridor and up the stairs. The apartment above the practice was bigger, brighter, and better equipped than the Bannermans might have hoped for. There were two bedrooms, one with a double bed and another a single. There was a decent-sized bathroom and a kitchen well equipped with an oven, fridge, and dishwasher. The cupboards were full of dishes and the drawers full of cutlery. Finally, there was a comfortable sitting room with a nice view of Main Street, armchairs with coloured cushions and even a relatively new TV.

Lily Bannerman looked on with puzzlement for a while and then the penny dropped; turning to Colin Campbell, she said, "There's something I don't understand, this lovely flat has the touch of a woman; who was last to live here?"

"You're very observant, Mrs Bannerman. My wife and I lived here until a year ago, when she died in a boating accident. I couldn't face living here alone, so I moved in with my father, who has the big family home near Machrihanish on the west coast."

There was no more to say and there and then Campbeltown acquired a new doctor and a new receptionist, and everyone was happy.

Chapter 9

Dr Bannerman's case book

Alastair and his mother started work at the Campbells' surgery the second week of September 1961. Lily Bannerman had demonstrated a metamorphosis from larva to butterfly. She had bought herself a second-hand navy-coloured suit with a pencil skirt, a new white blouse, and shoes with heels, and had applied make-up for the first time that her son could remember. Although aged 42 she looked 10 years younger. They had breakfast together in flat upstairs with victuals that Lily had bought on her first shopping expedition the day before. What with all this and the monthly payment for the Hillman, they were probably overdrawn at the local bank, but for the first time ever she was not worried as the household income was nearly £100 a month. Mother and son went downstairs at 8.00am to sort things out for their first surgery, which would start at 9.00am. Looking at his mother standing behind the counter, creating order out of the disarray of patients notes, Dr Bannerman felt very proud and for a moment lost his self-control, allowing a tear or two to dampen his cheek bones. On entering Dr Campbell senior's consulting room, the first thing he saw had him in a fit of laughter. It was an embroidery in a frame that you might expect to declaim a verse from the Gospels but instead carried this comical rhyme.

> *Dr Bell fell down the well and broke her collar bone.*
> *Doctors should attend the sick and leave the well alone.*

It was funny but in fact was the counterpoint to his

philosophy. In Glasgow the "well" didn't attend doctors and died young and he was determined to improve the health of the community rather than sticking plasters over the cracks. At this point he had no idea that within the next 12 months two NHS interventions would bolster his beliefs.

The schedule he had agreed to was as follows. He would attend morning surgery between 9.00am and 12.30pm Monday to Friday and afternoon surgery between 4.30pm and 6.00pm four days a week, with Wednesday as a half day. Apart from Wednesday he would spend the afternoon hours before the evening surgery doing house calls in town and within the nearby countryside. He would be on call every other weekend and would be allowed four weeks' holiday a year, covered by Dr Campbell senior, who was in semi-retirement.

Just before 9.00am he peaked round the door and was alarmed to see the waiting room full but then remembered that Dr Campbell junior was also going to share the workload. At that very moment his senior colleague burst through the front doors and warmly greeted the assembly, who replied in unison, "Good morning, Dr Campbell!" Instead of going to his consulting room he nearly pushed Alastair on the floor as he bulldozed into the room.

"Welcome to your first clinic, laddie. If you have any questions or doubts just press this button under the desk just here; it'll buzz in my room, and I'll pop in within a moment or two. This other button on the desktop is to call in your next patient. They'll come in the right order as they have been trained not to jump queues. Your mother will register them when they arrive and with any luck she might even find the patients' notes amongst the mess we've left behind. She'll take all the telephone calls and share out the afternoon house calls. Finally, if you and your mother survive the first day, we will gather in my room at 6.00pm for a wee dram or two." Without waiting for a response, he barged his way out and Dr Bannerman pressed the button on his desk, heard the buzzer outside, and welcomed his first patient, who timidly entered through the dust cloud left behind by his colleague.

In preparation for this moment Alastair had provided himself with a sturdily bound notebook to make a start on his project of recording the details of the four major causes of death in Scotland: lung cancer, cardio-vascular disease, cerebra-vascular disease, and the consequences of alcoholism. In the clinics that day he scored zero. In fact, he came to the opinion that learning medicine in a large city hospital was no place to teach a GP. Going from top to toe he listed a selection of cases he saw on his first day.

- Head lice in the hair of a 12-year-old child who lived in a caravan.
- A foreign body in the ear of a three-year-old child that turned out to be a dried pea.
- A sore throat and a nasal drip in a neurotic old lady.
- Abdominal distension in a fat old man with constipation (his notes described that he presented with this problem three times a year).
- Two patients with haemorrhoids.
- One woman with something "down there" who demanded to be seen by a lady doctor.
- One very old man who couldn't bend down to cut his nails and had developed onychogryphosis of both great toenails. In English that meant the nails looked like the horns of a griffin.

For most cases he had to buzz his boss and for the woman who would only see a lady doctor he called in his mother who instantly picked on what was happening and examined the lady behind a screen. His mother was able to reassure her that it was only a sebaceous cyst of the vulva, having experienced the same nodule herself a year ago.

His boss was very tolerant of his young apprentice and reassured him he'd pick it up quickly learning on the job.

His experiences on his home visits were more rewarding.

The first call was from a farmhouse up in the hills near the village of Stewarton. The view on the short drive was spectacular and the patient delightful. Tom Goodwin had been called up as a young man in 1918 and got into the habit of smoking the cheap cigarettes dished out to them along with their rations. After demob he was addicted to nicotine and smoking 40 a day. At the relatively early age of 65 he started to suffer from intermittent claudication because of poor blood flow to the lower leg. It progressed to gangrene of the left foot that required a below knee amputation. He apologised for not hopping down to the surgery, but he couldn't get his prosthetic leg on the stump because of a painful ulcer. Fortunately, Alastair was well prepared, and his doctor's bag carried dressings and an emollient cream. Whilst he was there, he thought he might as well check up on the old soldier. He was alarmed to note that the pulse in the right carotid artery was missing and that he was at risk of a stroke. He had recently read a paper in *The Lancet* that aspirin had anti-platelet activity and might be of value for preventing blood clots in the narrowed arteries of those suffering from atherosclerosis. He explained all this to the old soldier who agreed to be a "guinea pig". This was to be the first patient in Dr Bannerman's case book. Patient and doctor became firm friends, and the doctor was rewarded with a pint of best cream from the farm's dairy.

The afternoon clinic was very much the repeat of the morning clinic, with one unpleasant experience. The last man in at just before 6.00pm was a scrawny and filthy man, aged about 50, who stank of alcohol and demanded a sick note so he could go a watch the Glasgow Rangers the next day. Alastair refused on a matter of principle and the miscreant drew a knife and bellowed some expletives at the young doctor. The noise was heard by his colleague next door, who burst through the door yelling, "Not you again you idle idiot, put that knife down and get the fuck out of my sight or I'll have you locked up in the pokey before you can say Jack MacRobinson." He then grabbed the man's hand with the knife and twisted his arm behind his back before marching him to the door and literally threw him down the steps.

Wiping his hands on the back of his trousers, he turned to Alastair and said, "That's Tiger Taggart. He's a lazy layabout and gets violent when drunk. Take nae notice of him; he's a softy who never draws blood. You must be a bit shaken so gather your mother and join me for a wee dram of a 12-year-old Glen Scotia."

Lily Bannerman had just finished tidying up and had witnessed the fracas, thinking that Dr Campbell junior had just saved the life of her son. Shaking with alarm with her face drained of blood, she followed her son into the consulting room. Colin Campbell had his back to her, carefully pouring an amber liquid into a cut-glass tumbler. On turning round, he did a double take, and his ruddy complexion turned a deeper shade of red. Turning to Alastair, he said, "Dr Bannerman, is this your sister I see before me?" Lily's skin turned from white to pink in a blink of the eye; this was the first time in 20 years that a man had offered a compliment. All three burst out laughing as Dr Campbell toasted his new friends.

Alastair's days settled into a comfortable routine whilst his mother developed a flirty relationship with her boss. But all work and no play were an unhealthy way of life even for a young doctor. The first thing he did was to join the town's football club. They trained every Wednesday afternoon and he found himself in demand as a striker, so he played in the team every other Saturday when he was off duty. Every Wednesday evening after training a group of the team dropped into the Crown and Anchor pub for a pint of beer. Each time Alastair was disappointed not to see the landlord's daughter again. After some discreet enquiries he learnt that she was studying economics at Edinburgh University. His other recreation was to take his mother to the Wee Picture House once a week and occasionally they were joined by Colin Campbell.

★ ★ ★

Christmas and New Year 1961–1962 brought about some important developments in Dr Bannerman's professional and social life. To begin with the weather changed for the worse. Living on the coast in south-west Scotland you could expect the Atlantic storms drifting in from the west to hit their first landfall with fury, so gales and torrential rainfall was expected but snowfall of up to 14 inches on Christmas Eve was exceptional. The consequences were threefold for a GP working on the Kintyre peninsula. Firstly, the elderly and poverty-stricken men and women couldn't keep warm and there was a breakout of influenza and bronchial pneumonia. Many died consequently. The cold weather also provoked heart attacks for the elderly venturing outside to shovel the snow off the path. Next there was an epidemic of trauma. The ice on the road was traitorous and many falls ended up with fractures of the wrist and fractures of the hip.

Dr Bannerman found himself working all hours at the local cottage hospital, reducing Colles' fractures of the wrist and applying plaster of Paris. Fractures of the hip were beyond help and were in effect mortal injuries. Flying the patient to the Victoria hospital in Glasgow for a surgical pin and plate was unrealistic in the foul weather, so the elderly were confined to bed and least 50% of them died with hypostatic pneumonia.

Finally, because it was dangerous for many patients locally, and more so up in the hills, to make the journey to the surgery, the calls for home visits were overwhelming.

Dr Campbell senior came out of his semi-retirement to man all the clinics for those who could make it to the surgery, whilst the other two doctors were worked off their feet. The clapped-out Hillman owned by Dr Bannerman died a rusty death but the community got together to rent him a sturdy new Land Rover with extra-large tyres.

Despite all that, the hills and houses looked beautiful in the covering of snow, like a Christmas card. Festivities were cancelled, although many of the hardy Presbyterian faithful made it to the Lorne and Lowland Church for midnight mass.

Fortunately, the weather settled, and temperature rose above freezing point for Hogmanay to be celebrated in the traditional manner. The Campbeltown football club had organised a party in the function's room of the first floor of the Crown and Anchor, and Janet, the landlord's daughter, down for the holidays from Edinburgh, was at hand to serve the drinks and serve the haggis, neeps, and tatties.

One of the team began to molest the bonnie young lassie only to wake up on the floor having been knocked out by a punch to the jaw from Alastair Bannerman. Young Janet made a cute little curtsy to her saviour and ran out of the room in tears.

Chapter 10

Campbeltown
1962–1965

The years 1962–1965 were momentous in the evolution of the NHS as a contradiction for the comical injunction embroidered by decorative needlework in a frame above the fireplace in Dr Bannerman's consulting room. He was to treat the *well* with preventative interventions in the name of public health. These were the offer of the Sabin oral polio vaccine, the contraceptive pill offered *almost* free on the NHS for married couples, and the introduction of cervical screening in the prevention of cancer of the cervix. All three were controversial in one way or the other and each added to the burden of the GP. Yet to Alastair they provided interesting challenges and indirectly increased the numbers on their list of patients thus increasing the income of the practice.

The Sabin vaccine was a live attenuated virus that could easily be delivered to all children as a drop of fluid on a cube of sugar. At first parents were frightened off by the idea of a live vaccine but, with leaflets put out by the NHS and endorsed by their trusted family doctors, the population accepted this gift of science. The pictures of wards full of young patients in "iron lungs" were not easy to forget and the schools and playgrounds still being peppered with children or young adults walking with callipers supporting their legs were a constant reminder that prevention was better than the cures. The Campbell practice was allotted the role of vaccinating all the eligible children on the Kintyre peninsula. The vaccine had to be stored in a large refrigerator and only Campbeltown had that facility. To get the job done efficiently, Alastair gave up his half day and parents with children queued out in the street every Wednesday afternoon until the job was done.

The offer of the contraceptive pill provoked all sorts of arguments both religious and philosophical. These debates were conducted mostly by men on behalf of their womenfolk in the misogynist culture of that time. When it comes to sex, the religious hierarchy "get their knickers in a twist"! It's as if the fact that sexual intercourse, a necessary activity for the continuation of our species, happens to be pleasurable to such an extent that it must be a sin.

The Catholic Church had no doubts: oral contraception was not allowed and if confessed to the priest in his box behind the grill would be punished with a lot of Hail Marys and the threat of hell fires in the afterlife. The response of the Church of Scotland was ambiguous and involved a list of conditions that made it acceptable. The Anglican church was confused but agreed that it was a medical decision rather than the business of the clerics, although it was still in favour of virtue and fornication out of wedlock was still a sin. The *Daily Telegraph* and the *Manchester Guardian* were at loggerheads as if the pill was a political football in the game of right wing versus left wing. Most women were in favour of the pill and that, surprisingly, included some Anglican orders of nuns, who had witnessed again and again the tragedies of failed abortions of unwanted bastard children. In theory this development would make no difference to the incidence of children born out of wedlock but it soon became apparent to the GPs that many unmarried girls would borrow or buy a golden band to place on their fourth finger of their left hand. Most doctors turned a blind eye to this deception.

The emergence of the pill in Scotland also represented a distinctive example of patient consumerism within the NHS. The pill was the first drug given to a healthy population and first drug that required a modest sum of one shilling per prescription. Also, for the first time, instead of going to the doctor with a problem, thousands of women quickly turned to their GPs "demanding" a solution to their family planning tribulations. This altered the dynamic of the patient–practitioner relationship, which, in turn, resulted in a significant number of medical professionals resisting their new role in family planning. This was particularly heightened in Scotland, where many social and institutional barriers remained in place to restrict access to prescription contraceptives. Thus, healthy, contraceptive-seeking women entered into a negotiation with medical professionals, many of whom viewed themselves as judges of "deserving" and "undeserving" pill-takers.

The Campbell practice had no religious or ethical concerns about handing our prescriptions for the oral contraceptive. Quite the opposite: as a public health measure it made a lot of sense. Nevertheless, setting up the service required a lot of thought and diplomacy. Dr Campbell senior therefore set up an office conference for the three doctors and their receptionist. There were two conflicting issues to manage. On the one hand was the pressure on the practice by the patients playing the role of consumers demanding their rights, yet on the other hand there would be many women who would benefit from the pill being too embarrassed to approach the doctors or denied this freedom by domineering husbands. In the end they reached an elegant solution. All the women on the list under the age of 50 would be posted a form to complete with tick boxes about their health status and previous pregnancies. They would also offer an NHS leaflet describing the benefits and potential harms of the pill and a telephone number to book appointments to see the practice receptionist in confidence at an evening clinic on Tuesdays and Thursdays. These clinics would take place between the hours of 6.30 and 8.30pm and would be manned by Colin Campbell on Tuesdays and Alastair Bannerman on Thursday. Lily Bannerman would see all the clients first and, if there were no obvious counter-indications, pop next door for the doctor to prescribe the pill.

If there were any problems Lily would chaperone the client as she took them into the consulting room.

Although this would be an unrewarded task, they correctly predicted that when the word got out their list of patients would expand to a point they could increase the salaries for Alastair and Lily Bannerman. The plan worked wonders and within a few days their books were full for the next month or so.

Shortly before the Easter holidays, a drama played itself out one Thursday evening.

At 8.20pm, Lily knocked on the door of her son's room and let herself in with a worried look on her face, carrying a patient's file. "Alastair, I'm worried about this young lassie. She's in good health but unmarried and I suspect she is being coerced to take the pill. She is a bit tearful and has a heavy layer of make-up on her face that fails to hide a black eye; is there any way we can help her without breaking trust?"

After a minute or two of deliberation, a proverbial light bulb flashed above his head. "Tell her that all our clients need their blood pressure read and the doctor will see her now." Whilst waiting for the young lady to be ushered in, he took a quick look at her notes. Her name was Miss J. O'Connor, DOB 02/08/1942, with an address on the quayside. The only entries in her notes were the dates of her vaccinations against TB and smallpox. When his mother brought the young lady through his consulting room door, Alastair was overcome with multiple emotions that left him dumb for a moment. First, he thought himself an idiot for not realising that this was Janet the landlord's daughter; secondly, a sense of jealousy that this young bonnie lassie was already having sexual relations with a boyfriend; and, third, a sense of fury to note that she had a black eye badly concealed by a layer of cosmetics. He quickly controlled his emotions and introduced himself with a smile. "Welcome to my humble clinic. I see that you have a clean bill of health in your notes, and I just need to measure your blood pressure before prescribing the pill. By the way, is that a black eye you've got under the make-up? How did this happen?"

Blushing furiously, she replied, "Oh it's nothing, doctor, I just tripped on the doorsteps of the Crown and Anchor and fell on my face." Nodding as if satisfied, Alastair pulled the sphygmomanometer and rolled of the sleeve of cardigan. As predicted, he immediately saw the stigmata of thumb and finger bruises on her wrist and upper arm, confirming his suspicion that the visit was by coercion by a violent partner.

Without a word he exchanged looks with Miss O'Connor, who broke down in floods of tears and without restraint accepted the hugs of comfort from Lily, who gently steered her out of the consulting room and up the stairs to their living room. After a strong cup of tea, the appalling story burst through Janet's shell of self-control. Her father was a drunkard and most evenings after ringing the bell and bellowing out "time gentlemen please" he reverted his behaviour to that of a primitive ape. In Janet's absence at university, his wife suffered abuse but, when she was home during the vacations, he turned his attentions to her. It had now reached the point that his violence had progressed to sexual abuse and attempts at rape. He threatened to kill her if she told anyone about these happenings and he was too strong to fight off and so far out of control that he could easily fulfil his threat. Lily asked her to stay put as she and the good doctor would come up with a plan to deal with this evil man.

She then trotted downstairs and entered her son's consulting room, white of face and wet with tears. On hearing the story, Alastair nearly exploded with fury and disgust. Once he had calmed down, they agreed on the only possible way of dealing with this tragic situation. The two of them returned to their sitting room, where they found Janet had gained her self-control and was sitting on the edge of the sofa ready to hear what they had to say. Alastair was first to speak. "There is no way you can go back and face your father. If this story gets out, you will not be able to look people in their faces even though you are the innocent victim. Furthermore, if he finds out that you've spoken to strangers about his criminal conduct, he could indeed thrash out and cause you severe bodily harm. Do you have any relatives you could stay with and could trust to keep secret the reason you are running away from home?"

Janet answered immediately, "Yes, my mother's sister, Auntie Kate. She knows how violent my father can be and treats me like a daughter as she has no children of her own."

"Where does she live?" asked Lily and Alastair in unison.

"She lives in Belfast in a nice little house up in the hills looking over the docks."

Mother and son stood aside and conferred in whispers and with a nod, Lily turned to the girl and offered their solution. "Janet, my dear, this is what we suggest. Phone your Auntie Kate and say you would like to spend the rest of your vacation with her. Spend the night with us; we can easily make up a bed on the sofa. You and I are about the same size so I can put together a change of clothes and underwear and give you an old wash bag with a collection of toiletries. You will then take the first ferry to Belfast from the docks you face from the Crown and Anchor." She then turned to her son, who continued, "As far as your father is concerned, my partner, Colin Campbell, who can look like a prize fighter if he chooses, will accompany me for a chat with your dad. We will inform him that his daughter is in safe hands and warn him that, if this story gets out, we will report him to the police of being guilty of sexual abuse and grievous bodily harm. That will put him in the slammer for about six years, if I remember correctly."

And so it came to pass. Alastair accompanied her to the ferry terminal to catch the 7.30am Kintyre Express to Ballycastle on the Antrim coast, a bus ride away from Belfast.

As he waved his goodbye, he realised they would never meet again and was broken-hearted.

★ ★ ★

Over the next three years, the practice flourished. The exemplary way Alastair organised the polio vaccine and prescriptions for the pill enhanced applications to sign up from the whole length of the Kintyre peninsula. The reopening of two dormant distilleries attracted families from all over Scotland and the opening of a golf club with beautiful greens running along the west coast of the Mull of Kintyre attracted tourists from all over the world. Some of these tourists were wealthy Americans who added to their scant list of private patients. This was just as well: when cervical screening was introduced, they would be able to afford to appoint a practice nurse. All that aside, there was one case alone that would profoundly impact on Dr Bannerman's future.

In the early summer of 1962, he had a call from the cottage hospital from one of the midwives. She wouldn't explain what the problem was but sounded agitated and tearful, so he made this the visit after morning surgery. The midwife, Sister Anne, was from a nearby convent of the Anglican church. She was wringing her hands in distress and guided Alastair to a cot in a side ward where a tightly swaddled new-born baby was screaming to be fed. Sister Anne lifted the tiny bairn and unwrapped the bundle. She broke down in tears as she laid her burden on the nursery table. It took a moment or two to sink in before Alastair understood the midwife's despair. There was an absence of arms and in their place were two flippers attached to the baby's shoulders. Although never seen before, he recognised the syndrome and confirmed the diagnosis after reading the mother's notes. The association between the drug thalidomide and these deformities was reported in *The Lancet* in 1961. She had been prescribed thalidomide for morning sickness early in her pregnancy shortly before it had been withdrawn from use in the UK. Fortunately, the drug had not been prescribed by one of the doctors in his practice but that was of little comfort. Although it was not his responsibility, he agreed to accompany sister Anne with the baby to reveal and explain the deformities.

The mother was a young lass with an Ulster accent urgently waiting to empty her engorged breasts. When she saw the wee bairn, she screamed out loud and refused to offer her breast to the hungry new-born or speak to the doctor and midwife. Alastair had a heavy day ahead of him but promised to call again after the evening surgery. All the rest of the day he was haunted by the sight he'd left behind, wondering how the young mother would be able to raise her child without the help of the state. When he returned that evening, she was still inconsolable, but her husband sitting by the bed demonstrated more self-control and looked blankly at Dr Bannerman. It transpired that he was a newcomer to Campbeltown working at the Longrow distillery who hadn't yet registered with a GP. This was his first child and a doctor in Belfast had prescribed the thalidomide. Alastair took him aside and promised he would act as their GP and the best he could offer might be some compensation from the NHS. Although he would never regret that promise, it launched him on a clash with the Department of Health and the start of his political career.

Enoch Powell returned to the Conservative Party government in July 1960, when he was appointed health minister and became a member of the Cabinet until 1962. One of his first tasks on taking office was to deal with the thalidomide tragedy. During meetings with parents of babies that had been born with deformities caused by the drug thalidomide, he was unsympathetic to the victims, refusing to meet any babies affected by the drug. Powell also refused to launch a public inquiry, and resisted calls to issue a warning against any left-over thalidomide pills that might remain in people's medicine cabinets. Furthermore, he saw no reason why the NHS should compensate the parents to help cover the costs of bringing up their baby, as this was the responsibility of the pharmaceutical company, Chemie Grunenthal, in Germany, or Distillers, who distributed the drug in the UK. The BMA was appalled by the attitude of the health minister and Dr Bannerman volunteered to be one of the representatives of the Scottish branch of the association, who would make up a delegation to challenge

Mr Powell in his Westminster den. They were treated with contempt and recommended that they galvanise their patients to take out a legal suit against Distillers.

On his return home, one of Alastair's first tasks was to join the Labour Party and become an activist, at a time the party was consolidating its power in Scotland.

PART 3

Dylan Baddams 1962–1965

Chapter 11

Caerphilly District Miners Hospital

Caerphilly Castle remains a pure example of 13th-century military architecture and is the largest castle in Wales (three times the size of Wales's modern-day stronghold and home of Welsh rugby, the Principality Stadium) and the second largest in Britain after Windsor Castle. To this day this citadel appears like some mythical castle floating in an enchanted lake, an effect oddly enhanced by the Civil War gunpowder that left the south-east tower at a precarious angle. In fact, Wales's very own Leaning Tower, even wonkier than that of Pisa, is probably the castle's best-loved feature. During the 1700s, Caerphilly began to grow into a market town, and during the 19th century, as the South Wales valleys underwent massive growth through industrialisation, so too the town's population grew. However, the expansion of the population in the 19th century was more to do with the increasing market for coal. In 1895 the Windsor Colliery Company started to sink two shafts to a depth of around 2018 feet (615m).

The first coal was raised in 1902, The workings were connected underground to the Universal Colliery in Senghenydd for ventilation purposes. On 1 June 1902, a platform collapsed in the mine, tipping nine men into 25 feet (8m) of water, which had gathered in the sump. Three escaped drowning by clinging onto floating debris, but the other six died. On 14 October 1913, Senghenydd suffered the worst mining disaster and the single worst industrial accident in Britain's history, when a gas explosion occurred, resulting in the loss of 439 lives. Many of the surviving miners went back to help their workmates who were either trapped or buried alive. That disaster is memorised by a deeply moving sculpture of a miner holding a Davy lamp rescuing an injured colleague in the village that bears the name of the stricken mine.

Other major collieries around Caerphilly, Llanbradach, Abertridwr, Bedwas, Ystrad Mynach, and Nantgarw, came into existence in the years leading up to the First World War, and the need for better hospital provision for the injured and sick miners of the district became apparent. The competing pressure on beds in the Cardiff Infirmary from the casualties of war made the need more apparent. In 1917 the workmen, as members of the East Glamorgan District of the South Wales Miners Federation (known as the Fed), decided to pay a weekly levy of one penny towards the setting up of their own cottage hospital. Ten thousand contributed to this levy and by 1923 they had raised enough money to buy an old mansion house and convert it into a "cottage hospital". The hospital employed its own nurses and domestic staff. Local GPs looked after some of the patients but the consultant surgeons, based in Cardiff and Newport hospitals, visited as required and received their fees accordingly. In 1930 the hospital became a maternity hospital for miners' families and in 1942 it served the whole community. The hospital's wards were named after the local pits whose miners contributed to the funds that financed the building of the hospital – Nantgarw, Penallta, Bedwas, Llanbradach, Nelson, and Senghenydd. The collieries were nationalised and run by the National Coal Board from 1946, and in 1948 the miners' hospital was given to the NHS.

★ ★ ★

Dylan Baddams was back home to his birthplace, Heol Aneurin, a street lined with modest terrace houses at the south-west corner of Caerphilly, close to the Nantgarw Road. He was back in time for the festive season 1961/1962 and his family organised a party in his honour. The tall narrow house was festooned with bunting and "welcome home" banners.

He had his old room to himself because his brother, Gareth, with whom he used to share, was married, and lived at the top of the same road. His father, Owen Baddams, was 62 and short of breath thanks to his emphysema. He went down the mine for the first time when he was aged 16 when there was a desperate need for coal as so many young men were fighting in the trenches of Normandy. He was promoted to a foreman in his mid-50s and now worked above ground at the Nantgarw mine, in management and was the representative of the coal miners' union for East Glamorgan District of the South Wales Miners Federation. His first son went down the mines at the age of 18 and was proud to follow in his father's and grandfather's tradition. Gareth was big and tough like his brother, which meant he was soon promoted to be a "hewer", cutting away at the coalface. Gareth was also proud of his young brother graduating as a doctor and bragged about him at the nearby tavern, the Red Dragon, where the miners quenched their thirst after washing the coal dust off their face at the pit-top baths. As for his mother, Gwyneth, she was walking on air. She was five years younger than her husband and two inches taller. She had gone to grammar school and at the age of 18 was employed by the mine as a secretary and was now in charge of the staff above ground. She had always wanted to go to university, but her family were desperately poor and needed another income in the home to pay for the coal to keep them warm in winter. In addition to the immediate family, there were uncles and aunts and cousins, mostly employed by the coal industry. One of his uncles was famous for leading the Abertridwr brass band and his favourite cousin, Ken Jones, was famous for playing on the left wing for the Cardiff RFC. Outside the extended family was Bronwen Evans, Dylan's sweetheart since his schooldays. Much beer and port wine were consumed in honour of the first of the Baddamss to graduate from university.

On 5 January 1962, Dr Dylan Baddams started his job

as the medical SHO at the Caerphilly Miners' and District Hospital. There were only two resident medical officers in the hospital, one for medicine and one for surgery. The senior medical staff were based at the Cardiff Royal Infirmary. He looked upon this as a stepping-stone to whatever route he might take in his medical career. But, in addition, this also allowed for the flowering of three other loves in his life. He was a much more romantic and complex character than first impressions suggested; he even wrote love poems to his first love.

His first love was Bronwen Evans, who lived nearby. Bronwen in Welsh means white and pure-breasted, which could be considered an understatement. She had a voluptuous figure, beautiful blue eyes, golden locks, and a pure soprano voice. Dylan's second love was rugby football. Caerphilly RFC played in the division two east of the Welsh National League. That might be a good start, but his real ambition was the play in the front row of the scrum for the neighbouring team of Pontypridd. Their front row was notorious and legendary, leading them to be in the top three slots of the Welsh Premier League most years. His third love was singing in a male voice choir and the Caerphilly Miners were famous for that above-ground activity.

His work at the hospital was not arduous, consisting of two ward rounds a day, morning and evening, outpatient clinics each morning between 09.30 and 12.30 apart from weekends and assisting the visiting surgeon for any minor operations in the afternoon. Major surgery was performed at the Royal Infirmary in Cardiff. He was also on call for emergencies most of the time but that was rewarded by a nice little resident's cottage in the grounds for the two SHOs. This enabled him to enjoy singing lessons with Miss Evans, most evenings. In this way his work/life balance was perfect, and he could give almost equal time to his duties and three other loves. Caerphilly RFC welcomed him to replace their aged tight-head prop, the Caerphilly miners' male voice choir welcomed him to add strength to their baritone line-up, and Bronwen could pester him about plans to get married.

★ ★ ★

His three other loves punctuated his professional career like semi-colons and exclamation marks, but the establishment of his medical career was the first chapter of his professional life. Looking after the mining community of the Rhymney valley was very different to walking the wards of the Queen Elizabeth teaching hospital in Birmingham City. To begin with, most of the miners both employed and retired who sought his advice were suffering from respiratory disease, and he had only spent a few months as a medical houseman to study the problems. Fortunately, each outpatient clinic was manned by a local experienced GP, JJ Williams, who was in a consulting room next door, who taught him the fundamentals, but that was not enough for Dylan. He was interested in studying the subject in his own time, explore the working conditions of the miners and to learn what precautions were on offer to prevent the ubiquitous chronic bronchitis, emphysema, pneumoconiosis, silicosis, and lung cancer.

So, to begin with, he started reading the classical works of Professor Archie Cochrane, who was head of the department of epidemiology at the Welsh National School of Medicine in Cardiff. Then, to explore the working conditions of the miners, he would ask his brother, Gareth, to get permission to go down the shaft of the colliery and learn first-hand what kind of life the troglodytes lived below ground. An excellent review in a recent edition of *The Lancet* set him off on his way.

★ ★ ★

In the mid-1930s reports were accumulating from the British coalfields, particularly from the anthracite area of South Wales, that coal face workers suffered a disabling lung condition that was

not recognized as the (compensatable) silicosis of rock workers.
The Second World War was threatening, and discontent was rife.
Government, through the Medical Research Council, initiated a
medical and environmental investigation of chronic pulmonary
disease in South Wales coalminers to make a systematic survey.
The medical surveys, 1936-1942, were undertaken by a
member of MRC staff, Dr Philip D'Arcy Hart assisted by Dr
Edward Aslett of the Welsh National Memorial Association.
One colliery (Ammanford) was intensively investigated; fifteen
others less so; coal trimmers at the docks were added. The main
observations were to confirm and describe radiographically the
frequency of serious lung lesions apparently due to coal dust, and
distinguishable from classical silicosis. Among recommendations
accepted by Government, the lung condition became recognized
for compensations, and the generic term pneumoconiosis of Coal
Workers' was substituted for silicosis. At that time there were over
200 000 men employed at 250 pits in the Welsh deep mine coal
industry. The problem of coal workers' pneumoconiosis ('black'
lung) was extensive. Between 1931 and 1948 over 22 000
British miners were required to leave their work because they
had contracted pneumoconiosis, and 85% of them were living
in the small mountainous coalfield of South Wales. The high
incidence of disease in the area had been found to be related to the
type of coal mined, with the prevalence of disease being highest in
the anthracite seams. The many factors related to dust diseases,
dust measurement and dust control were poorly understood,
and in 1945 the MRC established the Pneumoconiosis Unit at
Llandough Hospital, Penarth, to research these issues. The first
director of this unit was Dr Archie Cochrane.

★ ★ ★

Having got this far in the small hospital library, Dylan was still
not clear about the prevention and treatment of the miner's
black lungs and determined to meet in person Professor
Cochrane, who headed the MRC unit a mere seven miles

away. He thought he might offer to join his research team using his patients in Caerphilly as subjects of any clinical or epidemiological research. But before that he needed to see what things were really like underground and what protection the miners were offered.

There is an old saying in South Wales: "If you can see the hills, it's going to rain and if you can't see the hills, it's raining already!" That cold November morning, Dylan couldn't see the hills because it was raining, and it was the unearthly hour of 6.30am as he waited with his brother on the Nantgarw Road for the miners' coach that would pick them up in time for the morning shift at the colliery. Nantgarw mine was opened in 1911 and boasted two large shafts at a depth of 856 yards or approximately half a mile. This was the deepest mine in South Wales. Until nationalisation in 1948, like most of the mines in England and Wales, they were plagued by strikes as the avaricious landowners above ground expected the workers below ground to work longer hours for less pay according to the fluctuations in the price of coal. Their working conditions were inhuman to begin with, the shifts were 12 hours without a break, and they were paid according to how much coal they cut free from the coalface. The work was dangerous with roofs collapsing and gas explosions, not to mention the lifetime risk of debilitating lung disease. As a result, the mines were opened and closed at intervals, with some strikes lasting 12 months whilst the families of the miners starved. During the Second World War, young men of fighting age were offered working down the pits instead of fighting on the front line. The wise amongst them judged it was safer to take on the Nazis than to attack King Coal. After the war and the start of nationalisation, conditions improved a little, and the mines were "modernised". Nantgarw mine had benefited from modernisation in the 1950s, with ventilation underground improved to reduce the build-up of methane and carbon monoxide. A surface bath house was built with lockers in a changing room so that the miners could shower instead of carrying home their sooty selves to be washed free of coal dust by their wives in cast iron tubs in front of a coal fire. The coal board also provided overalls to be worn underground instead of their own threadbare clothes that would also need washing at least once a week.

Dylan learnt all this from his brother on the 10-minute coach ride to the pit. On arrival he was warmly welcomed in the pithead office by the daytime gaffer in charge. Any son of the chairman of the local trade union chapter was treated like a prince. Dylan couldn't but notice the respect paid to his brother Gareth as well. He later learnt that his brother's work rate at the coalface was legendary and consequently his pay packet was the thickest in the box. He was then guided to the locker-room and offered an outfit that had seen better days.

The overalls were made of coarse denim baggy trousers with a bib over the chest to be worn over his own vest. He was to learn of the significance of the design half a mile down and a mile on the flat on his route to the coalface. Dylan was then taken to the lamp room and fitted with a helmet bearing an electric light linked to a heavy battery strapped to his waist. He was embarrassed to confess that he was expecting to carry the Davy lamp, the iconic image of the coal miner's history. Gareth, in addition to his battery, had his lunch box hanging from his belt carrying his sandwich and flask of cold tea. It was only when Dylan joined the morning shift on the way to the cage that would drop the men half a mile underground that he felt a little anxious.

The gate of the cage shut tight with 14 men squeezed side to side and without any warning the floor beneath his feet went into free-fall. He screamed out loud, to the amusement of his companions, but regained his composure once the cage slowed down about 100 yards from the ground. Still laughing, Gareth put an arm around his brother's shoulder and guided him out into a poorly lighted cave surrounded by stalls. Each stall had a name on a plaque that once belonged to a pit pony that had become obsolete after the modernisation and mechanisation after the government took control. One of the pit ponies, Dolly, was kept as a pet by the pit head manager.

From the stables Dylan was taken to the underground office and introduced to the shift's gaffer, who was responsible for the safety of the miners. It was well stocked with a first aid kit and the controls for guaranteeing the free flow of fresh air down the one shaft and the egress of foul air from the pit itself by another shaft. He then heard the least expected underground sound of a bird's cheep-cheep. And there she was, the brilliant yellow canary in a cage hanging from the ceiling, whose iridescence seemed to light up the monochrome grey background. Dylan has assumed that the canary in the coal mine was merely a manner of speech but here she was, still the best test for toxic gases giving her life to save the lives of miners. Gareth gave her a piece of orange peel he kept in his pocket.

The two brothers walked arm in arm into the maws of the long eastern tunnel heading to the coalfaces. Dylan immediately noted the flow of stale air on its way to the upwards shaft and started to cough as he inhaled coal dust. He turned to his brother, having just noticed the obvious that none of the miners were wearing masks, and yet this coal dust might be fatal in the long run. "Gareth, boyo, why are we not wearing masks or other protection from inhaling the coal dust?"

He was shocked by his brother's response, two words with no hint of irony: "Dylan, don't ask."

With that Gareth led his young brother along a tunnel that was ill lit and shrinking as they walked. An occasional jar on his helmet warned Dylan to keep his head down. The height of the roof was becoming very uneven; the floor was becoming very uneven as well, with pools of deep mud between the sleepers forcing him to vary his pace from step to step. The electric battery hanging on his hip became a weight to reckon with. The air was warm and stale and the unchanging current only half dried the sweat on his forehead and produced sticky discomfort. He was glad when a line of tubs came along, and they had to withdraw into a recess whilst it passed. "Is it much further?" Dylan gasped.

Gareth laughed. "Man, we are only just starting." They came to a crossroad where the roof heightened, and they could walk upright for a precious few minutes. Now they left the road where the trucks ran and turned into a gallery where the conveyor belt ran alongside them with the rustling sound like an underground stream and where the average hight to the roof was three feet and on the floor was three inches of thick, soft sucking mud. Bent double, Dylan found himself slithering all over the place and each time he slithered he grazed his backbone against the steel straps supporting the roof. They were now travelling through the actual coal seam itself coal formed the side walls of the gallery it seemed to go on intermittently. It took 10 minutes of his desperate scrambling on all fours before Dylan saw lights ahead; by that time, he was feeling that, if the gallery went on much longer, he would faint. Every muscle in his body was shrieking in protest.

"How far have we come?" he asked.

"Oh, about a mile and a half," said Gareth. After another 20 minutes they stopped, and Dylan lay down utterly exhausted full length in the black slime. Gareth was now kneeling on the uneven floor facing a black wall that was the coalface as left from the previous shift, who had left their pick-axes behind. The temperature and humidity of the enclosed space was intolerable, so he followed his brother's example and stripped down to the waist. Gareth then started wielding his axe against the black wall whilst in his kneeling position and great chucks of coal and dust fell to the floor. From out of nowhere another troglodyte emerged from the shadows and without a word shovelled up the black diamonds and tossed them onto the end of the conveyor belt nearby.

Gareth swung his axe like an automaton with a steady rhythm and remarkable strength. In the torchlight from Dylan's helmet his brother's broad muscular shoulders gleamed as the sweat dripped off. All this time Dylan could only watch with awe sitting against the side wall of the gallery whilst trying to catch his breath. Eventually he could take no more and begged to be taken back above ground. Gareth stopped and swung round on his knee pads and spoke these words. "I love you, Dylan bach, and proud that you won't need to work like this. We miners comfort ourselves by claiming that we are the aristocracy of the working classes and walk back to our homes after the shift with a swagger and holding our heads up high. We have the toughest trade union in the country, but we all agree in secret that this is no way to make a living and no one of us would want a son to follow us down the pits. All I ask of you is that your intelligence and the privilege of being a medical man will help you find ways of preventing our black lungs." He then turned to the man with the shovel and said, "Dai bach, show my young brother out of this hole so he can breathe fresh air again and tell his doctor friends how lucky they are." By this time in spite of his bravado, Dylan was in tears and retraced his way back to the "road" like a worm.

Once standing up straight he realised he needed to empty his bladder. Turning to the man with the shovel, he asked, "Dai bach, I need a piss, where's the nearest toilet?"

The other man clapped his hands with laughter and pointed to the wall against where Dylan stood. "There, boyo, that line where the wall meets the floor is your nearest toilet so piss in that corner and I promise yer I won't look."

Once Dylan had emptied his bladder he turned back to Dai, the miner with the shovel. "Seriously, man, if I wanted to have a shit where would I go?"

With a straight face the other man handed over his shovel and said, "You take this shovel and go into a recess along the rail track; you shit on the shovel and throw the turds on the passing conveying belt of coal. It mixes nicely with the other muck. There ain't no toilet underground! Now come along and sit with me on this block and share a sandwich."

Dylan had no appetite to share a cheese sandwich with

Dai but couldn't help noticing how all the miners taking a break for refreshment in this popular corner of the mine unwrapped their sandwiches, with greaseproof paper catching the ubiquitous coal dust in the passing air draft, so that the bread was soon covered with black pockmarks.

Chapter 12

The Five Nations match interrupted

The following day, Dylan started his clinic with his brother's words from underground ringing in his ears. He was more than ever committed to care for the mining community by treating and preventing their common ailments. He knew about the black lung, had his suspicions about lung cancer and by the end of the day would have added a possible new killer to make up a trinity of miners' mortal complaints.

His last patient of the day was Elwyn Williams. Elwyn could not hide the fact that he had been a miner for most of his 65 years, having gone down the pits for the first time at the age of 15. His nose, lips and back of his hands were covered with the miners' tattoos. These were black dots of silica or coal dust that had been ingested by the phagocytes just below the surface of the skin. Recent research had shown that macrophage cells had a half-life of 48 hours but as soon as the cell dies the immortal inorganic elements from the cell's cytoplasm are gobbled up by young macrophages at the precise same site. It is a miracle that these tattoos outlive the host intact after countless exchanges of phagocytic cells churned out from the bone marrow every day. These blemishes or stigmata are a gauge of exposure to the agents for diseases that add to the risk of premature death. A wise and observant doctor will always join up the black dots in making a diagnosis. Dylan had been treating Mr Williams since he first joined the hospital: a left-over patient with chronic bronchitis, but at a glance he knew something else was eating away this witty old man. He had obviously lost weight and his complexion had turned a paler shade of grey. He complained of a loss of appetite and dyspepsia. The clinical examination confirmed the diagnosis Dylan had made, as the man came through the door.

There was a hard and fixed lymph node just above the left clavicle in the angle the bone makes with the insertion of the sternomastoid muscle. This was known as Troisier's sign, a lymphatic metastasis from cells of a gastric cancer floating up along the cisterna chyli in the thorax to a lymph node at the junction between the lymphatic system and the jugular veins. Palpation of the abdomen revealed a craggy mass just below the angle of the xiphisternum. As his patient winced with the tenderness of pressure on his abdomen, his bloodshot eyes showed fear and tears as he read Dylan's face. "I've got stomach cancer doctor, ain't I?"

"I fear so, Elwyn, but I'm going to send you to the best surgical specialist at the Cardiff Royal Infirmary, Mr Huw Evans; he can sometimes work magic." There and then Dr Bannerman phoned Mr Evans's secretary, who was always kind and helpful, the daughter of a miner herself. She understood the urgency of the referral and added Mr Williams to her boss's overloaded clinic on Monday morning.

It was 6.00pm on the Friday evening and he was looking forward the match at Cardiff Arms Park on Saturday afternoon when Wales were playing at home against England in the Five Nations clash. Yet he couldn't help leaping out of his chair as something startling bubbled up in his brain. He remembered the last thing he saw the previous morning before leaving the pit. This was the coal dust settling on the miners' sandwiches. He then linked that to the tattoos on the face of Elwyn Williams. If the macrophages of the face can ingest silica and coal dust particles, then the same would apply to the macrophages of the lung and the gastric mucosa. These inorganic elements could provoke cancer not only in the lung but also in the stomach. He couldn't sleep that night over the enormity of his conjecture.

A Five Nations match day in Cardiff is a sight to be experienced, more like a carnival than a crowd going to watch a rugby match. All the roads leading to the Cardiff Arms Park are bursting with supporters from the competing nations. All the pubs along this route are allowed to open earlier than usual and beer consumption starts at 12.00 noon before kick-off at 3.00pm. The Wales versus England game is not just a local derby but more like a replay of the battles fought in the days of Owain Glyndŵr in the 15th century. It is also a battle of the classes, the workers versus the toffs. The Welsh supporters are obvious, the men wrapped in flags bearing the Welsh dragon, with some wielding giant leeks, the national vegetable of Wales. Many of the women wear national dress with a bonnet made up as a daffodil, the national flower of Wales. They all speak with that lovely lilting accent of South Wales, so as they talk they might as well be singing. The English supporters wrap themselves in the red cross of St George and some wear the white rugby shirt bearing a rose on the left side of the chest. You can also tell an English supporter by his accent. It is public-school posh. In England, rugby football is a game for hooligans played by gentlemen, whilst in Wales rugby football is a game for hooligans played by coal miners and steel factory artisans. Hence the hint of the class war played out with the elaborate rules of the game with an oval ball. There's also the joke by a famous stand-up comedian doing his rounds in the local pubs. He is an ex-steelworker and claims that his life was saved when his head was stuck in a steel press and a passing England supporter threw in his wallet.

Dylan and his brother Gareth and their dad had excellent seats for the match in the second row from the front almost on the halfway line. They were not under cover, so there was a 50/50 risk of getting wet in a cloud burst. Had they sat six rows back they would have been covered by the flooring of the upper stand. But that would have a 100% risk of getting wet from the urine leaking out of the empty beer bottles used by the supporters above who couldn't get through the packed crowds to the toilets in time. They were lucky to get these seats with the stadium completely sold out but that was thanks to the brotherhood of miners. Their best friend, Ken Jones, was playing for Wales on the left wing and the friends and families of the Welsh stars had first choice.

The two teams ran onto the hallowed ground at 2.50pm as the brass band of the miners' union marched off. They then lined up for the national anthems. The visiting team sang first with a lacklustre performance of "God Save the Queen". This was followed by the Welsh team and the whole stadium sung like a male voice choir the thrilling verses of the Welsh national anthem, "Hen Wlad Fy Nhadau" ("Old Land of My Fathers"). That alone was worth a three-point start but to add insult to injury the spectators spontaneously broke into unrehearsed harmony to sing the Welsh rugby anthem, a nonsense song "Sosban Fach" (Mary Ann has hurt her finger and a little saucepan is on fire). This was worth another five points, an unfair advantage when Wales was playing at home.

England had the kick-off at precisely 3.00pm, playing left to right from the Baddams' point of view. Their fly half kicked long and high with the wind behind him. It was neatly caught by the Welsh number 15, JPR Williams, within the five-yard line, who ran fast and straight into the face of the English forwards and at the last moment sent the ball spinning backwards to Ken Jones, running fast along the left wing. His opposite number came hurtling out of his traps and looked bewildered when Ken's side-step took him by surprise. Ken could run 100 yards in 12 seconds and flashed by Dylan on the halfway line into an impregnable line of English forwards. He neatly completing a chip kick over the heads of the defence and chased the ball ahead of the invaders who had to turn and run. Ken then collected the ball five yards from the line and, ball in hand, flew like a swallow to touch down only one minute after kick-off. The crowd went mad, and Dylan nearly fainted with excitement when suddenly he heard his name called out on the tannoy speaker. "Would Doctor Baddams please go immediately to the hospital for an emergency?"

★ ★ ★

Dylan jumped up and made his way through the crush to the office at the main entrance to the ground. He explained who he was and phoned the miners' hospital to find out what the crisis was. The telephonist who sent the message answered the phone and explained that the old miner he saw yesterday was vomiting up blood. Dr Baddams then calculated the most time-effective way of handling the emergency. Elwyn Williams needed a blood transfusion and urgent surgery and that entailed transfer to the Cardiff Royal Infirmary (CRI) as soon as possible. It would be a waste of precious time for him to go back to Caerphilly as he was only walking distance from the CRI. He knew the girl at the end of the line and knew she could be relied upon, so he instructed her to call an ambulance to take the old miner to the A&E department of the infirmary and alert the hospital that the patient and his doctor were on their way.

He then jogged up Westgate Street, round the castle and then a mile up North Street, arriving at the CRI in 15 minutes. He introduced himself to the SHO manning the A&E department and explained the problem. They both agreed that urgent surgery was required and as this might mean a total gastrectomy it would be best to call in Mr Huw Evans, who was also attending the match at Cardiff Arms Park. A second tannoy call to the stadium shortly after England had equalised with a converted try had the crowd wondering what the hell was going on.

Huw Evans was a kind and compassionate man but certainly looked disgruntled on rushing into casualty 30 minutes later just after the patient arrived. He quickly summed up the problem and congratulated Dylan for his prompt response. The patient's blood pressure had dropped to 90/50 so Mr Evans called for a drip to be set up, blood group tested and matched to four units of banked blood. In the meantime, a balanced electrolyte infusion was requested for starters. He then ran off to alert the theatre staff.

Dylan then set up the drip, trying his best to comfort the patient whilst the A&E SHO ran off with blood specimens for cross-matching. Once the patient was stabilised, he was wheeled into the lift to take him down to the operating theatre. They found Mr Evans already gowned and gloved and an anaesthetist standing by. As soon as the patient was asleep, his vital signs began to deteriorate, so the anaesthetist decided to take the risk of starting the blood infusion with a bottle of O group type. Mr Evans asked Dylan to scrub up and give him a hand. With a rapid and deft cut of the scalpel, the abdomen was opened in a straight line from xiphisternum to umbilicus. The peritoneum was cut, and Dylan took two retractors to pull apart the abdominal cavity. The surgeon then started to explore the interior with an experienced hand.

With his cap and mask on it was difficult to determine Mr Evans's expression but his voice said it all. "This man has a very advanced gastric cancer probably arising from the gastro-oesophageal junction. It is fixed and infiltrating the diaphragm as has also spread along the fundus to the spleen. There are widespread metastases to the liver and peritoneum. It is inoperable and the best we can do is to open the stomach and tie off the artery that is bleeding." He then turned to the theatre nurse and politely asked for a large hand needle with thick-gauge cotton. He then asked Dylan to hold the sucker in anticipation of the flood once the stomach was opened before making a slit big enough to slip in his hand. When he removed his hand, his fist was full of blood clots as Dylan frantically sucked up the stream that followed. Mr Evans then enlarged the hole and with further sucking the origin of the flood was identified in the base of an ugly cavity the size of a saucer that had completely replaced the mucosal lining of the fundus of the stomach. Arterial blood was squirting out but there was no vessel to be seen that could be caught in forceps and tied off. The surgeon took the large hand needle and tried to tie off the vessel by underrunning a suture deep into the base of the ulcer. But there was nothing for the needle to grip as it cut through the cheese like tissue of the cancer. But then like magic the bleeding stopped, and it took a moment or two before Dylan and Mr Evans realised that their patient had bled to death in front of their eyes. The anaesthetist with a morose tone of voice declared the patient's time of death as 16.45. The abdomen was quickly closed with a running stich of black silk and then the surgical team returned to the changing room, where hot coffee was awaiting them.

They hung their heads with remorse until with graveyard humour Huw Evans asked if anyone knew the score in the Wales/England game.

Chapter 13

Archie Cochrane and the MRC unit

Dylan finally got round to making an appointment with Professor Archie Cochrane at the MRC Department of Epidemiology at the University of Cardiff two weeks after his adventures down the coal mine and the catastrophe on the day of the Wales/England match. He was fired up with questions and ideas after his relatively short sojourn at the Caerphilly Miners' District Hospital. The differences in the clientele between a teaching hospital in a middle-class neighbourhood of Birmingham and a working-class neighbourhood in South Wales allowed him to see what others overlooked who lived in the locality. The day before taking the bus to Cardiff he thought it might be wise to look up the entry for Archie Cochrane in the thick book in the library that acted as the *Who's Who* of the medical profession. What he discovered was quite remarkable. To say that this famous professor had a colourful past was an understatement.

> *Cochrane was born in Kirklands, Galashiels, Scotland, into a family he described as "industrial upper middle class". He won a scholarship to Uppingham School, and obtained another scholarship to King's College, Cambridge, achieving first class honours in Parts I and II of the Natural Sciences Tripos and completing 2nd MB studies in physiology and anatomy in 1930. He qualified in 1938 at University College Hospital, London. During the Spanish Civil War, Cochrane served as a member of a British Ambulance Unit within the Spanish Medical Aid Committee. In World War II he joined the British Army and*

*was captured during the Battle of Crete and subsequently worked
as a Medical Officer at Salonika (Greece) and Wittenberg an
der Elbe (Germany) prisoner of war camps. His experience in
the camp led him to believe that much of medicine did not have
sufficient evidence to justify its use. He said, "I knew that there
was no real evidence that anything we had to offer had any effect
on tuberculosis, and I was afraid that I shortened the lives of some
of my friends by unnecessary intervention." As a result, he spent
his career urging the medical community to adopt the scientific
method. After the war he studied for a Diploma in Public Health
at the London School of Hygiene & Tropical Medicine. Cochrane
joined the Medical Research Council's Pneumoconiosis Unit
at Llandough Hospital, a part of Welsh National School of
Medicine, in 1948. Here he began a series of studies on the health
of the population of Rhonda Valley – studies which pioneered
the use of randomised controlled trials (RCTs). In 1960 he was
appointed David Davies Professor of Tuberculosis and Chest
Diseases at the Welsh National School of Medicine. He also
promoted the cohort study and was a key adviser in a highly
detailed Caerphilly Heart Disease Study.*

The last line in Cochrane's CV made Dylan sit up. There
was a precedent for MRC to collaborate with the denizens of
Caerphilly and that was precisely what he had in mind.

He arrived at the nice new building of the MRC unit that
had recently been built on the university campus in the centre
of Cardiff on the dot of 11.00am and shown into Professor
Cochrane's office, where a pot of coffee and a plate of biscuits
were awaiting his arrival. Apart from the refreshments, Archie
Cochrane's desk was empty. This suggested a man with a
tidy mind, although he looked like a tramp in his choice of
clothing. The great man oozed goodwill and spoke with a soft
Scottish burr that was welcoming as well. So, Dylan's first
impression was that Prof Cochrane was looking forward to
this meeting as much as he was, and his first words confirmed
that impression. "Well, laddie, it's kind of you to come down

from the hills to spend time with me. How can I help you? There is no rush; I've cancelled all my other engagements and, if you like, I'd like to take you off for a light lunch in the senior common room."

At that Dylan nodded with a big smile and drew out of his pocket at list of bullet points as an agenda. "Please, sir, I have a list of questions and theories about the health of miners in South Wales."

"For God's sake, man, don't call me sir! I haven't been called sir since I left the army. Please call me Archie. Also, I distrust the patient with the *petit papier*. If you've got a good, organised mind, you won't need notes; you should have no difficulty in remembering the sequence of events that brought you here. It is my task to take notes and summarise what you've said and, if it makes sense, I should be able to translate your observations and conjectures into a workable research programme."

Dylan immediately understood that he was dealing with an intellectual giant who had read his mind and could bring order to the windmills of his mind. Clearly understanding what was required of him, he had no difficulty in describing everything that had happened to him as a linear narrative ending up with a list of questions and suggestions that were by nature the offspring of his experiences since arriving in the Rhondda and Taff valleys.

All the time Archie was taking notes and when Dylan's torrent of observations and hypotheses was spent he took a pipe from a neat pipe rack, topped it up with flake of tobacco from the top draw of his desk, lit the pipe with one match from a box in his pocket, tilted back his chair, and drew smoke whilst gazing at the ceiling. After a few minutes of silence as the fragrant smoke drifted across his desk, Archie's eyes lit up as the pieces of the jigsaw fell into place. He then stood up and walked round the desk, puffing his pipe whilst talking to Dylan.

"Here's what we will do. We'll make a start from where

you finished, with your unified hypothesis that inhaled or ingested particles of inorganic matter penetrate the mucosa and are ingested by a cell of the monocyte/macrophage lineage. These particles are fixed in situ and accumulate over time. There comes a point when they provoke and inflammatory response that kick-starts the neighbouring mucosal cells to proliferate the first step to oncogenesis. It would be easy to design experiments on syngeneic mice to test this hypothesis in a short time. I have no faith in animal experiments but I'm a cynic. Number one, it will keep you occupied for the first 12 months whilst we are designing and setting up the clinical trials in human subjects. Secondly, any phenomenology with the murine species can be used to help persuade the funding agent to provide the salary of a research fellow and pay for office expenses and travel. My paper in the *British Journal of Industrial Medicine* in 1956, 'The Prevalence of Coal-Workers' Pneumoconiosis: Its Measurement and Significance', will provide the credibility of grant proposal to the MRC if I'm registered as your PhD supervisor.

"Although pneumoconiosis and silicosis are unequivocally linked to coalmining, we have a lot to learn why or how these progress to fibrosis and death. Your work on macrophages might give us a clue. Lung cancer is associated with coalmining but, as you will soon learn, *association is no proof of causation*. We have a possible confounding variable of tobacco usage, which I will come back to shortly. As far as gastric cancer is concerned, I think you may be the first to suggest this link. How we will address these questions will require a five-year programme grant and I have the green shoots of a proposal that will cover all bases; that comes back to your first observation on your visit to a coal mine regarding the use of face masks. This, incidentally, will address the hostile response from your brother. Before I do so, I want to inform you of some vital results regarding cigarette smoking and lung cancer and why this might be a confounding variable. You won't have had a chance to read it yet, but the Royal College of Physicians have just published a report, 'Smoking in Relation to Cancer of the Lung'. One example of the strengths of this report is the alarming example that a man aged 35 who is a heavy smoker has a one in 23 chance of dying of lung cancer before the age of 65 compared with a non-smoker's chance of one in 90. Furthermore, there are remarkable data concerning the change in smoking habits amongst male doctors. In 1950, Richard Doll and Bradford Hill published the first report linking smoking to lung cancer, since when most doctors have given up smoking and their risk of lung cancer has dropped precipitously to the risk of non-smokers. You can now understand why smoking must be judged as a confounding variable in your searching for links between coalmining and lung cancer."

Throughout all this monologue Dylan was surprised at Archie's forgone conclusion that all this work would be supported and funded by the MRC, and he was going to enjoy at least five years working as an epidemiologist in Professor Cochrane's team. He then interrupted the discourse whilst his mentor drew deeply on his pipe. "But, Archie, you are smoking as we talk! Isn't this irresponsible for a doctor like you?"

"Aye, laddie, that's a good question but what the data shows is that the risk applies only to cigarettes, whereas pipes and cigars don't seem to share that risk. That might be a dose–response phenomenon, but the question remains. I've spoken enough for now so let's go and get some lunch when I shall describe the plan for the clinical trials and the mystery of the missing masks in the mines."

The sun was shining as the pair left the MRC unit and walked across a quadrangle towards the central block of the gleaming white neo-baroque buildings of the university. The first thing Dylan noticed on entering the senior common room was the number of senior academics who were smoking. The room was panelled with mahogany wood and decorated with portraits of provosts, deans, and vice-chancellors from the past, livened up by colourful examples of contemporary works from the department of fine art. Archie guided him to a servery in a far-off corner greeting all and sundry on the way. He ordered cheese and pickles sandwiches and half pints of pale ale for the two of them and then at a small table in another, quieter corner of the vast room and took off from where he'd left off in his office.

"How do we know that masks would protect miners from developing lung disease, Dylan?"

"Well, it's obvious: they cover the nose and mouth so that coal dust won't get to the lungs."

"That's what I expected you to say but like most folk you've not been educated about 'unintended consequences', the curse of the epidemiologists. I will lend you a book written by Dr William Silverman, entitled *Retrolental Fibroplasia – A Modern Parable*, that illustrates this point in a way you will never forget. Do you know what retrolental fibroplasia is, Dylan?"

"I'm sorry sir, err, Archie. It rings a bell but, to be honest, I can't remember."

"Aye, laddie, you must always be honest with me. Well, RLF, as we call it for short, was an epidemic of blindness amongst premature infants in the period 1942–1954; 1942 was the year that incubators supplied with oxygen were introduced in the USA in paediatric units that happened to coincide with me becoming a prisoner of war. The survival rate of these tiny tots improved but at the same time many of them became blind as a fibrous curtain grew behind their lenses. It took 10 years to discover that the high concentration of oxygen in the incubator was the culprit. They considered all other variables faced by premature infants in a box, but oxygen was last of all because no one could believe that oxygen could be toxic. In the end it was only a randomised controlled trial, RCT, of high versus low concentrations of oxygen that ended this tragic epidemic. So, with that in mind, we need an RCT to determine what you think is obvious: that wearing a face mask down the mine will reduce the incidence of coal miners disease. Before we even start planning that RCT, you need to do some boring groundwork to try and support your intuition that coaldust contributes to lung and gastric cancer. Think about it for a week before we meet again and, meanwhile, I'll see if I can raise a grant for you for a five-year research programme, during which time I have no doubt you will have written your PhD."

Dylan left the university buildings walking on air and couldn't wait to tell Bronwen his good news. With a secure income for at least five years, they could plan their wedding.

Chapter 14

A rugby fixture, a wedding, and the Llangollen International Musical Eisteddfod

Rugby football is a mystery to the uninitiated. It's not really football, more like hands-and-feet-ball. Rugby football was created by William Webb Ellis, who picked up the ball and ran with it in his arms during a football game at Rugby School in England in 1823. The game is now played with an oval ball because it's easier to carry under the arm and when it lands after a long kick it can bounce in all directions, which adds to the fun. The game is played 15 a side, made up of eight forwards and seven backs. Forwards are built big and bulky, whilst backs are tall and slim and can run very fast. To the uninitiated, the game simply looks like an uncontrolled battle for the ball between two groups of gorillas after the first kick-off, who try to capture the ball and throw it backwards to the backs, who pass it backwards to other backs, who are running along the side-lines to try to touch the ball down over the goal line before being stopped by a defence line of forwards. Passing the ball forwards or accidentally bouncing it forwards off your chest is penalised by giving the opposing team the ball for the "put in" for the scrummage that follows. The scrum, as it is called, lines up the eight forwards on each side to compete for the ball after it has been "put in" by the scrum half, who is usually the smallest and most nimble of the team. Sometimes they are shorter than five feet, 10 inches. To protect the forwards from serious damage, the rules of the scrum are manifold and that's where the referee must be on his toes because in Premier League rugby the rules are there to be covertly broken.

The forwards are numbered on their backs, 1–8. Numbers 1, 2, and 3 are the front line, with 1 and 3 acting as "props" to support 2, who is the hooker, whose job is to hook back the ball to the next line, 4 and 5, who are called locks. They then heel the ball to the back row – 6, 7, and 8.

Numbers 6 and 7 are called flankers and 8 is called "number 8". Number 8 is usually the biggest and heaviest of the forwards. When the scrum is set up the referee tells them to bend over and for the two front rows to lock heads but not to push until he gives permission just before the ball is put in. Now, if you think this through you will realise that if six heads are locked together one on each side will suffer the crush of a head on each side. He is called the "tight-head prop" and that is the position played by Dylan, initially for Caerphilly RFC but later fulfilling his dream, after a talent scout from the nearby Premier League team Pontypridd recruited him. At six feet tall, 17 stone in weight and with well-developed neck muscles, he perfectly fitted the slot.

His first and, sadly, his last game in the Premier League was against Llanelli that November. Llanelli is a small market town north-west of Swansea with a population of only 25,000, yet they can field one of the best 15s in the world. They wear a blood-red strip from top to toe and play like demons. They were notorious for attacking all newcomers to the competing team and this time was Dylan's turn. Each scrum he had to put up with profanities from the other side until he lost his temper with his opposite number that ended in fisticuffs. He came off worst and suffered concussion and got a red card for starting the fight. That meant his team had to play the rest of the match with 14 men and lost by 40 points to 12.

As if that wasn't humiliating enough, as he was recovering on the touchline, a blonde bombshell appeared from the stands and ran down to give him a dressing down for all to hear. At half time a voice over the tannoy announced the engagement of Dylan Baddam to Miss Bronwen Evans. There were cheers all round and at the end of the match, Dylan was carried out on the shoulders of his team as if he was a hero but that was the last game he played.

★ ★ ★

Bronwen and Dylan then planned their wedding for the second week in July 1963 when the weather should be clement, and his three best friends could take time off to act as ushers whilst his brother was best man. Until then he could finish his contract at the miners' hospital and start working for the MRC. The wedding date coincided with the Llangollen International Musical Eisteddfod, where they intended to take their honeymoon. The wedding was at St Martin's Church, with fine views of the castle floating on its lake. The bride looked charming, having dieted to fit into a third-generation bridal dress made with silk, covered in white lace and pearls, with a fringe dropping down from the knee-length skirt. Her grandmother was the first to wear it in the 1920s. All the men wore their best Sunday suits, with the groom, best man, and ushers bearing carnations in their buttonholes. No one hired a poncy morning suit as they were all working class and proud of it. There were two exceptions to the label "working class": Peter Baring, of course, and the bride's father, who, although the son of a pitman, had made a fortune from selling household necessities door to door in the remote villages of the Taff and Rhondda valleys. Mr Evans had bribed the vicar and recruited the members of the Welsh National Opera, most of whom were amateurs, to open the proceedings with another famous Welsh anthem, "Cwm Rhondda", "Bread of Heaven – Guide Me O Thou Great Redeemer". As the hymn was echoing around the walls of St Martins, the father of the bride walked Bronwen up the aisle. Everyone turned round, and a loud sighing ahh burst spontaneously from the congregation as the beautiful bride glided by to be greeted by a very proud groom with muscles showing through the outgrown best suit. The service complete, the best man found the gold ring deep in a pocket, polished it on his sleeve and passed it to Dylan, who slipped it on Bronwen's ring finger and kissed the bride in such a hurry she hadn't yet lifted the veil off her face. The newlywed couple led the congregation out of the church to the sound of the chorus from the *Merry Widow*; only in retrospect did they think it might have been in bad taste.

The bride and groom were then transported to the Masonic Hall nearby for the reception, where the bride's father was worshipful master. Mr Evans had rented a Rolls-Royce, decorated with white ribbons, from a fellow Mason at a discount.

After the wedding breakfast was complete the best man stood up to speak. Dylan was sure that his brother had never spoken in public but was pleasantly surprised as Gareth delivered a speech from his heart without any notes. He congratulated his brother for following him down to the coalface to witness the hardships working underground and how Dylan had committed himself to doing anything the medical profession could offer to improve their conditions. He finished his speech by describing the mess his brother looked after crawling backwards for a mile in the mud and how the canary in its cage dropped dead with fright on seeing this spectre rising from the earth. That had all the guests laughing out loud, with Dylan joining in. Gareth then asked everyone to raise their glasses of champagne to toast the happy couple. There was then a moment of confusion and embarrassment as no one could find a glass of bubbly on the table. Gareth then shouted out in apparent fury, "Where's the head waiter, where's the champagne?"

A little man with a toothbrush moustache and a black apron ran forward and in a thick Italian accent almost in tears replied, "Scusi, signore, mi scusi" and then waved to all the waiters and waitresses to come forward with the full glasses on trays. He then broke out with opening bars of "Libiamo, ne' lieti calici", "Let's Drink to the Sweet Excitement of Love", the drinking song in the first act of *La Traviata*. Then all the waiters and waitresses joined in, and they also happened to be the chorus of the Welsh National Opera in disguise! By the time everyone had a glass in their hand and was toasting Dylan and Bronwen, there wasn't a dry eye in the house.

★ ★ ★

The journey from South Wales to North Wales by car takes three and a half hours whichever way you drive. The passengers in the hired car with a "Just Married" banner in the back window chose the scenic route of the barren hills of mid-Wales to the breathtaking views of Snowdonia. Turning east from the mountains, they followed the River Dee to the pretty little market town that hosted the annual Llangollen International Musical Eisteddfod. They had booked the bridal suite at the Pen-y-Dyffryn Country Hotel just outside the hubbub of the festival park looking down to the Llangollen Bridge. The festival had been active since founded in 1947 and some of the most famous singers or choirs had made their name by winning the competitions. Dylan was singing in the male voice choir competition with the Caerphilly Miners' Choir. They did well, coming third, with the Colne Valley male voice choir winning the competition for the third year running. Bronwen was singing in the famous Pontypridd female voice choir, who sang wearing traditional Welsh costume. They had to sing two songs. The first was "Linden Lea", set to the music of Ralph Vaughan Williams, which all choirs had to perform, and then a second song chosen by their conductor. She had chosen a choral version of Johan Sebastian Bach's "Ave Maria", giving the solo soprano intermezzo to Mrs Bronwen Baddams. They came second to the Oswestry Girls High School Choir, but Bronwen's solo was noted by a well-known music agency, which was the first step in her professional career.

The honeymoon was blessed by fine weather so for a week they walked the hills and sang in the valley. Coming home afterwards was no anti-climax as Dylan had waiting for him cages full of little brown mice who were going to help discover the cure for cancer, whilst Bronwen was to be auditioned for the part of Amneris, the Egyptian Princess, in the next production of *Aida* with the Welsh National Opera.

PART 4

Mathew Barnet 1962–1965

Chapter 15

Friday night dinner at the Barnets' house

One year had passed since the engagement of Mathew and Minxy. During this time, they had seen little of each other because of Mathew's duties as a houseman. Furthermore, the Barnet family, living in Edgbaston, Birmingham, had hardly got to know the KaMinxy family, who lived in Hampstead Garden Suburb, London. Now was the time for Mathew to plan his future career and for his parents and future parents-in-law to plan the wedding. According to tradition, these discussions would place on a Friday night at the home of the parents of the groom and, according to another custom, the wedding would take place in the synagogue attended by the parents of the bride. Both families practised Orthodox Judaism, leaving out many of the inconvenient laws and restrictions according to the family's traditions. For example, both families kept a strictly kosher kitchen at home, but apart from shellfish and porcine meat were more relaxed when eating out.

Mathew's paternal grandfather had escaped the pogroms in Poland and landed in the docks of London in 1911. He was sponsored by distant relatives who lived in Barnet, and, because he had no English and their name was something unpronounceable in Polish, they were registered with Barnet as their surname. His mother's origins were similar, but she was born in London, whereas Mathew's father was 10 years old on arrival in the United Kingdom. Both families were very poor and neither his mother nor his father continued their education beyond 16. His father ended up making a reasonable living in the "rag trade".

The KaMinxy family, in contrast, were very wealthy in addition to being very lucky. Minxy's parents were married in Vienna in 1937. Their forebears had made a fortune in banking and lived in a huge apartment on the first floor of a mansion on the Ringstrasse in the centre of the city. For their honeymoon, they made the grand tour of European capitals and fell in love with Renaissance art on their first visit to Florence. They arrived in London on New Year's Day 1938 and found a telegram from Vienna waiting for them as they checked into their hotel. The telegram bore no evidence of the sender. All it said, in capital letters, was: STAY IN LONDON UNTIL FURTHER NOTICE MARKETS ARE FALLING.

The Anschluss of Austria occurred in March 1938 and Mr and Mrs KaMinxy never heard any more from any member of their families. Fortunately for them, the assets of the London branch of the KaMinxy bank could not be stolen by Adolf Hitler and, when Rebecca was born in 1939, they were reasonably well off but shared the austerity of all British citizens throughout the war.

Returning now to the Friday night dinner, both mothers were delighted with their children's choice of partner. Mrs KaMinxy always wanted he daughter to marry a Jewish doctor, whilst Mrs Barnet always wanted her son to marry a Jewish princess.

Mathew's mother may have had no formal education beyond the age of 16 but her traditional *haimysher* cooking was legendary. Mathew's father also had a limited education but was bookish and a star player at the bridge club. He also played chess and could demonstrate his skills by playing 12 boards simultaneously.

It should be noted that one guest was missing: Mathew's brother Mike, who was serving in the RAMC somewhere in the Sinai desert.

Mathew's mother blessed the Sabbath candles with her face covered and then Mathew's father blessed the wine and the bread, after which they sat down to starters of egg and onion, followed by chicken soup with noodles and *kneidlach*. Once the guests had finished gushing over the chicken soup, the two sets of parents started to discuss Mathew's future and the details for the wedding. Mathew and Minxy held hands under the table and winked at each other as their plans had already been made. It was agreed that the wedding would take place before the school summer holidays so that all their friends and relatives would be in town.

The ceremony would take place in the Norrice Lea Synagogue, close to where they lived, which happened to have the best cantor in the country, a refugee who had used to sing in the Berlin Opera. To save face, the Barnets would pay for the *kiddish* after the ceremony, which would attract about 400 souls. The father of the bride would pay for the reception at the Savoy and each family could invite 150 guests. Mr and Mrs KaMinxy would buy the couple a modest house in their suburb and pay the rental for rooms in Harley Street for the first year until the young doctor got on his feet. At that point Mathew and Minxy couldn't hold back their laughter any longer. "This is all beyond the realms of generosity, Mr KaMinxy, but forgive me if I interrupt your plans for our future. My bride-to-be would be happy if you paid for our honeymoon in Florence, but we cannot accept your gift of a house. To show my worth, I will work to buy my own house. As for rooms in Harley Street, you misjudge me. The state paid for my education in medical school, and I intend to pay back that debt by devoting my life to the NHS. I wish to specialise in psychiatry because I have learnt to my cost that the workings of the brain are terra incognita." Mr and Mrs KaMinxy put their heads together and blathered away in Yiddish and then Mr KaMinxy turned to his future son-in-law and resumed in English. "My dear Mathew, I respect your honourable vords but vos is this terror in de night oh?"

"I'm sorry, Mr KaMinxy, I was showing off my Latin. It means unexplored land. The brain has fascinated me since I was a first-year medical student." He then entertained them with the tale of the brain in the toilet bowl and the terrified maid. The laughter that followed broke any tension and allowed for a change of topic of conversation as the roast chicken, stuffing, and roast potatoes were brought in by Mathew's very proud mum.

Once the main course was complete, according to tradition, the womenfolk carried the empty dishes into the kitchen to prepare the deserts and lemon tea. They used this time for gossip and decisions on minor domestic topics like who to invite as bridesmaids, who mustn't sit next to whom and whether the women should wear hats in the synagogue. At the same time, according to tradition, the menfolk would make serious decisions about stabilising the economy and sorting out the problems in the Middle East.

At the end of dinner, they all felt well fed and relaxed in each other's company, having agreed on the date of the wedding and the future for Mathew. He would study to become a psychiatrist in London to allow Minxy to complete her masters in the history of art at the Courtauld.

Chapter 16

A visit to the National Gallery
May 1962

Having decided on a career in psychiatry, Mathew then paid
a visit to see his old mentor, Professor Gunter Hoffbrand, to
seek guidance. He was warmly welcomed into the professor's
disorganised office, where he had to remove a pile of old
journals from a chair to sit down with the old man. Gunter
Hoffbrand spoke with a thick German accent that was quite
difficult to follow. They enjoyed a long chat over cups of
strong coffee and concluded that there was only one place for
Mathew to study for his diploma of psychological medicine
(DPM) and that was the Maudsley Hospital and the Institute
of Psychiatry at King's College Hospital, Denmark Hill,
Camberwell in south-east London. This would also give him
a chance to work at the Bethlem lunatic asylum, the oldest
and most famous facility in the country. Professor Hoffbrand
would act as a referee and provide a letter of introduction
to the head of the institute. Furthermore, he would provide
Mathew with a letter of introduction to Sigmund Freud's
daughter Anna, who inherited the house her father had lived
in on coming to England. The house was in Hampstead, not
far from Hampstead Garden Suburb, where the KaMinxy
family lived. Anna was also a psychoanalyst and had pioneered
the extension of her father's work to children. Mathew was
very happy to accept that guidance as it meant he could live
in London after his wedding and that would please his fiancée
and her parents.

Dr Barnet's interview at the Maudsley Hospital was scheduled for Monday, 28 May, at 10.30, so he was invited to spend the weekend before with the KaMinxy family. The weekend would start before the Sabbath came in on the Friday evening. He would then be expected to join the family for prayers on Saturday morning at Norrice Lea Synagogue, where he could be presented to the community. Saturday afternoon would involve a walk round Hampstead Heath and, after the Sabbath went out, they were free to spend the weekend as they wished.

On Saturday evening at about 8.00pm, Minxy had arranged for Mathew to meet some of her best friends at Jack Straw's Castle, a famous historic pub next to the Whitestone pond, the highest point of northern London. Mathew found them a delightful crowd with no hints of snobbery. Half of them were art students who dressed like you would expect art students to dress, and half were students or young postgraduates. The most interesting of the young men was Oliver Sacks, a young doctor about his same age, who was working in the Middlesex hospital and planning to train as a neurologist. They had much in common. The evening was a great success and Mathew felt at home with Minxy's circle of friends and the feeling seemed to be reciprocated.

On Sunday morning, Minxy dragged Mathew to the National Gallery in Trafalgar Square, where she was studying iconography for a dissertation towards her MA.

Mathew knew nothing about fine art but went along to please his beloved. What he would never have predicted was this visit would be one of the most seminal milestones in his career.

The National Gallery runs across the north boundary of Trafalgar Square, with breathtaking views of the Houses of Parliament at the end of Whitehall. It is always bustling with tourists as Nelson's Column, one of the must-see sights of London Town, rises from a fountain just in front of the National Gallery. The gallery is in the neo-Classical style favoured in the mid-19th century. The pictures are hung chronologically, starting with the Gothic gilt-covered religious paintings in the west wing and ending up with the irreligious post impressionists in the east wing. Mathew and Rebecca started at the west wing, standing in front of a painting entitled *The Baptism of Christ*. Minxy then switched into tour guide mode and assured Mathew that this was a famous and popular work by Piero dela Francisca painted in 1439. "Tell me, Mathew, what do you feel when you look at the painting?"

Mathew decided to play along and replied, "Well, it's very symmetrical, very quiet, with pale pastel shades and that makes me feel calm."

"Very good," Minxy responded. "So, the painting has a physiological impact on you?"

"Well, now you mention it, yes."

"What is that white bird that floats above the head of the Christ figure?"

"I suppose it represents the dove of peace."

"Very close but in fact it represents the 'Holy Ghost' in the trinity of Christianity. That is what I mean when I talk about icons. Let me show you another painting with hidden icons with a more secular interpretation."

Minxy then took him by the hand and led him to the next room, showing paintings from the early Renaissance. The picture of interest was gorgeous as well as sexy. The frame was a rectangle with the width about four times the height. On the left-hand side of the picture was a very pretty blonde in a white nightdress, lying obliquely across half the painting, looking directly at the viewer with a coquettish expression. On the other side of the frame was the deeply bronzed and muscular naked man who was fast asleep. You knew he was fast asleep because two mischievous young satyrs were blowing conches into his ears. Minxy then explained what they were looking at. "The picture is this shape because it was made for the front of a trousseau chest to stand at the foot of newlywed bed. The painting is by Botticelli, completed in 1483, just 40 years after the Piero della Francisco we've just seen. It shows Venus and Mars recovering from some feverish sex. Venus has had time to put on her nightdress again but Mars, the god of war, is a wimp, sleeping off the effort. The model for Venus is Simonetta Vespucci, the most famous pin-up girl in Florence at the time. She was the one who posed for *The Birth of Venus* in the Uffizi. The poor girl died of consumption, whatever that is, at the age of 24."

Mathew interrupted the lecture by stating, "Consumption is the historic word for tuberculosis."

"I take your word for that, doctor, but how can we know for certain that this is Miss Vespucci?"

Accepting that this was a rhetorical question, Mathew kept shtum.

"Well, if you look in the top right-hand corner of the picture above the head of Mars, you will see some wasps flying in and out of a nest. Italian for wasp is *vespucci*, hence the name of the motor scooter. Vespucci is also the name of the model, and the wasp was on the coat of arms of her aristocratic family. Now that is also an example of iconography." Mathew was somewhat unimpressed by this discovery but didn't show it as he was still trying to digest the fact that this beautiful young lady died at 24 for a disease that was curable today.

Minxy then took his hand again and was about to take him to this next gallery when he noticed a picture on the opposite wall to Mars and Venus, the same shape of a trousseau box, which captured his attention. He pointed across the room and asked her about this weird painting with a dead, near-naked girl lying across the foreground.

With exaggerated reluctance, Minxy walked across the room and showed off her scholarship.

"This is a work by Piero di Cosimo, who was a contemporary of Botticelli and even used Simonetta as a model, but that's not her in this painting. The gallery describes it as 'A Satyr mourning over a Nymph'. I describe it as a hideous misogynist wet dream.

"It has been suggested that this painting depicts an episode from the *Metamorphoses*, a poem by the ancient Roman writer Ovid. The dead beautiful nymph would be Procris, who was unintentionally killed by her husband, Cephalus, in a hunting accident. Satisfied?"

After a few moments studying the picture Mathew responded, "No, I'm not satisfied. This was no accident; this was murder! I've just done a rapid and superficial forensic pathological examination and look what I've discovered. The mortal wound is this knife stab in the neck, probably transecting the spinal cord at C2/C3 but before that she struggled hard to hold off her assailant. The bleeding cut on her left forearm suggests she tried to cover her face from the knife. Now look carefully at the palm of her right hand: there are bleeding cuts across her fingers. That tells you how, in desperation, she grabbed the knife. The mystery here is how and why the artist painted these details and where on earth did he find the corpse? I accuse the artist himself as the murderer!"

Minxy was gawping at him, opening and closing her mouth like a fish out of water and then took her turn to look closely at the details before conceding defeat graciously. "Bloody hell, Mathew, I think you're right, and do you know what this means? You and I are going to write a paper for the *Art History Journal*. It will be called 'Death of the Maiden' by Barnet M and KaMinxy R." She then rewarded him with a long kiss on the lips and, gasping for breath, continued, "OK, clever clogs, follow me to see a painting by Bronzino with Venus and her son Cupid behaving inappropriately. Let's see how many iconographs you can find."

Taking Mathew's hand again, she pulled him along through two more galleries until they reached the zone devoted to the mannerists of mid-16th-century Florence.

At the mid-point of the of the long wall of the gallery, Mathew's eyes were drawn to the most beautiful painting he had ever seen. A painting that would influence his career from the start. At first glance he thought it was an abstract painting because it was so busy with light pink against a background of cobalt blue but on closer inspection the details came into focus. There was a central figure of a beautiful mature woman with off-white, blemish-free skin. Her right hand was raised holding an arrow, whilst her left hand on her thigh carried a golden ball. She was leaning on a handsome young man aged about 14, who was kissing her whilst fondling her left breast. The two central figures are surrounded by a carnival of curiosities, while a bearded old man carrying a blue robe contributed to the background. Mathew then turned to Minxy and said, "My God, this is gorgeous and very sexy, what the hell is going on?"

Minxy replied, "Funny that your question carries the words God and hell. The picture is called *An Allegory of Sacred and Profane Love* and was painted by Bronzino in 1545 as a gift to King Francis of France from Cosimo de Medici, the effective ruler of Florence. It is stacked full of iconography and is the main subject of my dissertation. The central figure is Venus, and we know that because one of her 'attributes' is the golden apple. The young man is her son Cupid and to say the least their relationship is inappropriate and, if you believe Freud, he might grow up with an Oedipus complex. So, this must be described as profane love. Much of the surrounding images can be explained as warnings of sexually transmitted diseases, a consequence of profane love. And my research will interest you as I've deduced the warnings apply to tertiary syphilis. The man on the far left is pulling his hair out and screaming: the insanity of cerebral syphilis. The man's head in the top left-hand corner has lost his cranium, indicting loss of memory, another symptom of cerebral syphilis. The weird girl on the right-hand side in the background has the trunk and tail of a griffin. In one hand she offers honeycomb and in the other hand the sting in the tail of the monster's body. I think you can deduce what that means yourself. The masks at the bottom right-hand corner illustrate comedy and tragedy, carrying the same message. And, finally, the arrow in Venus' right hand is about to be broken, the iconography for impotence. Returning to sacred love, the old man at the top is Old Father Time, with his attribute, the sand clock, on his shoulder. He warns that all this beauty will fade with time as he's about to cover all this sexual activity with a robe painted with lapis lazuli, the attribute of Mary the mother of Jesus."

Mathew was blown away by the scholarship of his fiancée and spent a few more minutes examining the painting in detail before responding. "Minxy, my darling, that is brilliant, and I think I can confirm your theory about the painting from two other details I've spotted. If you look at the palate of the madman you will see a small ulcer; that is called a gumma, another sign of tertiary syphilis, but the other sign is so subtle I nearly missed it. If you look at the cherub handing roses to Venus, he has a big smile on his face, but then if you look at his right foot in the background you'll see he is standing on a bed of thorns, and one has penetrated his foot. Loss of sensory signals in the feet is called *tabes dorsalis*, another symptom of tertiary syphilis."

Minxy's response was ecstatic and suggested another paper by KaMinxy and Barnet.

Mathew's response was a Damascene conversion. "My darling, you cannot understand how much this means to me. This picture illustrates how insanity can be part of a systemic neurological disorder. In this case the culprit is the bacterium *Treponema pallidum*. Perhaps schizophrenia has an organic cause rather than a metaphysical concept like the Oedipus complex!"

Minxy then ended the visit by reminding Mathew to make sure that the walls of his hospital's wards were painted in the manner of Piero della Francisco, whatever the cause of their insanity.

Chapter 17

The Maudsley Hospital
28 May 1962

Attempts to label and explain insanity go back to the era of ancient Greece. For thousands of years, mental suffering was viewed as reflecting an imbalance of forces within individuals and between individuals and their environments. The overriding Hippocratic/Galenic medical tradition postulated that four basic temperaments corresponded to the dominant fluids (what were called "humours") in bodies: passionate and easily excited sanguine personalities with high levels of blood; assertive and determined choleric types with dominance of "yellow bile"; quiet and anxious temperaments with an overload of "black bile"; and, finally, introspective and even-tempered with high levels of "phlegm". Excessive or deficient amounts of each humour contributed to adverse mental traits such as impulsivity, aggression, melancholy, and apathy. (*Melancholia* is Latin for black bile.) Hippocratic conceptions of disease as disturbing the balance between society and the individual persisted among general physicians and the lay public into the early 19th century. From that point until the early 1960s, the most prominent constructs of mental illness included broad subgroups, such as "psychoses", "neuroses", and "neurasthenia", or the Freudian psychoanalytic concepts such as Oedipal or inferiority complexes, repression, and the id, ego, and superego.

Those diagnosed with a "psychosis" were incarcerated in asylums. Subgroups of these psychoses were just four conditions: mania (conditions marked by excitement and fury), melancholia (serious depression), dementia (incoherent thoughts), and idiocy (intellectual deficiency and organic dementia). The conditions were considered incurable, but futile experiments that included insulin coma injections, shock treatments, fever therapies, and surgical procedures such as lobotomies, added torture to their life sentence.

By the early 1960s, however, the population of mental hospitals was steeply declining at the same time as the number of people seeking voluntary forms of outpatient treatment was dramatically escalating. Simultaneously, psychoanalysis was losing its credibility.

As psychiatric practice shifted from the asylums to outpatient treatment mostly for the "neuroses" that embraced the symptoms of fatigue, sadness, anxiety, and other stress-related complaints, the poor patient labelled with a "psychosis", such as schizophrenia, bipolar disorder, and dementia, and those at risk of suicide, were remained locked up in an asylum.

Mathew knew little of this as he was on his way to his interview at the Maudsley and was completely unaware that he was joining a profession that was on the cusp of a revolution. In preparation for the interview, he made notes about the history of the institution.

★ ★ ★

In 1247 Alderman Simon Fitz Mary, provided both funding and land for the priory which was linked to a religious order. The priory was the earliest form of what eventually became Bethlem Hospital. Towards the end of the 14th century, people with mental illness were accommodated in the hospital for the first time. In 1403 Bethlem was first referred to as a hospital for "insane" patients, and since then it has had a continuous history of caring for people with mental health issues. In 1547 King Henry VIII granted the 'custody, order and government' of the hospital of Bethlem to the City of London, as one of the five "royal" hospitals re-founded after the Reformation. From Bishopsgate, Bethlem was first re-sited in 1676 to a magnificent baroque building in Moorfields. It was the first purpose-built hospital for the "insane" in the country. In 1733 William Hogarth painted "Bedlam", the last scene in his Rake's Progress. The series shows the fall of fictional character, Tom Rakewell, the heir of a rich merchant, who comes to London, wastes all his money on luxurious living, prostitution, and gambling, and is imprisoned in the Fleet Prison and ultimately Bedlam. (Apart from the amusing antics of the inmates, the painting also includes some fashionably dressed making a visit for morbid entertainment, waving fans under their noses, no doubt to cope with the stench from faeces spread across the floor by the demented.)

In 1908, Dr Henry Maudsley, an eminent psychiatrist, urged the London City Council to establish a "fitly equipped hospital for mental diseases". He offered them £30,000 towards the costs. His vision was for an urban centre for a hospital rather than an asylum and for university psychiatric teaching and research.

The hospital offered treatment for both early and acute cases and had an outpatient clinic. It also housed teaching and research. The Maudsley had a good reputation for training nurses and applicants even travelled overseas to train there. Within 10 years, the associated Maudsley Hospital Medical School was officially recognised by the University of London. The school awarded one of the first diplomas in psychological medicine in the English-speaking world, thereby formalising psychiatry as a specialist discipline of medicine in the Commonwealth. In 1930, the Bethlem Royal Hospital relocated to Beckenham in the London Borough of Bromley, where it is still based today. In 1948, the Maudsley joined with the Bethlem Royal Hospital to become partners in the newly established NHS as a postgraduate psychiatric teaching hospital. The Maudsley Medical School became a founding member of the British Postgraduate Medical Federation and changed its name to the Institute of Psychiatry.

★ ★ ★

Minxy insisted on joining Mathew for the journey to the terra incognita of south-east London, not only to give him spiritual support but also out of curiosity. The furthest she'd ever travelled in London south of the River Thames was Waterloo to see a play at the Old Vic. The journey involved the Tube on the Northern Line from Golders Green, changing to the Bakerloo Line to the Elephant and Castle. From there they took a bus along the Walworth Road, Camberwell Road, and Denmark Hill. The view from the upper deck of the bus was squalid and seedy, with soot-covered tenements and ramshackle shops. Not a decent gown shop in sight. "So, this is how the poor people live and shop," she said to herself. Things brightened up a bit halfway up Denmark Hill, where the bus stopped outside the Maudsley Hospital, with the campus of King's College Hospital facing them on the other side of the road. They were in good time for Mathew's interview and Minxy decided to walk down the hill to Camberwell Green. She wished him good luck as he disappeared under the portico of the handsome red-brick neo-Classical building; she turned around and, with her crocodile skin handbag swinging on her right arm, sauntered down the busy street. When she arrived at the Green, the first thing she noticed was that there was no green left. It was covered in rubbish, cardboard boxes, and stinking rotten fruit and vegetables. Some of the boxes were inhabited by the homeless and some of them were obviously drunk, surrounded by empty beer cans and empty bottles of vodka. Those who were walking around the Green looked like tramps and children who should have been at school, were filthy and threatening, walking four abreast, blocking the pavement to other pedestrians. She was just about to turn round and walk back to the Maudsley when she was tapped the back by a little urchin with the face of a cherub. "'Av you got the time, missus? I ain't got no watch." Like a knee-jerk she looked at her watch on her left wrist and quick as a flash her handbag disappeared into the custody of a group of juvenile delinquents, who ran off laughing. She gave chase but other passers-by seemed to intentionally block her. It was like a scene from *Oliver Twist*. There were no police in sight, so she slid down the railings that encompassed "the Green", slumped on the pavement, and sobbed whilst kicking herself for her own stupidity.

It was no compensation when she met Mathew coming out of the Maudsley smiling ear to ear with thumbs up. She sulked all the way home and the thought of living anywhere near that cess pit horrified her.

Chapter 18

Maresfield Gardens to Dulwich Village

Once Mathew and Rebecca had returned to the KaMinxy home in Hampstead Garden Suburb, the normal pacific climate of the house was disrupted as a low-pressure weather system settled above the roof. Minxy ran upstairs weeping and locked herself in her bedroom. Her mother went hysterical without knowing what the problem was and summoned Mr KaMinxy to come home at once. His office was in a building on the High Street in Hampstead, so he was home in 20 minutes, sweating and out of breath. His first assumption was that the wedding was off thanks to some misdemeanour of his future son-in-law. Mathew calmed him down and poured two glasses of scotch from the crystal decanter on the sideboard and recounted the story. Mr KaMinxy, soothed by the reassuring words of Mathew and two fingers of 18-year-old Talisker, listened carefully. He dismissed the loss of the handbag but was concerned that he might have to change the locks on the door, congratulated Mathew on the outcome of his interview, and had the perfect solution of where best to live that was in easy reach of Denmark Hill. He summoned Rebecca to come downstairs and she meekly obeyed, red-eyed and miserable, and sat down on the settee next to Mathew. "Boobala, trust me, you have no reason to fret," her father said in a soft voice. "First thing, were the house keys in the bag?"

"No, Daddy, they are in my pocket," she replied.

"*Baruch HaShem*. Was there anything of value in the bag?"

"About £10, a powder compact, lipstick and gloves."

"*Gutt*, so the only thing of value you lost was the bag. I shall replace it and deduct the cost from your allowance."

Minxy smiled at that, knowing full well that her father would forget, so she simply nodded her consent.

"Now, young lady, I understand you do not vant to live in Camberwell. Well, neither would I. However, if you continue to drive further south for 10 minutes you would arrive at Dulwich Village; that would be more to your taste. I understand there is a famous little art gallery there and one of the trustees is a close friend. I suggest that tomorrow you take my car to visit Anna Freud, who happens to be an old friend of mine from Vienna, and in the afternoon continue driving to Dulwich Village. It will take an hour, but it will be worth the effort."

★ ★ ★

Number 20 Maresfield Gardens is a handsome house in a long road of other large and impressive properties at the southern border of Hampstead, one of the most fashionable districts of London. Many of the distinguished intelligentsia, authors, and artists live in this area, which boasts the largest unspoilt urban green parks, known as Hampstead Heath. You can walk for an hour without being disturbed by the noise from traffic on the roads. From the highest point of the Heath, Parliament Hill, you can see the whole of the city spread across the horizon, and yet by bus or the Underground train you can be in town in 20 minutes. No wonder the wealthy and well-connected choose this sanctuary. Anna Freud's house has a pretty front garden and to the left of the large porch a very large bay window, but the feature that distinguishes it from all the other grand houses is that it appears to have a nursery school where others would have a garage. Mathew and Minxy deduced this by the coming and going of mothers with their infant children at 9.30am.

Anna Freud opened the front door immediately after

they rung the bell, as if she was waiting for them. She greeted them both with triple European kisses on the cheeks that left Mathew off balance. On first sight, Sigmund Freud's youngest daughter looked like he imagined Minxy would look in 20- or 30-years' time. Petite, slim, dark brown eyes with the spark of intelligence and dark brown curly hair. Whilst Mathew was gathering his thoughts, Anna was first to speak. She had a soft voice with a distinct Austrian accent. "Miss KaMinxy – Rebecca, if I may – I remember your father from my childhood, and it is a great pleasure to welcome you to my father's house. Doctor Barnet, you are twice blest, first to be engaged to this beautiful young lady and second for the exceptional letter of recommendation from my old friend and colleague Professor Hoffbrand. Please follow me; we will have some coffee first and then I will show you round the house." They followed her to the kitchen at the back of the house that looked over a very well-cared-for garden. The entrance hall was huge and flooded with sunlight from all the surrounding windows, with a wide staircase covering two sides of the atrium with bannisters suggesting a minstrel's gallery.

After coffee and *kuchen*, they started the tour on the ground floor with the biggest room on the northern side of the house, which was brightly illuminated by the large bay window overlooking the front garden and French windows overlooking the back garden. This was Sigmund Freud's office, which doubled up as the therapy room. Anna had left it exactly as it had been when her father died in 1939. Her manner and the tone of her voice suggested that the young couple were being privileged in visiting the shrine to the memory of the man who gave birth to psychoanalysis.

The first thing they noticed was Freud's iconic psychoanalytic couch. The couch was covered with an oriental rug and cushions. The next thing that caught their attention was Freud's collection of ancient artefacts, which gave the office the look of a room in the British Museum. There was a cabinet full of ancient Greek vases and a wall covered with

African and Asian masks. But the most extraordinary sight was that Freud's desk, bookshelves, and every other flat surface were covered with terracotta idols, bronze figures with wings, statues of Greek gods and goddesses, and ancient Egyptian shabits linked to the burial ceremonies of high-ranking servants of the pharaohs. There was barely enough room on his desk for the writing pad upon which his wire-framed glasses were delicately placed. Anna then tried to make sense of the over-furnishing of her father's office. "After my father's death in 1939, my mother made no changes to the study for the rest of her life. After my mother's death I maintained that tradition. The psychoanalytic couch was brought to London from Vienna and can be seen as a functional item of furniture; it also has a metaphysical identity. Psychoanalysis represents a negative defined space: it is neither medicine nor psychiatry, neither a religious confessional nor artistic creation. The collection of artefacts bearing the images of men, women, gods, goddesses, and chimaera – half men, half beasts – illustrates his lifetime obsession in his search for the ego, superego, and id. In addition, some have exaggerated phalluses next to some of indeterminant gender. They all reflect the raw materials of psychoanalysis fleeting and invisible, associations of ideas, dreams, slips of the tongue, and even silence." Minxy had no idea what this minestrone soup of words meant but decided to keep quiet. Anna continued with her monologue. "My father's work was the first to have given the key to the understanding of human behaviour and its aberrations as being determined not by overt factors but by the pressure of instinctual forces emanating from the unconscious mind." The tour continued over most of the house, which was also full of bizarre artefacts and drawings or photographs of Sigmund Freud himself.

When they arrived at Anna Freud's study, which appeared to be a miniature version of her father's study, Minxy built up the courage to ask Anna a question that was bugging her. "Anna, I understand that you specialise in psychoanalysis of children. How can ego, id, and sexuality apply to children?"

"That's a good question, Rebecca. When infants develop from suckling to rational eating, the attitude to food itself reflects to the relationship between mother and child. The female breast that can arouse an adult man in one way has an impact on an infant in another way. At puberty for a male child there is a period of cross-over and that gives birth to the Oedipus complex." Minxy was none the wiser but politely smiled and nodded her head. As they were leaving Anna's room, Mathew spotted an alcove with a wooden weaving loom. Anna noticed his interest and turned back. "I'm glad you noted that, Mathew. Weaving is my hobby and my therapy. I find it very comforting and some of the rugs downstairs were made by me. My father was sceptical of its therapeutic value and dismissed it as the unconscious effect of 'penis envy'. Weaving imitates the pubic hair concealing the genitals; hence it is associated with shame and acts as a substitute penis." Minxy struggled to restrain her laughter until they left the house, waved goodbye, and got into their car.

Once Minxy had caught her breath, sharing her uncontrolled laughter with Mathew, her first words were, "You don't believe that do you? It sounds like bullshit to me."

"NO, I do not," he replied and then started a rant that almost took them to the Vauxhall Bridge en route to Dulwich Village. "Psychoanalysis is not psychiatry; it is a bogus set of ideas with no supporting evidence. Pundits say that the 20th century's three greatest thinkers, who all happened to be Jews, were Karl Marx, Albert Einstein, and Sigmund Freud. To put Freud alongside Marx and Einstein is an insult and an embarrassment. There are no controlled data that suggest psychotherapy cured anybody and without controls it might have made things worse. The patient was almost a prisoner of the therapist; furthermore, the treatment was only relevant to the wealthy with time on their hands. Some therapists suggested that the exchange of coins was symbolic of the valued link between patient and therapist. You bet! As a youth I read Freud's *The Interpretation of Dreams* and was taken in at first, but once I'd grown up I realised it was all a hoax. Most of his written work consisted of anecdotes of disturbed individuals, perhaps attention seekers or, worse, figments of Freud's imagination. Take the famous 'Wolf Man'. He was a wealthy aristocrat from Odesa in the Ukraine. He was suffering with constipation and depression and his physician recommended him to see Freud in Vienna. Freud's treatment centred on a dream this nobleman had as a young child. If I remember it correctly it went something like this. His bedroom window suddenly opened, and he was frightened to see some white wolves sitting under a tree in his garden. He was terrified he would be eaten by the wolves and screamed out loud and his nurse ran in to see what was wrong. Freud's eventual analysis was that the young boy had witnessed his parents having sex the doggy way. The patient continued with analysis for six decades before he was declared cured. This was considered one of the most important dreams in the development of Freud's theories. You can't make it up. You called it bullshit, I call it delusional, and the one who needed treatment was not the guy with constipation but the therapist himself."

"Yet Anna was right about one thing, Mathew," said Minxy, "she clearly described the relationship between Venus and Cupid in the Bronzino painting in the National Gallery."

After crossing to the south side of the Thames, Mathew had to guide Minxy, driving her father's car, using an A–Z of London. The transition from Camberwell Green to Dulwich Village was sudden and unexpected, like many districts in London. From squalor to Regency elegance by crossing from Denmark Hill to Redpost Hill. They drove along a charming line of little specialist shops, some with windows displaying fashionable ladieswear! There was a book shop that doubled as a post office and an old-fashioned cobbler's shop. A grand Victorian pub called the Crown and Greyhound dominated the parade, flanked by a coffee shop and a smart restaurant. Leaving the shops behind, they entered a wide stretch of road with black steel chains on posts, marking off the pavements that were built with cobblestones. Most of the houses were flat-fronted and three stories high with perfect Georgian symmetries of windows and doors. The walls painted white, and the doors painted red, blue, or black, took you back in time to when horses and carriages predated the motor car and crinolines predated the miniskirts. Just beyond the grand houses was a row of cute one-storied cottages, with pretty front gardens and roses all over the porch. They all had white wicket fences and gates. One of them had a plaque saying that this was Mr Pickwick's cottage as dreamt up by Charles Dickens. Further on were playing fields and impressive red-brick building of Dulwich College, one of the most famous public schools in England. Opposite the school were the high and elaborate gates at the entry to Dulwich Park. Next up on the south end of the college's playing fields was, wonder of wonders, a perfect low-rise, early-19th-century Palladian building with a large banner at the entrance announcing "Dulwich Picture Gallery. Entrance Free." They parked outside and Minxy couldn't believe her luck. The interior was silent like a chapel, beautiful in its proportions, with a bizarre extension that looked like a mausoleum. The plaque on the wall nearby read:

Dulwich Picture Gallery is one of the finest examples of gallery architecture in Britain. Open to the public in 1817. It was designed and built by the leading architect Sir John Soane (1753-1837) at the personal request of his friend Sir Francis Bourgeois who had left a fund of £2,000. He estimated that this new building would cost in the region of £11,270, substantially more than Bourgeois had provisioned. The deficit was generously met by the College, as well as Margaret Desenfans. Bourgeois and Margaret Desenfans are buried here.

Minxy was in her element and was ecstatic about the beauty of the building and couldn't believe that this picture gallery was open to the public before the National Gallery at Trafalgar Square.

Chapter 19

From Paradise to Bedlam
August to September 1962

Dr and Mrs Barnet felt rather smug as they walked past the long queue waiting to enter the Uffizi Gallery. They had the wisdom to book a timed entrance on this beautiful and hot morning in Florence. To get this far they had flown from Gatwick to Pisa, intending to catch the train to Florence, only to find the Italian railways were on strike. Instead, they splashed out a million or so liras for a taxi all the way. The Tuscan countryside was a delight, dotted with green hills bearing ancient citadels and clusters of tall, pointed cypress trees. They were dropped off at the Grand Hotel Baglioni Firenze, where Minxy had stayed on a previous visit with her parents. It was early evening and the first thing Minxy wanted to do was to take her husband onto the roof garden to see the city before the sunset. Comfortably seated, with a glass of pink Campari orange in hand, the view was breathtaking. The cathedral, with its dome and lantern, held centre stage, together with Giotto's bell tower standing upright on the side. Red tile roofs and church towers occupied the rest of the nearby scene, whilst the tower of the Palazzo della Signoria could just be seen to the right of their field of view. In the distant horizon the hills of Fiesole could just be seen in silhouette as the sunset exploded in all colours of the rainbow and a few stratified clouds, underlit by the setting sun, reflected a golden yellow. Exhausted from their travels and the exertions of their wedding ceremony, they chose to have a light supper and go to bed early, to be fresh the next day for exploring the epicentre of the Italian Renaissance.

Mathew had only the vaguest memory of his wedding because the evening before he enjoyed a "stag party" that included Peter, Dylan, and Ginger, and involved visits to several nightclubs under the sophisticated guidance and deep pockets of Dr Baring. This ended up at the Marquee club, where they enjoyed one of the first gigs played by the Rolling Stones. He got to bed stoned at about 3.00am. The wedding *chuppah* and the reception were held at the Savoy hotel on the Strand. He began to sober up just in time for the traditional ritual of the breaking of the glass in memory of the fall of the second Temple. This demanded that he stamp down his right foot with accuracy and without falling over. The crack of broken glass triggered an insane whirligig of traditional Eastern European Jewish dancing, with men and women segregated to opposite ends of the riverside hall of the hotel. The next thing he remembered was being held up in the air sitting on a chair by a circle of strong young men to meet his new bride face to face. She was also sitting on an elevated chair making decorous connection with the groom by holding the opposite corners of a white sheet. He nearly threw up on the crowd below and had only blurred visions of the rest of the evening. The moment the young couple got to the bridal suite, Mathew fell asleep flat on his face and fully dressed, unaware of the beautiful boat-shaped baroque bed he was sharing with his bride. He never got round to consummating his marriage until about 4.00am, when he was woken by his distended bladder.

Waking up on their first morning in Florence, with the sun shining in through their east-facing windows, Mathew found Minxy dressed already, eating croissants and drinking dark coffee ordered in from room service with a ticked-off menu they had hooked on the door before going to sleep. She chivvied him out of bed as if there were some urgency and Mathew was alarmed to find it was already 9.00am, having forgotten to change his wristwatch to the new time zone. Their timed entry passes for the Uffizi gallery were for 10.00am, so he washed, shaved, and dressed as quickly as possible, gulped back a mouthful of coffee, and was on the street within 20 minutes. Minxy led the way with confidence. Turning left out of the hotel, they immediately saw the dome of the Duomo looming up at the end of a narrow street. At the door of the cathedral, they turned right and skipped along the narrow footpath between Giotto's campanile and the baptistry bearing Ghiberti's golden gates to paradise. They jogged along the diagonal across the Piazza della República, past the Palazzo Medici, pushed their way through a crowded open air market, past the Palazzo Vecchio, resisting to stop and gawp at Michelangelo's gigantic statue of David, ignoring the sculptures in the Loggia dei Lanzi and entering the Piazzale degli Uffizi just as all the bells in Florence chimed 10 o'clock.

Once inside the gallery, they caught their breath and Mathew treated himself to a small thimble of black espresso coffee whilst Minxy checked the map of the gallery to remind herself of her favourite paintings. After a two-hour guided tour by Mrs Barnet, there were four pictures that had a profound impact on him and ignited his love for fine art for the rest of his life. The first two shared a windowless room with grey walls. They faced each other as if competing for attention. The brilliant colours suggested that the light was transmitted not reflected thanks to the expert mounting of artificial lights. There were no other pictures in the room. They were both by Botticelli; on the left as you entered was the iconic *Birth of Venus* and on the right the less famous picture of equal beauty, *Primavera* (springtime).

In both he recognised the model, Simonetta Vespucci, naked at her birth on the left and wearing a see-through full-length dress covered in dainty flowers, representing springtime, on the right. They were huge panels, with the star model almost life size. The composition of the painting of Venus was simple but the composition of springtime was so complex that it drew you in, to wander round the woodland with all the pretty young maidens. Minxy had difficulty dragging him away to visit other masterpieces. The next painting that Mathew found unforgettable was in the octagonal room, hanging a group of portraits by Agnolo di Cosimo who was known as Bronzino, his old friend from the National Gallery. It was a painting of Lucrezia Panciatichi, the wife of a very wealthy nobleman. Whereas Simonetta was young and beautiful like a modern catwalk model, Lucrezia, was a mature woman in her early thirties. She had grey-green eyes that looked you in the face, her hair was set in a complex coif, her lips were full and kissable, and her neck was long and wreathed with a pearl neckless carrying a medallion bearing an inscription. She was dressed in an elaborate ruby-red silk costume and her right hand rested on an open book. She looked intelligent and the book was intended as an icon of her scholarship. Her overall impact on Mathew, he was embarrassed to say, was love at first sight. Minxy drew his attention to the engraving on the medallion on her neck that read, "Amour dure sans fin", translated as "Love is everlasting". He gazed on Lucrezia as if hypnotised until Minxy broke the spell. "For God's sake, Mathew, pull yourself together, she's been dead for 500 years. I hate that woman. All the men with any taste fall in love with her. Forget her and save all your love for me!"

Mathew never forgot Lucrezia, and her ghost haunted him for the rest of his life. He often wondered if this was like a Pygmalion syndrome.

The fourth painting that had a lasting effect on Mathew came as a shock. It was not on Minxy's list, and he could understand why. It was horrid and gratuitous in its brutality, yet beautifully painted. Why would anybody take so much trouble to illustrate such torture? The central figure was a woman, naked above the waist. On each side of her was a brutal torturer bearing long-handled iron instruments that looked as if they were designed to cut through the lock on your garage doors. In the foreground, within reach of the henchman on the right, was a long knife you might use for cutting sugar cane. The pliers are grasping her nipples, pulling the breast off her chest wall, and Mathew had no doubt what was going to happen next. The label below the picture announced that this was St Agatha, and the artist was Sebastiano del Piombo. He summoned Minxy back, demanding to know what the hell was going on. She was quick to spit out the answer. "That, dear love, is St Agatha, patron saint of the breast. A young virgin in the 3rd century, who resisted the advances of the Roman governor and was punished by having her breast cut off. This image of misogyny was very popular for artists between the 13th and 17th centuries as an excuse to provide some pornography for the celibate monks and bishops. In backward Catholic countries, women with breast cancer pray to these sacred icons." Mathew was instantly reminded of the radical mastectomy he watched as a medical student and came over nauseated and was quick to leave the gallery for some fresh air, leaning over the wall above the River Arno at the back of the Uffizi.

The rest of their honeymoon flew by, and every day was like paradise. They explored all the sights and galleries of Florence, enjoying Florentine wine and cuisine, which included steaks of dinner-plate size, not to mention the pasta dishes that were totally unlike the heavy, lumpen, and tasteless equivalents in London. They had a day out in Sienna, a perfect unspoilt city looking as if it was built yesterday but had in fact survived for 500 years.

Finally, they drove back from inland Tuscany for a week at the seaside at the fashionable resort Forte Dei Marmi, not far from the airport at Pisa. By this time Mathew was looking forward to starting work at the Royal Maudsley Hospital and Bethlem two days after they got home.

Chapter 20

From the sublime to the ridiculous
September 1962

Like most academic institutions, the Maudsley and Institute of Psychiatry accepted new staff at the beginning of the academic year in the first week of September. This particular year, the Jewish high holy days, Rosh Hashana (New Year) and Yom Kippur (the Day of Atonement), were early, which meant Mathew would have to request a few days off duty only one week after starting the job. He was terrified to find himself facing the fury of the clinical director of the Maudsley on the one hand or the fury of the creator of the Universe on the other hand. It was a close call and he decided that God outranked professor, Sir Aubrey Julian Lewis, his new boss. He was scheduled to meet the great man at 11.00am on his first day, where he would be instructed on the rules and regulations of the institute as well as his timetable of work. He would be one of three joining up as a senior house officer on that day. Shaking at the knees, he sat in the anteroom to the Holy of Holies of his terrestrial lord and master, waiting for the call. Sir Aubrey's secretary took pity on the young man and assured him that his bark was worse than his bite, at which point he heard the bark, just one word, "COME", and the secretary opened the double doors and ushered Mathew into the sanctuary.

Sitting behind a huge mahogany table was a fierce-looking, bald-headed, and moustachioed gentleman who looked to be in about his mid-sixties. Sir Aubrey did not lift his head for a while whilst signing off some letters before looking up and welcoming his new house officer with one word, "SIT". And lo! Mathew sat. Sir Aubrey then grabbed Mathew's file and started reading it, looking up at times with a quizzical expression, as if he doubted what he had read applied to the man in front of him. Then he spoke with a surprisingly friendly demeanour with a hint of a twinkle in his eyes. "Well, young man, you seem to have an excellent academic record and very good references from colleagues I respect. You are most welcome, and I have high expectations of your career, but you will find the work hard and paradoxically a threat to your own sanity. With your personal welfare at heart, I've arranged for you to visit our staff counselling unit every Friday morning at 9.00am.

"You will be working on our two sites, Monday, Wednesday, and Friday here and Tuesday and Thursday at the Bethlem Infirmary. You will join one of our three clinical firms and be on duty one weekend in three. We have regular case conferences and teaching seminars and one of our psychoanalysts will take you under her wing both to teach you the skills and keep an eye on your sub-conscience morbidity." Sir Aubrey stopped to take a sip of his coffee, whilst Mathew decided to keep shtum about his scepticism of psychoanalysis. "My secretary, Miss Blumenthal, will give you your timetable and you are scheduled to meet one of our consultants, Dr Isaac Zietman, who is chief of your firm. Any questions?"

With sweating armpits, and full fight-or-flight adrenaline release from his adrenal glands, Mathew responded in a squeaky voice, "Excuse me, sir, but can I have a few days off next week for the Jewish high holy days, please sir?"

Sir Aubrey's response was not quite what Mathew was expecting. He burst out laughing and once he caught his breath replied, "My dear young man, I had predicted that question. I too will be taking off time for Rosh Hashana and Yom Kippur. I'm Jewish and so are half my senior staff. We might as well shut down in this period. Do you know why so many psychiatrists are Jewish?" Then without waiting for an answer he continued, "Well in my opinion the history of the Jews tells us that we as a race have been culled by every despot and every autocracy over the last two millennium, so that only the wisest of our tribe have survived. Join the club." Mathew left the room totally confused, yet with a big smile on his face. In the anteroom Miss Blumenthal handed over his weekly agenda and then guided him to meet Dr Zietman on the first floor.

★ ★ ★

Mathew rapidly settled down into his routine and loved his work with a few serious caveats. He much preferred the days he worked at the Maudsley Hospital but became phobic about his days at the Bethlem asylum. In broad terms, most of the cases he looked after on Denmark Hill were "neuroses" like anxiety, depression, mild versions of bipolar disease, personality disorders, and the early stages of dementia. The latter often sent from over the road at King's College Hospital if picked up by chance, having been admitted for conventional medical and surgical disorders. Mathew was too junior in his post be aware of a trend amongst psychiatrists shifting their activities away from the psychoses toward milder conditions in the hope that early treatment of functional but distressed individuals would ultimately diminish the incidence of the more serious disorders. The role of factors such as difficulties in parent–child relationships and marriage, emotional immaturity, and the inability of individuals to adjust to their environments being responsible for triggering mental illness.

In contrast, the Bethlem asylum was for people with serious mental illness, in broad terms the psychoses, such as schizophrenia, schizoaffective disorder, advanced bipolar disorder, and major depressive disorder, and other severely disabling mental disorders, such as post-traumatic stress, who had many needs and might be a danger to themselves and to their families or society in general.

Mathew learnt quickly on the job. The most common conditions presented by patients at the Maudsley were anxiety and depression and he became to enjoy helping the sufferers because there was much to offer. Anxiety cases frequently complained of insomnia and panic attacks. The latter could be terrifying, with sensations of impending death. They would often run out of a gathering of friends or family without any excuse and run round the garden or around the block as if being chased. They would even harm themselves by way of distraction. They would repeatedly develop agoraphobia and avoid shopping malls and other crowded places.

The depressive patient was pathologically sad, but the sadness was much more than feeling down at heart. One of his patients described it very imaginatively with these words: "Doctor, I feel like a lump of shit, a turd hiding in a corner, I am worthless and a blot on the landscape. I think my family and the world at large would be better without me." He was a tall, handsome man with a successful legal practice.

Often the anxiety and depression went on side by side to the point that his consultants treated them as one disease described in the notes as *anxiety/depressive* illness.

The first visit of such patients was spent exploring their family history, lifestyle, relationships, sexuality, and financial affairs. Mathew felt genuinely sorry for them as they often had tragic stories to tell and problems that they thought were unsolvable, which would make the toughest of us crack up or break down. In other words, they were "reasonable" responses to intolerable circumstances. If they were judged suicidal, they would be admitted to hospital like any other life-threatening disease. Those that could be treated as outpatients had three or four options. First, simple counselling might help that could involve a sympathetic bank manager, marriage guidance, family therapy, or visits to the headmaster to find out if there was a problem at school that could explain a child's extremely bad behaviour. Finally, if the patient was a member of a faith there was always a role for a reassuring chat with a vicar or rabbi. Community groups, like churches and synagogues, provide companionship for the lonely and support for the struggling, in addition to being houses of prayer.

The next step for cases with no obvious exogenous causation fell into the hands of the psychotherapist. At first Mathew played along with this, not wishing to disclose his scepticism, but very soon he realised that to be completely dismissing of psychotherapy was bigotry. Under such circumstances unblocking "blocked" memory might be advantageous; often, the problem was linked to the patient's sexuality. A good example was Mr X, the lawyer who thought he was a blot on the landscape. He had no obvious or admitted problems and Mathew suspected he might be a homosexual. Between the first and second visit, he looked up the correlates said to be linked to homosexuality according to the teachings at the Maudsley.

> *The most significant factor which correlates with homosexuality is "gender nonconformity" or same-sex peer isolation. Another factor closely associated with homosexuality is an imbalance in parent–child interaction, notably forms of over-influence of the opposite-sex parent in combination with a deficient relationship with the same-sex parent. The third well-established correlation is with inherent, rather than discrimination-produced, "neuroticism" or emotional in stability/immaturity.*

He found that remarkably unhelpful. Freud's opinions were equally opaque, relying on the superego, which was but a metaphysical construct.

> *Freud's theories relating to male homosexuality and the development of the super-ego. These hypotheses are (1) relatively little father–son contact during early childhood increases the probability of homosexuality; (2) under a condition of relatively high father*

contact, increased sexual attachment to the mother decreases the
probability of homosexuality; (3) relatively little father–son contact
during early childhood impedes the development of the son's
super-ego; and (4) there should be a negative zero-order correlation
between homosexuality and the super-ego development.

The problem was not helped by the fact that the Wolfenden Committee, in 1957, recommended the decriminalisation of private homosexual activity between consenting adults over the age of 21, but with heavier penalties against homosexual activity in public places. The laws against homosexual activity remained unaltered, however. In the end Mathew had to develop his own method to cope with blocking. At the next appointment the analytic process went like this.

"Mr X, do you find yourself more attracted to men than to the opposite sex?"

"Yes, doctor, how did you guess? I assume I can trust you not to share this knowledge with anyone else."

"Absolutely, Mr X. I'm bound by the Hippocratic oath."

"I trust your word, doctor. Wasn't Hippocrates a bit of a hypocritic? I understand that all those ancient Greeks were queers." At which he burst with laughter and Mathew joined in with gusto. After a few minutes Mr X's laughter turned to tears. Once he had controlled his emotions he said, "Doctor, you know that's the first time I've confessed to being a homosexual and, what's more, I think you may have cured my depressive state. I *am* of some worth, my partner loves me, and my clients respect me, and my wife looks after me well despite suspecting my aberration. Our love is platonic, if you'll forgive me for that pun." He then stood upright, grabbed Mathew in a bear hug, and walked out with his head in the air. Not all cases were that easy, but he could always fall back on medication like the benzodiazepines Librium and Valium, which had recently been marketed for the relief of "anxiety and tension".

★ ★ ★

In contrast to his work at the Denmark Hill branch of the institute, Mathew dreaded his sessions at the Bethlem branch in Beckenham. On his first visit for induction, his was shown padded cells and taught how to dress a patient in a straitjacket with the help of a porter built like a bouncer. The interior of the building was enormous and looked as if there was space for over 1,000 inmates. His team were allocated a male and a female ward that included Nightingale units with long central corridors with patients' beds curtained to offer some privacy. There were also additional units with locked doors for those patients needing restraint. The colour scheme was nothing like that of Piero della Francisco but had a standard institutional appearance, with dark green tyles halfway up the wall and white painted bricks above, beyond the patients' reach. The smell of carbolic acid antiseptic was ubiquitous. It was made clear to Mathew that care was more important than cure, so his main responsibility was checking that the patient was kept clean, well fed, and free of the stigmata of self-harm. He was unaware that he had started work in the era that where "shock therapy" was starting to be replaced by drug therapy. Electroconvulsive therapy (ECT) was still in use as standard of care for schizophrenics but fortunately insulin coma therapy had just been abandoned. The first drug therapy that was effective for psychotic patients with schizophrenia or bipolar disease, chlorpromazine (Largactil), became available in 1956 in the UK, somewhat later than its introduction in France, where the drug was invented in 1951. The British psychiatric establishment was deeply sceptical of drug therapy for the psychoses as it was locked into the mindset of early-20th-century Viennese metaphysics of the mind. Nevertheless, despite the successes of Largactil, Mathew was burdened with three ECT sessions a week and each session involved up to 20 patients. From the patients' point of view, each course consisted of usually six to 12 treatments, with up to three treatments given each week. At that time, ECT was also used as a "treatment" for homosexuality, then considered by some psychiatrists to be an illness. The procedure looked barbaric but was delivered in a way considered humane and in good faith. The patients were given general anaesthetic and strong muscle relaxant to virtually paralyse them and stop dangerous physical convulsions. Their skin was smeared with gel for electrical conduction, and electrodes were taped to the forehead. The patient was then strapped on their back to the flat table, which had pivots so patients could be turned upside-down if they vomited. The psychiatrists then increased the voltage until they got a twitching toe – a sign that, despite paralysing drugs, the body's nervous system was in major convulsion. The electrical storm raging through every synapse of the brain was meant to cure patients, although all concerned had to admit they had no idea how. The main lasting side effect was loss of memory. In 1962, a novel was written by Ken Kesey, *One Flew Over the Cuckoo's Nest*, who drew on his experience working at a hospital in California to describe how ECT was used as a disciplinary tool to tame unruly patients at the time. Mathew read the book in 1963 and thought it was unfair to extrapolate the behaviour of doctors and nurses on the west coast of America to the practice in south-east London. Never had he witnessed ECT as a disciplinary tool and all the nurses he worked with were kind-hearted and saw their role as to protect and care for their patients. What upset Mathew, nonetheless, was the crudity of the technique. He looked upon it as akin to kicking the TV set if it wasn't performing well, when all that was wrong was a loose contact between a wire and a screw. In fact, there was an unkind definition of a mentally sick person having "a few loose screws". The suggestion that there was indeed a biological abnormality in the brain linked to schizophrenia was the success of chlorpromazine. The drug was originally developed as an antihistamine but there was still a lot of research required to fully understand its effect on the brain. Furthermore, although easier to deliver than ECT, it was not free of serious side effects that included sedation, weight gain, hypotension leading to dizziness, and a foul taste in the mouth. It was, as they said, to be a "dirty drug".

Chapter 21

A paradigm shift
1963–1965

Whilst Mathew was settling into his routine, Minxy was exploring the neighbourhoods. She loved Dulwich Village but found the surrounding boroughs alarming. Camberwell was squalid, Brixton was full of gangsters and prone to riots, and Clapham was clapped out. There was no Underground station within walking distance and buses, and overland trains took forever to get north of the river to the West End or Hampstead. She therefore decided to build up a new life within the green and appealing bounds of her village. This proved easier than she anticipated. First, she was within a five-minute walk of the local picture gallery and, with her MA in the history of art, was soon recruited as a guide and assistant curator. Amongst the collection there were two famous Rembrandts, *A Girl at the Window* and *Titus*, a portrait of Rembrandt's son. Both these paintings were notorious for having been stolen in the past and were to be stolen a second time the following year. Many of the visitors to the gallery were young mothers pushing babies in buggies, filling in the time until their husbands came home, who lived nearby. She often got into conversation with them and found they had much in common. They were mostly the wives of professional men, either lawyers in the City or consultants at King's College Hospital. Before long, invitations to coffee mornings or dinner parties came rolling in. Minxy's charm and vivaciousness made her very popular. Come spring 1963 she missed two periods and was declared by her local GP to be pregnant. Mathew was overjoyed by this development and developed morning sickness and abdominal distension in sympathy. He thought he must be going mad but soon learnt that this was a common psychosomatic phenomenon, worthy of research. His wife glowed in her pregnancy, and he fell in love with all over again. As far as his work was concerned, he was less than happy. By the mid-1960s, the population of mental hospitals was steeply declining at the same time as the number of people seeking voluntary forms of outpatient treatment was dramatically escalating. These were predominately the neurasthenic package of fatigue, sadness, anxiousness, and other stress-related complaints, victims of "outrageous fortune". But the major psychoses – schizophrenia, bipolar disorder, and melancholia – were the most easily recognisable psychiatric disorders. They were marked by behaviours, thoughts, and emotions that seem disconnected from reality and often accompanied by delusions and hallucinations, and patients who suffered these remained in the Bethlem sanatorium. As far as Mathew was concerned, using syphilis as an example, this implied a condition that appeared to be a mental disorder but was essentially an organic medical disease. It gave him hope that many other psychiatric conditions might also have organic causes and, if identified at an early stage through an objective test, might be prevented from progressing in severity. Furthermore, the limited successes of ECT and chlorpromazine reinforced his conviction. Things came to a head when, by chance, his social life collided with his scientific life in the early summer of 1964, at a dinner party organised by Minxy in honour of a lifelong friend who was visiting from the USA. This happened to be Oliver Sacks, who he had met at Jack Straw's Castle just after they got engaged. He now lived in California and was completing a residency in neurology and neuropathology at the University of California Los Angeles. The other guests were colleagues of Mathew from the Maudsley who lived in Dulwich Village and their wives. What the women had in common were babies in carrycots, who would join Shoshana Barnet in the spare bedroom upstairs.

The evening started well, with everyone enjoying champagne cocktails or a dram of whisky on arrival. Oliver fitted in very well as a Londoner and a brilliant raconteur. The men shared an interest in psychology and the women shared an interest in lactation and nappies. Seven of those present were Jewish and three of the couples weren't. To add a dash of colour, one couple, Dr and Mrs Vaidya, were Indian and Mrs Vaidya wore a peacock-coloured sari. Apart from the Hindu guests, who were quite happy with fruit juice, by the time they sat down everyone was very merry. The first course was a gazpacho soup with cream and croutons and the main course was Minxy's speciality, salmon *en croute* with a handmade mayonnaise. This was accompanied with a nicely chilled French Sauvignon Blanc. Before the guests arrived, Mathew had knocked back a double Johnnie Walker scotch to build up Dutch courage, so, what with the French, Scotch, and Dutch, by now he was a little inebriated. Despite dirty looks from his dear wife, he embarked on one of his favourite harangues. Psychotherapy was bogus, and had a great future behind it, ECT was no better than kicking the TV, and psychiatrics was just a branch of medicine rather than stand-alone metaphysic. This went down like a lead balloon and the reaction was like touching the blue fuse of a firework. The shouting got louder and louder until the babies upstairs started crying. Minxy was close to tears as her lovely dinner party was at the point of collapse, when Oliver intervened with a soft voice of authority that, like magic, attracted attention. "My dear friends, why do you fight when you are all agreeing with each other? True, our host framed his question with an unfortunate choice of words that sounded like an assertion but was in fact they were meant to be words of enquiry. His question is a fundamental challenge, and your passionate responses are a credit to your profession. Let me frame this debate in another way. Consider the brain as a grouping of three separate units that sit in comfort with mutual support within the cranium. These are made of two hemispheres, the right and the left, and the cerebellum. Since the original work of Broca in the 1890s, we know that the left hemisphere is responsible for all motor control of the body and the five senses, touch, sight, hearing, smell, and taste. The cerebellum's functions are maintaining balance, coordinating movement of multiple muscle groups, timing muscle contractions so that the body can move smoothly, coordinating eye movements, and helping the body to learn movements that require practice and fine-tuning. For example, the cerebellum plays a role in learning to ride a bicycle or play a musical instrument. So, what does the right hemisphere do? Well, to use Mathew's favourite cliché, it is terra incognita. That then leaves us all free to postulate its role. We, seated around the table, think it is the home for the mind. Note my use of the word *mind*. Not soul; that is a metaphysical construct. The mind is what makes us what we are. It controls the memory. We know that because loss of memory is a side effect of ECT. Beyond that it is difficult to judge. For example, Korsakov's syndrome, which is not only associated with loss of memory but also linked to confabulation and hallucinations. It is the consequence of alcoholism but also with tertiary syphilis or on rare occasions, with advanced cerebral tumours. But memory does not in itself make a person with desires, love, faith, truth telling, or criminality. Catatonia, a symptom of advanced schizophrenia, is also a symptom of sleeping sickness, a viral disease. We use the words psychopath or sociopaths but are there many organic foci that determine virtue, vice, or personality. Unlike other components of the body, superficial anatomy tells us little about functions, microscopic anatomy is so complex we can't make sense of it, X-rays are of no value and the electro-encephalogram, EEG, is helpful in diagnosing epilepsy but nothing else. It is left to our generation to explore this mysterious and tantalising land, and this demands approaches from all different standpoints and technologies." At the end of this brilliant deposition, there was silence in the room that was followed by a different type of debate of mutual respect and the evening was a great success and the last guests left at midnight, Minxy went upstairs to attend to Shoshana, leaving Mathew and Oliver talking through the night. It was a memorable event for all those fortunate to be there, but for Mathew it had life-changing consequences. Psychiatry and neurology were like Janus, the two-faced god, and should be practised and researched as one set of pathologies effecting the brain. The following morning, he built up the courage to visit Sir Aubrey Lewis, to request a transfer to the Department of Neurology at King's College Hospital across the road.

PART 5

Peter Baring 1962–1965

Chapter 22

Bedlam at Steelhouse Lane 1962

Peter started his surgical career by being thrown in at the deep end in the Birmingham General Hospital, Steelhouse Lane. It was his misfortune to start working as a senior house officer in the Accident and Emergency department (A&E) on Friday, 3 August. Friday was the day that the poorest workingmen received their brown envelope with their humble pay. Their priority before coming home for the weekend was to visit their local hostelry to drown their sorrows. Sadly, this was a vicious circle as this only added to their sorrows once they handed over their pay packet to "her indoors". Drinking two or three pints of best bitter ale led to three types of trauma: a punch in the face in a brawl, a fall on their face as they staggered outside, or a black eye from his missus after she has inspected what was left of her housekeeping money. Whatever the source of the trauma, they ended up at the A&E department of the General. This gave the department the appearance of Hogarth's *Bedlam*, more so than what Mathew was experiencing at the Bethlem asylum. In fact, when the fisticuffs spilled out into Steelhouse Lane, the ambiance was more akin to Hogarth's *Gin Lane*. Amongst the apparent chaos indoors there was an element of order as the toughest of the nurses at the reception zone carried out a triage. Walking wounded were sent to a waiting room to take their turn, those with arterial haemorrhage taken on a trolley to the A&E operating tables for a ligature and sutures, and those who were moribund admitted to the hospital and if it was a surgical emergency whisked to the main theatres for the surgical registrar on call to deal with. As the new man in the block, Peter was given the task of suturing the minor wounds and assessing those who had suffered concussion in case that were at risk of intra-cranial haemorrhage. Scattered amongst the Friday night specials there were the run of the mill "acute abdomens". These were commonly acute appendicitis, a perforated duodenal ulcer, cholecystitis, diverticulitis, aortic aneurisms, and the odd gynaecological emergency such as an ectopic pregnancy or acute salpingitis. In such cases the SHOs in A&E would send for one of the resident surgical registrars. According to the best advice from his mentor, Professor Iain McGregor, Peter should have been studying for part 1 of the FRCS whilst acting as a demonstrator in the Anatomy Department and only then spend a year as an SHO in the A&E department at the General. But Peter was a man in a hurry; he thought he could study for part 1 of the FRCS in his spare time whilst working in the A&E department. This spare time was the evenings he was not in residence on call and two out of three weekends. Mrs Baring was not happy with this arrangement. During his first Monday, after a frenetic weekend, Peter experienced the pace of work in A&E slowing down, yet in many ways more interesting. He was now observing the worst of the real world and for the first time realised that he had a privileged upbringing that protected him from witnessing the foulest behaviour of mankind. He soon deduced that many of the "accidents" he saw were not accidents at all but stigmata of bestial criminality. Babies or toddlers were brought in by distressed parents because they had fallen down the stairs and broken a leg. A closer look would disclose bruising on other parts of the body or even 1.0cm circular burns that could only have been made by the red-hot tip of a cigarette. Prepubescent girls would be brought in with bleeding fissures in their anus or vagina, having fallen from a chair onto a sharp object. These crimes should have been reported to the police, but the Hippocratic oath was ambiguous on this matter. Yet the police were no better. Steelhouse Lane was also the address of the Birmingham Central Police Station and lockup. On two occasions in his first month a prisoner was brought across by a uniformed officer with massive lacerations of the scalp so that flaps of skin and hair were covering their ears. They had apparently fallen down the stairs to the basement of the lockup. On one of these occasions the police officer had the chutzpah to give Peter a nod and a wink. Other "accidents" were the consequence of sexual deviation and, sad to say, quite comical. There was an epidemic of men falling off ladders and landing on an ebony statuette of Napoleon wearing his cocked hat, which got stuck up his anus. These and other foreign bodies were difficult to remove and often needed a general anaesthetic. The most extreme of these perversions was a man who degloved the skin from his penis whilst making love to his vacuum cleaner.

All that aside the work was rewarding. Correcting a dislocated shoulder gave instant relief and gratitude. Straightening out the wrist of a Colles fracture and applying plaster of Paris for an elderly woman who slipped on the pavement or doing the same for a minor fracture of the ankle was also instant gratification. At the other extreme, doing a rectal examination for an elderly man passing blood and mucus, and finding a cancer, reminded Peter of the importance of his training.

By any standard he was a good doctor learning quickly on the job and winning the respect of the nurses and the head of the department. He was an attractive young man who was more than popular amongst the nurses, who were bitterly disappointed to learn he was married. Working night and day, seven days a week, he completed his year at A&E and passed the primary FRCS with flying colours. All this time, Fiona, his long-suffering wife, did not complain and as a reward was treated to a holiday in the Bahamas in August 1963.

Chapter 23

The making of a surgeon
1963

There are general surgeons and specialist surgeons. Most surgeons consider themselves physicians who incidentally happen to have been trained in cutting things out or sewing things up. Putting it another way, few surgeons spend more than half of their time in the operating theatre; most surgeons spend more time in outpatient clinics selecting cases that might benefit from surgery by improving their length of life and quality of life.

Doctor Baring wanted to be a general surgeon. A general surgeon is defined by what he or she doesn't do. This is where the specialists come in. A list of specialists can be documented from head to toe.

- Brain surgeons
- Ear, nose and throat (ENT) surgeons
- Cardiothoracic surgeons
- Urology surgeons
- Vascular surgeons
- Obstetric and gynaecology surgeons
- Orthopaedic surgeons

You might be surprised to learn that urology was a speciality, but it happened to be the first of the specialities amongst the barber surgeons at the time of King Henry VIII. These were experts in "cutting for stone" in the bladder, a very common problem in the 16th century because of their poor diets. The stones were removed by entering the bladder via the perinium, the gap between urethra and anus, or via the urethra with a frightening-looking device that could crush the stone in situ. No anaesthesia was available, 50% died of septicaemia, and most of the survivors squirted urine from their backsides.

General surgeons do the rest that includes a variety of procedures that have little in common, as follows:

- Thyroidectomy
- Breast surgery
- Oesophageal and gastric surgery
- Gall bladders and bile ducts
- Small bowel
- Large bowel and appendix
- Hernias in the groin
- Haemorrhoids
- Varicose veins
- Lumps and bumps all over the skin

To become skilled in those areas takes some time but the general surgeon also has to spend some years witnessing what the specialists are doing. For this reason, it is rare to be appointed a consultant general surgeon under the age of 35. If you also want to follow the academic route via senior lecturer to professor, you need to add two additional years for original research towards a higher degree such as PhD, ChM, or MD.

Peter was ambitious and wanted to end up with a "chair" in the Department of Surgery. The word "chair" in this context refers to the impressive cathedra sat upon by the masters of the guilds in medieval times. He embarked on this long journey in September 1963 full of self-confidence that was, in this case, fully justified.

★ ★ ★

Professor Iain McGregor warmly welcomed him on his first day in his office on ward West 2, at the Queen Elizabeth Hospital. Although it was 11.00am he was offered a glass of sherry instead of the cup of coffee he had expected. As was the convention, professors had honorary contracts with the NHS and received their income from the university. As such he was denied a private practice, being on a full-time contract. That was why most of the professors of surgery had been trained in Scotland, where there was very little private practice in Edinburgh, Glasgow, St Andrews, or Aberdeen. Furthermore, their Presbyterian tradition frowned on extreme wealth when caring for the sick. The first assistant to the professor, known as a senior lecturer, was also paid by the university. The incumbent of this post was Mr Andrew Sutcliff, a blunt Yorkshireman who took Peter under his wing. The firm also had a senior registrar employed by the NHS, Patrick Cullum, an Australian from Sydney, who became Peter's best friend. At the bottom of the pecking list were two housemen, one of whom was a woman. Peter's role as the junior registrar was to monitor the behaviour of these "housepersons", attend outpatients to look after the follow-up cases, assist his seniors in the operating theatre, and learn to do the simple procedures at the end of every operating list, such as inguinal hernias, varicose veins and, at the very bottom, thrombosed haemorrhoids. They were a happy crew reflecting good leadership at the top and Peter loved his work even though he often spent an 11-hour day and was on call at night twice a week and a weekend every three weeks. His weekend on call, Friday to Sunday, effectively started on a Friday morning and finished at 6.00pm on the following Monday. That was very tiresome for Fiona, who was now expecting their first child.

They had operating lists on Mondays, Wednesdays, and Fridays. That implied patients for Monday's lists how to be admitted on a Sunday evening, "clerked" by the housemen, who took their case histories, ordered chest X-rays, tested urine, and took bloods for haemoglobin, white cell count, electrolytes, and cross-matching in anticipation of a blood transfusion for the major cases. There were often seven or more cases on a list. All this had to be checked by Peter on a Sunday evening even if he wasn't on call; the alternative was coming into work at 06.30am on Mondays before kick-off in the operating theatre at 08.30am.

The operating lists were notionally in the names of the two consultants, the professor, and the senior lecturer, but Peter was expected to help on all lists. He soon noticed an eccentricity with the professor's lists. They were always started by Patrick Cullum and, after making the first incision of the day, Professor McGregor would poke his head around the door and say, "Patrick, would you mind starting the list for me? If you have any problems just get one of the nurses to give me a call." Peter assumed that the head of the academic department of surgery was overwhelmed with work, managerial, teaching, and scientific, but the truth was more disturbing. Early on in his appointment to the professorial unit, Patrick invited him to share a beer in the doctor's mess at end of play on a Friday evening when they were not on duty.

They found a cosy corner where their conversation could not be overheard, then Patrick lifted his glass and started off his disclosures. "G'day Bruce, here's to your health. Can I have your promise not to tell a soul what I'm about to say?" Peter nodded sternly, whilst downing a half pint of ale. "You most have noticed by now that our leader always avoids operating. That suits me fine as I'm learning on the job and I'm sorry to say that might include learning from my mistakes. Sad to say, he is an alcoholic and has a tremor that makes it difficult to operate. He took to drink about two years ago after his wife died of a brain tumour. Now, we all love our Prof and Andrew Sutcliff and I are doing our best to cover things up. He's a kind guy and will do anything to promote our careers. He's also done some good research on the treatment of peptic ulcers. His basic physiological work has established the technique of vagotomy and pyloroplasty that has pioneered the end of gastrectomy for duodenal ulcers."

At this juncture, Peter intervened. "Pat, I have already suspected this might be the case when he had me starting drinking alcohol at 11.00 in the morning all my first day and you can rely on my integrity. You must remember I only started my training in general surgery three or four weeks ago; I look forward to you teaching me how to do a vagotomy and pyloroplasty when next it's on our list."

"Will do, but first you need to learn the simple procedures, like repair of an inguinal hernia, before I let you loose in the depths of the abdominal cavity."

By chance, such a case was admitted the next Sunday evening.

★ ★ ★

Mr William Ramsbottom was an obese, jolly old man aged 65. He looked like a stereotype of the landlord of a public house. He was in fact the very popular landlord of the Star & Garter hostelry often frequented by medical students. He had been complaining of a swelling in the right groin for about three years. It was obviously a hernia as the swelling fell back into the abdomen when he laid down but popped up when he stood and swelled even more on coughing. His GP had prescribed a truss but that no longer held the herniating bowel in place.

It was a particular encumbrance when "Old Bill" was lifting heavy casks full of beer. He was seen by Mr Sutcliff in outpatients two weeks earlier, who thought there was some urgency in operating as the small bowel was getting stuck all the way down to his scrotum and was at risk of intestinal obstruction. It was third on the list on Monday morning, so Peter got out his textbook, Bailey and Love's *Short Practice of Surgery*, to revise the subject. The title of the book always made young surgeons laugh as it weighed 4kg and carried 1,350 pages.

The anatomy of the inguinal canal reflected the embryology of the testes.

*The first appearance of the gonad is essentially the same in the
two sexes, and consists in a thickening of the mesothelial layer of
the peritoneum. This is termed the gonadal ridge. The gonadal
ridge, in turn, develops into a gonad. This is a testis in the male
and an ovary in the female. At an early period of foetal life, the
testes are placed at the back part of abdominal cavity, behind the
peritoneum, and each is attached by a peritoneal fold, known
as the mesonephros. From the front of the mesonephros a fold
of peritoneum termed the inguinal fold grows forward to meet
and fuse with a peritoneal fold, the inguinal crest, which grows
backward from the antero-lateral abdominal wall. The testis
thus acquires an indirect connection with the anterior abdominal
wall. Also, in the inguinal crest a structure, the gubernaculum
testis, makes its appearance. This is at first a slender band,
extending from that part of the skin of the groin which afterward
forms the scrotum through the inguinal canal to the body and
epididymis of the testis. This band grows into a thick cord
known as the gubernaculum. By the end of the eighth month the
testis has reached the scrotum, preceded by the vaginal process,
which communicates by its upper extremity with the peritoneal
cavity. Just before birth the upper part of the vaginal process,
at the internal inguinal ring, usually becomes closed, and this
obliteration extends gradually downward to within a short
distance of the testis. The process of peritoneum surrounding the
testis is now entirely cut off from the general peritoneal cavity
and constitutes the tunica vaginalis.*

All that gobbledegook simply means that the testis starts on
the back wall of the abdomen and ends up in the scrotum.
Peter assumed there had to be some evolutionally advantage
to this strange voyage. The textbook then went on to suggest
two possibilities.

*Since descent of the testes into a scrotal pouch subjects the animal
to enhanced risk of accidental damage and/or vulnerability from
predators and rivals, presumably there must be some evolutionary*

adaptive advantage to testicular descent. It has been proposed
that the scrotum may act as a form of sexual decoration. A scrotal
location also exposes the testes to a reduced temperature below that
of the body, which has been suggested to reduce the spontaneous
rate of germ cell mutations.

Peter favoured the second hypothesis as he had never been aware of an instinct to expose his gonads to attract a member of the opposite in the way a peacock exhibits his amazing colourful fan of tail feathers. Whatever the reason may be, the inguinal canal is the Achilles heel of the abdominal wall, the commonest site for a hernia to burst through so that loops of small bowel can follow the passage into the scrotum.

When Peter was assisted to do his first inguinal hernia the next morning, he found it surprisingly easy. One oblique incision across the groin, opening the anterior wall of the inguinal canal, identifying and retracting the testicular artery, vein, nerve, and spermatic cord, then repairing the posterior wall with a line of silk sutures. Silk had recently replaced catgut because the latter dissolved over time and the hernia would recure.

Later that week he was taught to carry out an appendicectomy as an emergency and that he also found easy.

As his education proceeded over the year, he discovered that other procedures were not only difficult but terrifying. Terrifying because of the medico-legal consequences if anything went wrong. Top of the terror list was a parotidectomy and second in the league was a thyroidectomy.

The parotid gland sits above the angle of the jaw and is the major source of saliva. This gland is notorious for developing large, yet benign tumours that are quite disfiguring and sporadically can turn malignant. The problem in removing them is the five branches of the facial nerve that run through the middle of the lump. These nerve branches are as thin as the cotton used to sew on your buttons; if any branch is accidentally divided, you then get paralysis of a group of

172

muscles that are used for facial expression and the patient is left forever with a one-sided downturned mouth or an eyelid that can't blink or enhance a smile.

The thyroid gland needs to be removed if the patient has an overactive gland and complains of weight loss, sweating, and agitation. They also become popeyed for no clear reason. The other indications are for benign goitres or malignant tumours. Behind the thyroid are the very fine nerves that supply the vocal nerves and four tiny glands that control the metabolism of the skeleton, known as parathyroids. If you accidentally damage one of the nerves to a vocal cord, the patient will lose their singing voice. If by chance you remove the parathyroids, then the patient cannot control the calcium levels in the blood, with dire consequences.

Most other operations Peter had to learn were relatively simple and you didn't need the skills of a violinist to perform providing there was adequate exposure. For example, a radical mastectomy was easy because the organ of interest was on the surface, whereas a cholecystectomy for gall stones could be difficult if the patient was obese and your assistant wasn't strong enough to retract the right upper quadrant of the abdominal wall for 30 minutes.

Peter worked hard and studied hard, determined to present himself to the Royal College of surgeons for the fellowship final exam within three years.

Chapter 24

The golden bough calamity

Peter's mother-in-law, Lady Pauline Berkeley, was a charming and attractive woman in her fifties. As a debutante she adorned the front cover of *The Tatler*. She mixed in high-society circles but was not a snob. She always made Peter feel welcomed and listened with interest to his tales from the operating theatre. One evening, when Peter was on call at the hospital, he had a distraught call from Fiona who was in tears about something or other that involved her mother. Once Peter had calmed her down, he deduced that his mother-in-law had just been diagnosed with breast cancer but had refused treatment and could he come at once? He explained that he was on call and that breast cancer was not an emergency, but he could get off work the next day at about 4.00pm and the two of them could drive up to Berkeley.

They arrived at the Berkeleys' stately home at 6.00pm and were ushered into the library by the butler. Fiona's parents immediately leapt from their chairs, gave their daughter a hug, and shook Peter's hand vigorously. Lord Berkeley looked worried but Lady Berkeley looked like a plate from a fashion magazine. Tall and slim with a tight-fitting dress and fresh make-up, she was in some way making a statement, but for the moment Peter was at a loss to understand.

Fiona's father already had a cut-glass dram of whisky in his hand and poured another from a decanter for Peter without asking. He then asked them to sit down and then said, "Thanks for coming over so quickly, you two. I'm hoping Peter can help us sort things out for Pauline; tell him your story, darling."

Taking a sip of port from a tulip-shaped glass, Lady Berkeley started to speak. "About six months ago I noticed a lump in my left breast. I thought it was just a cyst like I had before my menopause, so I left it for a month or two, but it seemed to be growing. I went to our GP, and he wanted to send me to see a surgeon. Well, I refused because I remembered what happened to my Aunty Mildred. She had a mutilating radical mastectomy and still died less than five years later. I respect my body and have no intention of swapping one of my boobs for a bean bag. One of my closest friends is a lady in waiting to Queen Elizabeth, and recommended I went to see Sir John Weir, the royal homeopathic physician, in London. I found him at the Royal Homeopathic Hospital in Queen Square. He was very charming and reassuring and has been treating me with something called Iscador 40C. I think it's working as there is now a hole in the centre of the lump, but my husband thinks I should have a second opinion. Can you suggest someone, Peter?"

Her son-in-law, speechless, had no idea what homeopathy was and had never heard of a drug called *Iscador*. He would have to do some homework back in the hospital library and speak to the Prof. He then remembered Mr Alex McKenzie, who had taught him in medical school. He was kind and gentle and reluctant to carry out radical mastectomies. So, he pulled himself together and replied, "Lady Berkeley – Pauline, if I may – I know just the man for you."

He then embarked on an anecdote from his first clinical year as an undergraduate comparing the brutal Mr Duffield with the gentle Mr McKenzie and had them laughing as he mimicked their way of speaking. Having lightened the tone but feeling sick inside, Peter and Pauline exchanged smiles. The butler then entered and declared "Dinner is served" and the rest of the evening was free of medical discourse. On the way home Fiona asked Peter what homeopathy was. He confessed he hadn't a clue but was going to find out tomorrow.

★ ★ ★

The following day he was able to track down Professor McGregor, Mr Sutcliff, Patrick Cullum, and Mr McKenzie. The first three more or less said the same when asked about homeopathy: that it was quack medicine or herbalism. Mr McKenzie had something interesting to say in addition to the vagueness of his other three senior colleagues. He described his experience of attending to German prisoners of war after the liberation of the Belsen. Those who survived with their first aid packs intact had vials of liquids labelled *Homöopathisch*, in addition to bandages and dressings. He learnt from a German doctor that this was a German invention favoured by the Führer, but he had no idea what it contained. Peter then explained why he was interested and asked whether Mr McKenzie would kindly see his mother-in-law. The outpatient appointment was arranged for the following week and Peter was invited to sit in on the examination provided Lady Berkeley agreed. In the meantime, Peter set out to find out more about this mysterious Germanic medicine. His next visit was to the hospital library. He looked in the indices of all the standard textbooks of medicine and surgery but found no reference so as a long shot he took down the volume E–H of the *Encyclopaedia Britannica* and there it was:

> *Homeopathy is a system of alternative medicine. It was conceived in 1796 by the German physician Samuel Hahnemann. Its practitioners, called homeopaths, believe that a substance that causes symptoms of a disease in healthy people can cure similar symptoms in sick people; this doctrine is called **similia similibus curentur**, or "like cures like". Homeopathic preparations are termed remedies and are made using homeopathic dilution. In this process, the selected substance is repeatedly diluted until the final product is chemically indistinguishable from the diluent. Between each dilution homeopaths may hit and/or shake the product, claiming this makes the diluent remember the original substance*

176

after its removal. Practitioners claim that such preparations, upon oral intake, can treat or cure disease.

He then learnt that the "potency" of the remedy was inversely related to the concentration. The "potency" was described in terms of the number of dilutions the remedy had experienced. C40 was more potent than C10. In mathematical terms, this can be shown as $C^{-40} > C^{-10}$. Peter couldn't believe what he was reading: homeopathy was a topsy-turvy world where less is more! He then looked for examples for the treatment of common disorders. Top of the list was Arnica C40. Arnica was made from the petals of a flower that grows on the Swiss Alps, *Arnica montana*. If you rub these petals on your forearm, they leave a purple stain just like a bruise, *ergo*, this is the treatment for bruises. Furthermore, a concentration of 10^{-40} is beyond Avogadro's constant (number), which is the approximate number of nucleons (protons or neutrons) in one gram of ordinary matter. This would mean, in the real world, that it would be highly unlikely that there would be a single molecule of the blue petals to be found in the amount of ointment you could carry on your fingertip.

He then searched for Iscador, the treatment his mother-in-law was taking for her breast cancer. It turns out to be an extract of the white berries of mistletoe, the "golden bough" of the Druids. Why mistletoe? Well, it's obvious. Mistletoe grows on an oak tree like a cancer grows on the body! And the recommended potency is C100 (10^{-100}), which translates to one molecule in the volume of the universe. Well, if you are to believe the homeopath that the remedies carry the memory of water, and you know that the volume of water on the planet earth is constant, then you are more likely to get the memory of a molecule from the piss of Julius Caesar than from a molecule of mistletoe in Iscador C100. In other words, Lady Berkeley's treatment for breast cancer was the square root of nothing. By this time Peter was fulminating: homeopathy was fraudulent and those practising it were charlatans and should be put on trial. And yet, and yet... the treatments are endorsed by the royal family; does he really intend to take them on? He decided to postpone starting his campaign until he had seen his mother-in-law's cancer next week, remembering the words of Hamlet:

There are more things in heaven and Earth, Horatio, than are dreamt of in your philosophy.

The following week, with the approval of his in-laws, Peter joined up with Mr McKenzie in the outpatient clinic, with Lady Berkeley as the last patient on the list at 5.00pm. The last slot was chosen to allow the consultation to carry on as long as the patient wanted. His mother-in-law arrived looking glamorous as ever, although she had dark rings under her eyes, whilst his father-in-law looked as if he had aged since they had last met. Mr McKenzie quickly demonstrated his communication skills in putting his patient at ease from the start. He started to take her medical history, listening carefully and making eye contact. Peter was impressed that this consultant made no notes, focussing on the patient rather than the notepad. He also picked a variation in her story from what she told him the previous week: the lump had first been noticed 12 not six months ago. Once that was complete, the clinic nurse guided Her Ladyship into the examination room and helped her to disrobe and sit upright on the couch. As Peter followed McKenzie once the nurse beckoned them in, the first thing he noted was a foul smell. He then joined his senior colleague to the foot of the couch to observe the breasts before palpating them. That confirmed the diagnosis and prognosis at a glance.

The left breast had been eaten away by the cancer and the stink came from the purulent ulcer in the centre. There were also metastatic nodules around the perimeter of what was left of the breast. Peter had difficulty in not throwing up and turned his head away to perform the act of sneezing into his handkerchief. For McKenzie, this was not the first time he had seen the consequences of a neglected cancer of the breast, but this was one of the worst. He maintained his *sangfroid* and asked the nurse to provide with a pair of rubber gloves and a kidney dish with saline and a bunch of gauze swabs. Before touching the left breast, he examined the healthy one on the right side, and palpated both armpits and the supraclavicular region to check for enlarged lymph glands. He then cleaned out the ulcer with gauze swabs soaked in saline and noticed that the cancer had eaten through the muscles on the chest wall to expose a centimetre or two of rib. He then ripped off his gloves and carried out a careful examination of the abdomen to see if the liver was palpable.

He turned to the nurse again and asked to dress the wound with honey, cover the ulcer with iodine impregnated mesh, place a pad of cotton wool on top, and then bandage the lady's chest to hold everything in place. Peter and the poor nurse had difficulty in controlling their expressions to maintain a professional demeanour.

McKenzie then turned to his patient and said, "I can see that the homeopathy has removed the centre of the cancer so there is no question of a mastectomy. The honey dressing is a natural treatment to absorb pus, but I will explain the allopathic treatment on offer that has a good chance of clearing things up."

The two doctors walked out of the examination room with white faces and grim expressions that merely reinforced the presumptions of Lord Berkeley, who was no fool. He was about to speak when McKenzie interrupted, "Why don't we wait for Her Ladyship to come out, so I don't have to repeat what I have to say?" Once Pauline Berkeley had returned, settled in her chair, and turned to face the surgeon, he continued.

"First of all, Your Ladyship, that dressing needs to be refreshed every day, but I will organise a district nurse to visit you and I would like to see you again next week to check on progress. Once the ulcer is clean, I would like you to see Professor Brinkley, who is head of our Radiotherapy

Department. She is an expert in this field, and I think there's a very good chance of clearing up the cancer on your chest wall with about 12 fractions of treatment over a two-week period. I'm going to send you for some blood tests and a chest X-ray, and I'll discuss those results when I see you again next week. Do you have any questions?"

"Yes, how long have I got?"

"I'm often asked that question and, contrary to what you see in hospital TV dramas, it's not that easy. I'm not ducking the question; it's just that breast cancer has a very unpredictable natural history. Once I've got your blood and X-ray reports I might be able to give you some idea but with broad confidence intervals."

The patient and her husband seemed satisfied with that and as they left the room Pauline Berkeley gave Peter a hug and a kiss on the cheek.

Once they were out of hearing Peter turned to Mr McKenzie, who had his head down, searching for something in the lowest draw in his desk. When he came up for air, he had a bottle of Johnnie Walker Black Label and two cut-glass tumblers in his hands.

"Before you say a word, laddie, have a dram of scotch. It's therapeutic at times like this."

"Thanks, sir, I thought you handled that very well. What more is there to say?"

"Please don't call me sir, but thanks for the compliment. I haven't seen a case like that for years. As they say, a radical mastectomy is better than uncontrolled cancer on the chest wall. This gives you an idea of the natural history of breast cancer if left untreated. It will be no surprise to you that her axillary supraclavicular nodes are enlarged. I can't feel the liver, but I suspect by now that the seeds of this disease are scattered widely. I think that radiotherapy will control the local disease but there's nothing that will increase her chances of survival. I see you are red in the face with controlled fury; finish your whisky and then let it out."

Peter took Mr McKenzie's advice and felt the fire as the scotch went down his throat dampen the fire in his belly, and then said, "I'm furious for two reasons. First it was the fear of the mastectomy that turned her over to the quacks and, secondly, I now know that homeopathy is bogus. How are they allowed to get away with it? They are all charlatans and those with medical qualifications should be struck off the register."

"I couldn't disagree with what you say but I suggest that you don't go after the homeopaths as they are very powerful, endorsed by the royal family and frequented by those in the House of Lords. It may seem courageous to speak truth to power but, if you value your career, hold off until you have a leadership role of your own. As far as the first suggestion, I will put you in touch with Sir Geoffrey Keynes. He was my senior officer when I was a captain in the RMAC in 1944–1945. He published some good papers on breast conserving procedures just before the outbreak of World War II but retired from medical practice at the end of the war. I'm sure he'd be delighted for you to continue his work from where he left off and it would be an excellent topic for your thesis."

★ ★ ★

When Peter got home that evening, he had to tell Fiona the full story, and she was inconsolable. Things were even worse the next week when the chest X-ray showed secondary deposits and the blood tests showed dysfunction of the liver. Over the remaining months of 1964, Fiona's mother deteriorated but at least the course of radiotherapy allowed the malignant ulcer on her chest wall to heal. Just before Christmas, Pauline Berkeley had her first epileptic fit and died with brain secondaries early in the New Year.

Chapter 25

A visit to Sir Geoffrey Keynes
1965

On the first Sunday of the New Year, Pauline Berkeley was buried in the family mausoleum in the grounds of Berkeley Castle. The short and dignified service at her funeral was in the small chapel attached to the castle that had a history dating back to Tudor times. Only family and close friends were invited as there were only seats for 20 mourners. Lord Berkeley delivered the eulogy, which was perfectly judged in content and length. Fiona Baring was beyond consolation and spent the whole service wrapped in Peter's arms. Much to his alarm and with no warning, Peter was invited to say a few words after the eulogy. To his own surprise the words came easily. "Dear family and friends, it is difficult for me to say anything more about the beautiful soul of the deceased, after Lord Berkeley's eulogy. I sincerely loved my mother-in-law and will miss her badly. I will never forget the courage with which she tolerated the symptoms of the evil disease that tortured her in the last few months of her life. As a doctor and a surgeon, I felt ashamed that I couldn't do more to prolong or alleviate her suffering. All I can do in her memory is to dedicate the rest of my professional life to help other women to avoid the torment that Pauline Berkeley endured in the last year of her life. These are not empty words as I will begin this journey next week."

★ ★ ★

The following Sunday morning Peter made the difficult journey to Brinkley in Cambridgeshire, taking the Cambridge train from New Street Station and then the branch line to Newmarket, where he found a taxi to take him to Brinkley. Lammas House was a beautiful, rambling early-19th-century building with an inviting porch carrying a blue Wedgwood design around its jutting square cornice. Sir Geoffrey and his wife, Margaret, greeted him warmly at the door. He was shown into a warm and cosy sitting room. The room was hung with alarming, flame-coloured, insane-looking original works of William Blake. Peter knew virtually nothing of Blake's work, but it was love at first sight. Sir Geoffrey, obviously delighted with his enthusiasm, sent Margaret off to prepare tea and then conducted him around his collection of watercolours, woodcuts, and framed handwritten poems of this mystic genius whose greatest claim to fame, to Peter's knowledge, were the words to the hymn "Jerusalem". Sir Geoffrey was very tall and as a result walked with a slight stoop, a habit derived from coping with the low lintels above the doors of a Georgian house. He was grey-haired, with a grey bristling moustache that balanced his lantern jaw, and his pale blue eyes sparkled with intelligent enquiry. Tea arrived and the two of surgeons arranged themselves around the fire, with tea, hot scones and butter, and some slices of fruitcake. Peter told him about his mother-in-law's experience and his interest in his paper in the paper published by his host in the BMJ in 1937, the first paper ever published with data supporting breast conserving surgery. At that point his host eagerly launched into his story, explaining the logical inconsistencies of the radical operation in a way that Peter had yet to organise in his own mind – the ideas had been just out of reach. The greatest inconsistency of them all, he said, was that the disease kept stubbornly recurring almost anywhere in the body, however perfectly and completely it had been removed. He uttered the words "perfectly" and "completely" with heavy irony. The logical conclusion, therefore, was that by the time of diagnosis cancer cells had already disseminated throughout the body via the bloodstream, planting the seeds that in due course would grow into lethal metastases. If so, the therapeutic consequences were obvious: nothing could ultimately improve survival so the best we could offer was to remove the malignant lump and control any residual local disease with radium. If nothing else, this offered a better quality of survival than that offered by radical surgery. "As my brother Maynard once said, 'When my information changes, I alter my conclusions. What do you do, sir?'" He then went on to explain the details of the technique he had pioneered and how he had patiently collected a large series of cases treated in this manner and compared them favourably with a similar series treated by radical surgery by Sampson Handley at Middlesex Hospital. He then told his story of how he had been invited to talk on the subject by the American Association of Surgeons in New York just before the war. He was so shocked by the hostile reception he received there that he truncated his lecture tour and returned home. He continued his work despite the criticisms from his own colleagues but warned his students not to repeat his heresies in front of their examiners in surgical finals. The war intervened and in anticipation of enemy bombing raids he buried his set of radium needles in a lead-lined box, effectively burying the technique for another 20 years.

He clearly enjoyed recounting his story to an attentive audience and the time flew by until Margaret interrupted us, saying, "Darling, I think we should let Mr Baring go if I'm to drive him to Newmarket in time for the 17.50 to Cambridge."

They exchanged goodbyes and Sir Geoffrey's last words to Peter were, "Thank you for your interest, Baring, but be very careful how you make use of this knowledge." Despite Peter's protestations, Lady Keynes insisted on driving him to the station and along the way told him how much her husband must have enjoyed his visit as almost no one had shown any interest in his work on breast cancer since he was discharged from the RAF in 1945.

Peter would never forget his pledge at Lady Berkeley's funeral, but the first pragmatic step was to pass his final FRCS exam. For the rest of the year, he worked hard and studied hard. His routine on the days he was not on call, was to get home at about 6.00pm and have a sherry with Fiona, eat his dinner between 7.00pm and 8.00pm, and then study his books and notes for three hours before crashing out to sleep at 11.00pm. His long-suffering wife was very tolerant as she was still suckling their baby girl, Lucy, but they often met on the stairs for a chat; Peter coming up stairs to bed after having saved a life in the hospital or after completing his studies for the day, whilst Fiona and Lucy were walking down the stairs for the midnight feed. It was all worthwhile.

In September 1965 Peter presented himself for the final FRCS exams at Queen Square examination halls in London. There were three days of written papers and *viva voce* exams. Ironically one of the questions read as follows:

Explain the rationale and describe the technique used in the treatment of early breast cancer

Remembering the cautionary words of Sir Geoffrey Keynes, he wrote an essay that would have delighted Mr Morgan Duffield, even though he didn't believe a word. The tradition at the Royal College of Surgery was for all the examinees to gather in the entrance hall of the college in Lincoln's Inn Fields, where the secretary of the college, standing on the grand staircase, would call out the results and one by one the fortunate would climb the stairs to shake the hand of the president of the college and be handed a certificate signed by all the members of the college council. When Peter heard his name called out, he felt himself floating up the stairs, then, gripping his certificate in its protective cardboard tube with its red ribbon, floating down again. The first action on finding a telephone was to call Fiona. The call went something like this.

"Hallo, who is this?"

"This is *Mister* Peter Baring!"

"Does that mean you passed, and you are now FRCS?"

"Yes indeed, I'm now Mr Baring, MB, ChB, FRCS."

"*Sob, sob, sob.*" Deep breath. "Sob, sob, sob."

PART 6

1966–1970

Chapter 26

Alastair's story continues
A wedding, a funeral,
and a general election
1966

After the harsh winter over Christmas and New Year 1965–1966 the doctors in the Campbeltown surgery were exhausted and old Walter Campbell needed to retire. Alastair Bannerman and Colin Campbell decided to take on a locum pending the recruitment of a new trainee. Alastair was invited to replace Dr Walter Campbell as an equity partner and his mother, Lily, was given a pay rise. They advertised for a locum in the BMJ and were astonished to receive many applicants with Indian-sounding names. This should not have been surprising because the founding of the NHS and the independence of India and Pakistan almost coincided, and the demand for doctors for the NHS exceeded the number of homegrown GPs. Doctors from the subcontinent came in large numbers in response to an appeal in the early 1960s by the then health minister Enoch Powell. They decided to choose the locum by the CVs of the applicants rather than interviewing them all, as it was only a six-month appointment. They chose Dr Suni Ramanakumar, MB, BS, University of Bombay, who had just completed a rotating internship at the Goa Medical College. The choice was made because his application was perfectly typed out and he included a photograph of himself wearing a big smile, suggesting Suni by name and sunny by nature. He was wearing the same smile as he bounced into the Campbeltown surgery. His accent was thick, and he had that strange Indian habit of shaking the head side to side, expressing enthusiasm rather than dissatisfaction. He won Lily Bannerman's heart by calling her memsahib. Alastair was given the task of taking him under his wing and quickly learnt that the young man was extremely intelligent and could quote pages of famous textbooks off by heart, but at the same time was lacking in much experience and with little knowledge of British culture.

As his surname was a mouthful, he suggested they all called him Dr Raman or just Suni.

Dr Campbell and Dr Bannerman wondered what their patients would make of this young Indian doctor, but it was only a stopgap appointment until they were ready to employ a new trainee. They needn't have worried; the good people of the Mull of Kintyre treated him as an exotic curiosity with not a semblance of racism.

Dr Walter Campbell had a leaving party with all their patients invited. He was loved by the community and the surgery ended up knee high in wrapping paper from all the gifts of thanks and enough bottles of Springbank and Glen Scotia fine malt whisky to open his own tavern. Meanwhile, Dr Colin Campbell was behaving strangely. He seemed to be losing weight and avoiding eye contact. Alastair was beginning to think he might be suffering from a mortal affliction, but all became clear when he called a meeting of the staff at 6.00pm on Friday night, 1 March. In addition to Alastair and his mother was Dr Raman, practice nurse Katie McPherson, and the retired Dr Walter Campbell. Colin Campbell had a new suit on and looked rather dapper. Everyone was offered a wee dram of an 18-year-old Springbank, but Dr Raman politely declined.

He then put on a formal voice, cleared his throat, and turned to Alastair: "Dr Bannerman, we are all gathered here to witness me formally seeking your permission to ask your mother to accept my hand in marriage." Alastair was flabbergasted and delighted at the same time and chose to play the role of the father of the bride. "Dr Campbell, can you keep Lily Bannerman in the comfort to which she is accustomed to?"

"That I can promise, Dr Bannerman, sir."

Alastair then turned his attention to his mother, who by now was laughing and crying at the same time, and said, "In which case you have my permission." Colin Campbell then got down on his knee in a way he couldn't have managed six months before, took a small red leather box out of his pocket, flipped the lid, and displayed a diamond of significant diameter. Lily continued the pantomime of the *ingénue* receiving her first offer of marriage, nodded "yes please", and helped Colin get off his knees and gave him a big kiss.

★ ★ ★

The next day another development added to the excited atmosphere in the surgery as the news came out that Prime Minister Harold Wilson was calling a snap election on 31 March. The reason was that the Labour Party only had a four-seat majority, making it nigh on impossible to get important legislation through Parliament. On the same day Dr Bannerman received a letter from the offices of the Argyll and Bute Council Labour Party inviting him to stand as the candidate for Kintyre and Islands ward. It was a double-edged compliment because the Argyll and Bute parliamentary seat and control of the local councils had always been with the Tory Party. Yet at the same time it meant he had been noticed and this might be his first step in his political career. Not bad for a man aged 31. The next month was a flurry of activity, with Colin and Lily planning their wedding and Alastair preparing speeches and travelling all over the geographically large ward. This left Suni Raman replacing Alastair on the days he was travelling. It also meant that Dr Walter Campbell coming out of retirement to hold Dr Raman's hand.

Fortunately, Suni was quick to learn.

Colin and Lily decided to postpone their wedding until after the general election as they wanted to help Alastair posting leaflets all over the Mull of Kintyre and the Islands of Islay, Jura, and Arran. Apart from that they thought that April, the start of spring was more romantic, so they booked the Lorne and Lowland Parish Church for the first Sunday in April and published their banns a month beforehand.

The hustings for the council election were to be in the town hall in Campbeltown on 29 March and Alastair was determined to make himself known all over the ward, planning to visit the Islands along with his mother and Colin Campbell and then travelling north to visit the small towns en route to the Labour HQ in Argyll and Bute.

Their first outing was taking the ferry to Port Ellen to the Island of Islay, world famous for their peaty single malt whiskies. They booked a B&B for one night as they thought they might pay a visit to the Ardbeg, Lagavulin, and Bowmore distilleries as well as the medical clinic in Port Ellen, which served a population of 3,000. Dr Bannerman had never visited Islay but was very familiar with their legendary produce. Their host, Dr Angus Fraser, who ran the clinic, had arranged a dinner party in his house for the local dignitaries on the evening of their sleep-over. He would also take them on the tour of the distilleries. Dr Fraser met them off the ferry and gave them a warm welcome despite admitting he was a member of the Scottish National Party. They had great fun on the tour and learnt that this was the first time a candidate for a seat on the council had taken the trouble to visit them. After tasting many wee drams of some of the finest malt whiskies in the world, they checked in to their B&B to freshen up and sober up in time for the dinner party. Dr Fraser opened the door to them wearing his full Scottish national dress, with a kilt of the Fraser clan, a sporran and a *scian dubhs* dagger in his long sock on his right leg. This was all topped off with his shaggy red beard looking like a character from central casting.

Although his smile was somewhat lost within the shrubbery, the twinkle in his eyes signalled his genuine pleasure of hosting the dinner. Mrs Fraser was obviously excited to welcome these distinguished guests and had obviously gone out of her way to cook a traditional heavy Gaelic dinner. The other eight guests were all men of a certain age who measured up the three strangers with suspicion. However, within 20 minutes and plenty of the golden spirit everyone was warm, friendly, and slightly drunk.

By this time Lily Bannerman had lost all her inhibitions and was guilty of a *faux pas*:

"Dr Fraser, what will all this whisky swilling around the island, is there a high level of alcoholism amongst your patients?" Suddenly there was a dead silence and Alastair saw his chances of winning over the community dissolving like a snowball in hell.

Angus Fraser then exhibited his qualities as a fine gentleman and a good doctor by saying, "That is a very good question, Lily, if I may; the simple answer is no, there is little alcoholism in Port Helen or the rest of Islay. The difficult question is: why is that the case? Can anyone come up with a plausible explanation?" Instantly there was a hubbub that replaced the silence with everyone talking at once until Dr Fraser banged his fist on the table and demanded silence before turning to Alastair. "Well, Dr Bannerman, I'm interested in your explanation."

Alastair was prepared for that question, having asked himself the same after a year in Campbeltown. He was oblivious that he had stood up to speak. "I have often asked myself that question as it relates to my experience in my practice on the mainland. Let us start with our experiences today. This afternoon my mother, Dr Campbell, and myself were taken on a tour of three distilleries nearby. All the employees we met seemed healthy if not a bit bucolic, we *tasted* many of the malts and enjoyed that experience. I emphasise tastings as the intention was *not* to get drunk. This evening, thanks to the hospitality of Angus and Mrs Fraser, we've enjoyed fine food and fine whisky. I look around the room and what do I see? We are all smiling, a little flushed, and fully relaxed. You all look prosperous, well fed, and comfortable in your skins. Like me, we are all employed in worthwhile work and enjoy a reasonable level of self-esteem. I would imagine that, like me after a stressful day in the surgery, you may take a wee dram to settle you down before enjoying a healthy evening meal. We may not be wealthy but a least we live in warm, waterproof homes that protect us from the wind and snow at mid-winter. We have no reason to seek oblivion from the real world by abusing the goodness of fine malt whisky to get blind drunk. My mother and I grew up in Glasgow and my father was made redundant at the steelworks. We lived in a slum that was not inured to the wind and the rain. We had not enough money to feed ourselves and, without wishing to embarrass my mother, I was aware that she smoked to stave off her hunger as there was only enough food for two in the house. My father was sucked into a vicious circle. His self-esteem was lost, humiliated that he couldn't provide for his family. He took to drink to block out the real world and then became an addicted dipsomaniac. The more he drank, the poorer the family, and after nearly 10 years he died from cirrhosis of the liver and bleeding oesophageal varices. We tend to blame poverty on alcoholism, but we have the direction of causality reversed. It is poverty and loss of self-esteem that drives a man to drink.

"With respect to our host, as much as I'm proud of my Scottish identity, seeking to break away from the union with the United Kingdom won't correct this problem; voting for the Tory Party would suggest complacency; only the Labour Party will address these problems: poverty and austerity are the number one cause of premature death and the best we doctors can do is sticking plasters over the cracks!"

He sat down sweating, with his mother looking at him with alarm. There was a moment of silence and then all those around the table stood up and applauded his rant. Once everyone had sat down again, Angus Fraser stood up and said, "Well, my dear colleague, that was some speech; 'twas if I'd ignited a firework. You have convinced me. The SNP can wait. At least you've won my vote." All around the table expressed their concordance in one way or another. Alastair could barely believe his own rhetorical skills; it was if he had been possessed by a friendly incubus. He then realised that he was ready for the hustings on 29th March simply by speaking from the heart rather than speaking from his notes.

★ ★ ★

The Labour Party did very well at the general election, increasing its majority to 98. Alastair won his ward by a landslide, although the turnout was only 60%. As important was the collateral damage to the local Tory candidates as his words spilled over the boundaries. All this did not go unheeded at the party HQ in Argyle and Bute.

★ ★ ★

Alastair's celebrations were short-lived when Dr Walter Campbell dropped dead following a myocardial infarct on 8th April and a black cloud settled over the Campbeltown practice and its environs. Colin and Lily's wedding was postponed and the whole town gathered at their church for the funeral ceremony. Colin asked Alastair to deliver the eulogy as he knew he could not hold back his tears. The vicar and several dignitaries of the town also wanted to say a few words as they all had been patients of Dr Campbell senior and had all loved and respected the old man.

★ ★ ★

Colin and Lily were married six weeks after the funeral. The event was low key and went off for a weekend honeymoon

195

at the Gleneagles Hotel in the countryside midway between Stirling and Perth. On their return the married couple set up home in Machrihanish, the family home of generations of Campbells, leaving Alastair on his own. He rejected the idea of Suni taking his mother's room, who continued living in a boarding house halfway up the main street. Everything settled into place and Dr Raman was formally appointed the trainee post; apart from learning quickly, he was so good natured that many of their patients specifically asked for appointments with him.

About six months later, Suni sheepishly asked for a staff meeting one evening. He then explained that his parents had chosen a suitable girl to be his wife, he had seen her photographs and she looked very pretty, and they were planning his wedding in Goa after the monsoon season in January 1967 the following year. They were all invited at his father's expense. Colin, Lily, and Alastair were left speechless. First, they had never heard of arranged marriages and, secondly, they couldn't believe the generosity of Mr Raman inviting them all; he must be very rich. Dr Campbell responded on their behalf.

"First, Suni, on behalf of all of us, congratulations. Next, we couldn't possibly accept such generosity from your parents, and someone has to look after the shop. Finally, do you intend coming back?"

"Of course, Dr Campbell, I'll be coming back. I love working here and I'm learning so much. Scottish people very nice." said Suni, wagging his head furiously.

"But where will you live with your new wife?" asked Lily.

"No problem, Memsahib Campbell, my father very rich, he will buy us nice house nearby."

"Does your future wife speak English?" asked Alastair.

"My parents say she speaks very good English and has just completed her training as a paediatrician!"

Chapter 27

The health centre established and happiness ever after
1967–1969

Early in the spring of 1967, Suni Raman returned to Campbeltown with his new bride, Anushka. She was a pretty young thing with large brown eyes, about five feet, two inches, who looked about 16. She wore a colourful sari that exposed her midriff and carried with her certificates confirming that she had graduated MBBS from the Goa Medical College and had also been accepted as a fellow of the Royal College of Physicians (FRCP), specialising in child health. She spoke perfect English with a cut-glass accent, having studied at the North London Collegiate secondary school for girls. She came bearing gifts of small bronze sculptures of Ganesha, the Hindu god of scholarship. It transpired that her father was a professor of medicine who was leading the campaign to make the state of Goa tobacco-free. Suni was obviously delighted in his parent's choice of bride.

Anushka won Lily's heart by sitting on the floor at her feet whenever the family gathered to plan their future. Their future had, to an extent, already been plotted by the young Indian couple, but happily reflected Alastair's embryonic ideas exactly.

The shop next door to the practice was for sale along with the living quarters on the first and second floors. Anushka would use her generous dowry to buy the building whilst at the same time share equity partnerships with Dr Campbell and Bannerman. The two buildings next to each other would allow the development into a health centre that went beyond simply diagnosing and treating disease but also involved in "public health" for the prevention of disease in addition to the treatment of disease. With Alastair as a councillor representing the district, the health centre would become an extension of local government that would promote immunisation and healthy exercise as well as well campaigning for a healthy environment and educating the community on the hazards of alcohol and tobacco. This model was common in Goa and Kerala in South India, whilst despite the NHS having been founded in 1948 there was no equivalent in the UK; organised public health responsibility had been overlooked.

Leaders of the profession were well aware of this deficiency. For example, Frances Albert Crew, professor of public health and social medicine at the University of Edinburgh, published this in *The Lancet* in 1962:

> *The average individual, not being sick, resists all attempts to protect him against the hazards of disease and refuses his cooperation, without which there is much that must remain undone. Since public health has always dealt with environmental, social and bacteriological phenomena in communities rather than symptoms in individuals, its foundations are more scientific than those of most branches of curative medicine. There is a crucial difference between the position of the clinician in charge of the sick, responsible and empowered to take such action as he thinks appropriate to treat an individual patient and the medical officer of health whose role is almost entirely non-executive and advisory.*

Furthermore, Sir George Godber, chief medical officer of health, published this in the BMJ in 1965:

> *Everyone says that prevention is better than cure and hardly anyone acts as if he believes it, whether he is attached to Parliament, central or local government, or the commonalty of*

citizens. Palliatives nearly always take precedence over prevention. Treatment – the attempt to heal the sick – is more tangible, more exciting, and more immediately rewarding, than prevention. There were those who believed that the regionalisation of curative medicine had swung the balance of power so violently towards cure rather than prevention that to survive successfully public health would have to undergo a similar reorganisation and separate itself from local government.

Totally unaware of these trends, the Campbeltown Health Centre pre-empted the ruminations of the great and the good of the medical profession and embarked on an ambitious endeavour that many others would imitate.

The allotment of roles was almost self-evident. Dr Campbell would be the director and continue his work as the senior partner as in the past. Dr Bannerman would act as the liaison between the health centre and local government, with 50% of his time in his past role as a general practitioner. Young Dr Suni Raman would be a junior partner, with 100% of his time spent in clinical duties. Dr Anouska Raman would of course run a clinic for mothers and children and be responsible for running the vaccination programme. Lily Campbell would continue acting as receptionist but share the role of the public health campaign with the practice nurse. The local council was very supportive as most of them were clients of the practice and Alastair was very popular.

Anoushka's dowry was sufficient to rebuild the ground floor of the shop next door into a handsome set of consultation rooms and a modern-looking waiting room. The second and third floors were refurbished into a comfortable apartment for the newlyweds. There was even enough money left over to do the same to the waiting room next door, but Colin and Alastair liked the old-fashioned look and mahogany panelling of their consulting rooms to remain untouched.

Five months later they had a formal opening ceremony where the provost cut a ribbon and the Springbank distillery provided the refreshments. The local newspaper sent a reporter, and the story next day was picked up by the nationals.

Professor Crew at the University of Edinburgh read the report and had mixed feelings. On the one hand, he was jealous of being pre-empted but on the other hand he reckoned how to exploit this uppity GP to the advantage of his Department of Public Health and Social Medicine. A week later, the great man, accompanied by his PA, came to visit and had to confess that the Campbeltown Health Centre was a blueprint for a network all over Scotland. He then made an offer to Colin Campbell and his team that was difficult to refuse: the University of Edinburgh would like this health centre to become a satellite of his medical school, to receive undergraduate students for monthly placements, and to encourage research on the impact on public health in the future, using Dr Bannerman's casebook as the baseline reference. His department would set up a similar programme in the poorest part of Glasgow, where the baseline reference would be as low as could be.

To make this happen, the University of Edinburgh would offer them a £10,000 grant. This was an offer that was hard to refuse.

★ ★ ★

The next day at the "happy hour" the health centre team gathered to celebrate their triumph and plan how best to spend the grant. Colin Campbell, as a graduate of Edinburgh University, was quick to suggest an outlay of a modest sum to commission a large painted board to run across the entrance announcing the imprimatur of the University of Edinburgh for their regional health centre.

Everyone agreed with that idea, but more important pragmatic needs were discussed at length. In the end they decided that that needed another member of staff who would deal with financial issues and act as a data manager for research.

The salary would have to be at management level as the ideal applicant should hold a degree.

A small advert was placed in the local newspaper and in the back page of the BMJ. A few applications arrived in dribs and dabs and the choice for interviews was left to Colin Campbell. In the end, there was only one who fitted the requirements for the job, having gained a first-class degree in economics at Edinburgh University with an address in Belfast but willing to move to Scotland. The interview was arranged for the following week, with Colin, Alastair, Lily, and Anouska in attendance. Suni met the candidate at the front hall and announced her at the door of the refurbished waiting room. "Miss Janet O'Connor MA, please let me introduce you to Dr Campbell, Dr Bannerman, Dr Ramanakumar, and our receptionist, Mrs Lily Campbell." Suni was totally unprepared for the response from the committee, as was his wife. Lily leapt up and hugged Janet tightly and the two of them burst into tears. Colin jumped up with a big smile on his face, whilst Alastair sat down, pale in the face as if he'd seen a ghost. Once everyone had settled down and with the permission of their guest, Lily explained Janet's backstory.

In Alastair's eyes, she was more beautiful than he remembered, very fashionably dressed in a dark blue business suit, a Vidal Sassoon bobbed hairstyle, and a demeanour of self-assurance. She explained that her father had died of cirrhosis of the liver a week ago and she had returned to Campbeltown to look after her mother.

Her appointment to the job of manager of the health centre was unanimously agreed, and Alastair decided that life was worth living after all.

* * *

The Department of Health and Social Security (DHSS) was created in November 1969, merging the Ministry of Health and the Ministry of Social Security. The first meaningful decree of the Secretary of State for Health, Kenneth Robinson, was banning adverts for tobacco on TV.

Chapter 28

Dylan's story continues
Fags and phagocytes
1966–1970

In the first week of the New Year 1966 Dylan had confirmation from Professor Cochrane that he had been funded as a postgraduate student at the MRC unit in Cardiff. He would keep an honorary appointment at the miners' hospital to have access to human "guinea pigs", although the first year he would spend more time sacrificing murine "guinea pigs".

He also remembered the last words of wisdom from Archie as he left his office a few weeks earlier.

We need a randomised controlled trial (RCT) to determine what you think is obvious, that wearing a face mask down the mine will reduce the incidence of coal miners disease. Before we even start planning that RCT, you need to do some boring groundwork to try and support your intuition that coaldust contributes to lung and gastric cancer. Think about it for a week or so before we meet again.

As charity starts at home, he thought he would meet up with his father and his brother to do some boring groundwork concerning the acceptability of a trial. His brother was a local hero of the coalface, and his father, Owen, was the head of the coal miners' union's chapter for the Rhondda Valley and Merthyr Tydfil region.

He chose his time carefully and they agreed to meet at their local pub on the Saturday night after Wales beat Ireland in the Five Nations rugby union fixture. Once they had settled in a cosy and relatively quiet corner of the Red Dragon, Dylan started the conversation. "Dad, Gareth, you know I'm starting this new job next week and I swear that my research work will be planned to improve the length and quality of your mining brethren. I know that this is a sensitive subject, but I can't understand the objections for planning a clinical trial to see if face masks could protect coal miners from the black lung and early death from silicosis or pneumoconiosis, whatever you choose to call it. Can you enlighten me?"

At that point Gareth went red in the face and looked as if he would punch Dylan in the face until his father intervened. "Gareth, sit you down. It's a fair question and Dylan needs to understand the matter for his own sake as well as ours." He then turned to Dylan. "Son, you know we are proud of you and would do anything to help your career, so I'm glad you asked that question and I'm sure that you will not share what I'm going to tell you. You've witnessed first-hand how hard your brother works at the coalface. He strips to the waist and still he sweats like a pig. The sweat dripping down from the scalp is blinding but essential to maintaining normal body temperature.

"You're the doctor and I'm the uneducated miner but there are many things I learn on the job that never reach your textbooks. The face masks that can filter out the fine particles in the coal dust are uncomfortable to wear and carry eye shields to redirect the sweat. To wear them is so uncomfortable that compliance amongst the workers would be very low and then, if you can prove that the masks work, those who refuse to wear them will be penalised and denied their right for compensation if they develop pneumoconiosis.

"That brings me on to the second point, which is very sensitive and again I plead with you not to pass it on. Many miners *welcome* the diagnosis of the 'black lung'. It allows them to take early retirement on half pay. Many of my comrades are glad to escape from the pits at the age of 50 or so and start some other activity to make up the shortfall. Furthermore, the new recommendation of annual chest X-rays might increase these numbers." Dylan felt mortified taking this in and there was a deadly silence round the pub table.

Gareth broke the silence. "It's my round. I assume we'll all enjoy another pint of best bitter whilst my young brother takes this on board." There was quite a crush round the bar that gave Dylan the chance to prepare his response. The tall glasses of the amber liquid were plonked on the table and that provided the cue for Dylan's response.

"Right, Dad, there'll be no clinical trial for facemasks. Instead, I shall use all my energy to confirm my hunch that stomach cancer is another industrial hazard that deserves compensation. I'll do the laboratory work to come up with a plausible mechanism and I'm sure that it would be in the enlightened self-interest of the miners' union to help me to collect data on the incidence of stomach cancer in coal miners. One last question. Why do you use the expression 'sweat like a pig' when you should know that pigs don't sweat at all?"

Gareth and Owen Baddams burst out laughing and when they could catch their breath. It was Dylan's brother's chance to speak. "Well, boyo that's the advantage of a university education, don't you agree, Dad? Porky pigs don't sweat? Mmm, I must remember that. Except the pigs we had in mind wouldn't make for good bacon; we had in mind pig iron. When molten iron in the Welsh steelworks cool, they make shapes that look like porky pigs and piglets. These pigs and their steelworkers sweat like armpits in a sauna!"

★ ★ ★

In the second week of 1966 Dylan met up with Archie Cochrane to start planning his programme of research that would be submitted to the university for a doctorate. They met at 6.00pm and the boss thought it appropriate to toast the New Year with a dram of his favourite Islay. Once they had settled down, Dylan started with the bad news about the chances of a RCT for face masks. Archie's response was not what was expected.

"Well, Dylan, you've merely confirmed what I deduced myself in the past. There are some trials that are not possible, but, to paraphrase the great philosopher Bertrand Russell, 'Our science teaches us to live with uncertainty', in which case we don't waste our time planning to carry out trials that are doomed to fail. You were right to use that pathway to win their support for observational studies on the links of coal dust to lung and stomach cancer. Note my careful choice of words: *links of coal dust to lung and stomach cancer*.

"Remember lesson one: *association does not mean causation*. Can you come up with the flaw in the simple description of the study?"

Fortunately, Dylan was prepared for that question. "Well, sir – sorry, Archie – say we do find an excess of lung and gastric cancers amongst miners; the title of the study presupposes that the coal dust is the culprit. For all we know, coal miners smoke more than steelworkers after work because they can't smoke underground. I believe that's what you call a confounding variable." Professor Cochrane was dumbfounded by that answer. "My God, Dylan, you already have the makings of a fine epidemiologist! Now, my next question is more difficult. Sticking with lung cancer, say steelworkers and coal miners smoke the same amount; how does that affect the interpretation of any results concerning incidence and mortality of lung cancers?"

That gave Dylan pause for thought but after a minute or two, whilst Archie was enjoying a sip of his 18-year-old Ardbeg, a light bulb in his head flashed twice. "I've noted that your comparative population are the South Wales steelworkers and I understand that choice avoids the biases of social class. It is more than likely the miners and steelers smoke the same number of fags a day. In fact, I've done some groundwork already with my dad and brother, drinking beer whilst observing the other customers' fag consumption. Say miners and steelers smoke 40 a day. They then have a 30-fold risk of dying of lung cancer. To then recognise an additional risk from inhaling coal dust would need huge number for sufficient statistical power."

Archie almost choked on his scotch and with a chuckle responded, "Have you got your eyes on my job, laddie? You are spot on. So, accepting what you've just said, you will understand why it might take two or three years to see if coal miners die more often from lung and stomach cancers than the average population balanced for age, sex, social class, and cigarette consumption. Setting up observation studies like this are our bread and butter. There are two designs. The first is easy: that's a retrospective review of death registries. That is a makeshift technique and full of biases, but the best way of looking for truth is a cohort study, where you recruit thousands of miners and follow them up until enough have died. You will also have to recruit a similar number of a control group, balanced as I've already described.

"In the meantime, I'll introduce you to our chief technician tomorrow morning, who will then introduce you to some friendly rats who will provide answers to your theories in the short term."

★ ★ ★

The laboratories of the MRC were new and state of the art. The chief technician was Huw Williams, who had been at school with Dylan and even played in the school's first XV, so they made an excellent team. Professor Cochrane left the young scientists to get on with the job having briefed Huw the day before. After a brief tour of the labs, Huw took Dylan into the experimental animal facility to meet the rats. There were several species available varying in colour from dark brown to white. Many of them were albinos with white coats and pink eyes. They were kept eight per cage and fed by a sliding tray and water was delivered via a bottle and narrow rubber tube. Dylan had never handled a rat nor considered the husbandry or ethics of animal experimentation. Like most scientists he was not imbued with sentimental anthropomorphism but believed that, if the research was to find a cure or prevention of cancer, and the animals were not allowed to suffer, then it was alright with him. He was of course fearful of a rat bite but was reassured by Huw. "The rats we're going to use are called Lewis rats, named after Margaret Lewis, who reared the first colony about 10 years ago and are ideal for your experiments. Here they are and you can see they are albinos; they are also quite docile, although we usually use leather gloves when handling them. The Lewis rat suffers from several spontaneous pathologies: for example, they can suffer from high incidences of neoplasms, including the Lewis lung cancer. The females develop mammary gland tumours and endometrial carcinomas, so that's why we will use the male of the species. The other advantage of these rats is that they are syngeneic and can therefore have any cancers they develop transplanted onto any of their brothers or sisters. Rats are expensive to buy and care for, but your grant should cover at least one year of animal experiments. Let's go into my office and plan your experiments."

After two strong cups of coffee, they derived and elegant design that could answer the two questions at the same time with an economy of rats. It was a design used in agriculture and described as 2×2 factorial planting plan. In practice it was very simple.

The rats would be divided into four cohorts. Group A would be controls kept in the lab as normal, Group B would be kept in the lab but have coal dust added to its feed, Group C would be kept in the coal mine close to the fans, and Group D would be kept in the coal mine but have coal dust added to their food. Each group would have three cages and each month one of the cages would be transferred to the benches of the lab and the rats would be humanely killed by inhaling CO_2 and then dissected. As well as looking for lung and stomach cancers, they would take biopsies of the lung and stomach to see if there were any inflammatory or pre-malignant foci compared with the control group.

Dylan then wrote out the research protocol in detail and had it approved and signed off by his professor. Setting up the experiment was not too difficult, although Dylan almost had a panic attack descending into the mine again, but at least he didn't have to crawl along to the coalface this time.

Once that was set up, he turned his mind to implementing the two epidemiological studies. The coal miners' union were very helpful in activating the cohort study as it was in their enlightened self-interest, but it still involved Dylan traipsing all over the coalfields of South Wales to recruit and complete a questionnaire for 2,000 men. The second study of the death registries involved tedious and frustrating hours in ill-ventilated libraries searching old dusty tomes. He estimated that it would take about five years to complete that work but for instant gratification he always had the Lewis rats to turn to.

★ ★ ★

The first four cages of rats came back to the lab on 1 February. They were put to sleep in bell jars in an atmosphere of CO_2 and then splayed out on cork boards. A single slice from neck to pubis displayed all the internal organs. The first observation was unpredicted: apart from the control Group A, all the rats had spleens nearly double the normal size. Dylan and Huw had no idea at this stage what this meant but were at least encouraged to learn that one or more of the contents of coal dust stimulated the reticuloendothelial system. They then removed the lung and stomachs of all four groups and found no obvious foci of cancer, having sliced the organs into 2mm sections. These sections were fixed in wax, and then stained with haematoxylin and eosin – dyes that stain nuclei and cytoplasm – and studied with bifocal microscopes. What they saw was quite spectacular. Groups B, C, and D demonstrated that all tissues examined were infiltrated with monocytes and macrophages, the latter having ingested black particulate matter.

What was puzzling was Group C, who had been exposed to the fans underground without adding dust to the feeding box yet exhibited the same overload of dust particles in the gastric mucosa.

A month later they repeated the autopsies. No cancers were found but microscopy of the lung and stomach demonstrated phagocytes bursting with particulate matter surrounded by the cells of chronic inflammatory reactions in groups C and D but only in the gastric mucosa of Group B.

One month later, 1 April, "All Fool's Day", the third batch of rats were sacrificed in the lab. The results were spectacular. Group A had no cancers to show but Group B came up with six stomach cancers: four visible to the naked eye and two seen on microscopy. Group C and D developed both lung and gastric cancers.

Archie Cochrane was delighted with the results but added a cautionary note. Coal dust was a complex substance, and this was the beginning of the story, not the end. He then went on to quote a line from Bernard Shaw's play *The Doctor's Dilemma*: "'There is at bottom only one genuinely scientific treatment for all diseases, and that is to stimulate the phagocytes.' Well, my boys, these rat phagocytes have been over-stimulated, and you might by chance, found the explanation for the lethal dense fibrosis in pneumoconiosis!" Nevertheless, they were in a hurry to publish, and *Nature* was happy to take it. The title and abstract were as follows:

Gastric and lung cancers in coal miners:
A hypothesis of coal mine dust causation
Baddams D, Williams H, and Cochrane A. Nature,
Friday, 21 October 1966
A hypothesis is proposed to explain the anecdotal evidence of

elevated incidence of lung and gastric cancers among coal miners. Inhaled coal mine dust, especially the larger particles, is cleared from the lung and tracheobronchial tree by mucocilliary function, swallowed, and introduced into the stomach. Organic and/ or inorganic materials in the dust can undergo intra-gastric nitrosation and/or interaction with exogenous chemicals to form carcinogenic compounds which in turn may lead to precancerous lesions, which may subsequently develop into gastric cancer.

Sadly, this important scientific paper was completely overlooked because of more important events that coincided with its publication.

Chapter 29

The Aberfan disaster and its lasting heritage

On the morning of the publication of his first scientific paper, just as Dylan was starting an outpatient clinic at the miners' hospital, he was interrupted by a noise that sounded like a Boeing 707 landing in the Taff valley just north of the hospital. Out of curiosity, he and some of the patients waiting to be seen rushed to the window. A rumbling noise could still be heard but there was nothing to see. They were just about to return the consulting rooms when Dai Williams, an 80-year-old survivor from working in the pits in the Merthyr Tydfil coalfields, cried out whilst pointing to the mountain range on the horizon, "Oh my God, oh my God, Jesus, son of God, please make this not true. The spoil tip number 7, just above Aberfan, is no longer there. My kids and grandchildren live there. Has anyone got a car that can take me up the valley, for Christ's sake?"

There was a moment of silence and then they all heard the wailing of sirens from ambulances and police cars coming from all directions. A few minutes later, Gareth Slater, the hard-nosed senior executive of the Caerphilly Miners' District Hospital, came rushing in, red in the face and crying like a child. "Major incident, major incident, all nurses and doctors come with me, all others return home." He then left the room followed by the two SHOs, a local GP, six nurses, and two visiting medical students. They gathered in the entrance hall with the entrance to a small A&E facility on one side and the

212

one operating theatre on the other side. Once Mr Slater had regained his breath, he explained the catastrophic event that had triggered the major incident procedures. "One of the spoil tips sitting above the village of Aberfan has collapsed and buried half the village and the schoolhouse under mud, sludge, and slag. All hospitals in the region can expect a flood of the wounded survivors. God alone knows how many have died. We must set up a triage in the hall. Dr Evans is the most experienced doctor in the neighbourhood and will lead the triage with the support of Matron. Our visiting medical students will take care of the walking wounded in A&E and our two senior house officers will do the best they can in the operating theatre to save life and limb. I hear that the worst cases that need thoracic, cranial, or major intraabdominal surgery will bypass us and go straight to the Cardiff Royal Infirmary." The first two victims then arrived, a boy and a girl aged about 11. The boy had multiple bruises and lacerations, but none were life-threatening, so he was sent to the A&E room, where the nurses offered comfort and reassurance, cleaned him up and passed him to the medical students to sew up the lacerations. The girl had a compound fracture of the left femur and seemed to be suffering with concussion. She was sent to the operating theatre, where Dylan did his best to save her leg with the assistance of one of the nurses, whilst his new colleague, Dr Jamal Aziz, helped by another nurse, acted as anaesthetist. From that point for the next 48 hours, both teams worked nonstop in a blur of activity. They didn't even stop to eat and drink but sucked water up a straw whilst still in cap and gown. Many of the victims were dead on arrival and a few others died on the operating table, so Mr Slater had to collect some volunteers to make up a team to handle the corpses. The nearby church was quick to offer their services for this morbid task and clergymen from all branches of the Christian faith were quick to appear and to offer comfort to the parents and loved ones of those who did not survive their burial under a filthy, stinking mountain of slag.

After two days and nights at the operating table, Dylan fell into bed and slept for 12 hours. It was only then that he got round to reading the local and national press.

This is how it was reported in the *South Wales Evening Post*, whose reporter was first on the scene.

At about 9.15am on Friday 21 October 1966, spoil tip No 7 – one of seven slag heaps that loomed like a mountain range high above the south Wales village of Aberfan – started to move. Then, almost in the blink of an eye, the entire edifice was transformed into a 30-feet-high tsunami of sludge that slid downhill at over 80mph. Seconds later, a wave consisting of half a million tonnes of liquefied coal waste crashed into Aberfan. The wave swept across a canal and over an embankment before bearing down on the village primary school.

The children and staff of Pantglas Junior School were about to start their lessons on the last day before half-term. Suddenly they felt a deep shuddering and heard a deafening roar like a jet plane taking off close by. Before anyone had a chance to react, the walls and windows of four of the school's seven classrooms were violently breached and the school was inundated almost instantly by a powerful surge of cloying black sludge – over 1.4 million cubic feet of liquefied slurry. By the time the slithering mass came to a halt a few seconds later, dozens of children and adults had been engulfed where they stood or sat. The final death count was 116 children and 28 adults.

What Dylan would never forget was the very articulate description of the event, by a youth whose life and limb he saved. The boy was 12 years old and called Jeff. He was concussed, suffering from an extradural haemorrhage that Dylan drained through a burr hole in the skull. He had never done that procedure before, but it looked easy from the illustration in his textbook. His limb was saved by the rapid treatment of a compound fracture of his left leg, where the fractured end of the tibia bone was sticking out through the skin. He cleaned all the debris round the wound and trimmed the edges of the cut to fresh pink bleeding skin flaps. He then manipulated the bones so they clicked into place and encased the whole leg in plaster of Paris. This was the story from the boy's point of view.

When I woke up, I was surrounded by bricks and sludge, there was shouts and screams from all the kids in the classroom. I had a dead girl lying next to me, on my shoulder. I knew who the girl was, but I will never reveal that, obviously, because of her parents. I was one of the last children to be rescued alive from the building. I was lucky because the only reason I survived was the fact that I had a pocket of air around me. The others who died, they either died through being crushed by falling debris or the tip itself – or from drowning, being buried in the rubble, they couldn't breathe. It was just fortunate for me that there was a pocket of air around me, so it enabled me to breathe.

Dylan never really recovered from this event and went into an acute anxiety/depressive state. He was advised a six-week period off work but he was determined to continue his research, albeit accepting a leave of absence from clinical work at the miners' hospital. His best medicine, however, was the love and pampering of his wife, Bronwen. She even sang him to sleep during his bouts of insomnia or night terrors. His laboratory and epidemiological research went well and after three years was awarded a PhD with honours for a thesis entitled "The Mechanisms for and the Incidence of Lung and Gastric Cancer of Coal Miners in South Wales: Causal Proof of Two New Industrial Diseases".

The MRC, the coal miners, and his immediate family were delighted and proud by his achievement, but Dylan's interior voice did not share these accolades. You still couldn't prevent or cure pneumoconiosis, lung cancer, or gastric cancer; all you were gifted with was an early retirement with pay whilst you suffered a premature death. On top of that were the ghastly and dangerous working conditions that took lives every year and the ever-present slag heaps because it was cheaper to pile up the waste on the surface than to try to return it whence it came. He never shared these views with family and friends but looked forward to the day that the country's economy would no longer be dependent on "black gold".[1]

<hr />

1   Oil was discovered offshore in the North Sea in 1969 when Phillips Petroleum drilled a successful well in what later became known as the Ekofisk field in the Norwegian sector.

Chapter 30

Mathew's story continues
A window on the brain
1966–1970

The night after the dinner party in honour of his wife's friend, Oliver Sacks, Mathew couldn't sleep. He'd reached the rock-solid belief that psychiatry and neurology were like Janus, the two-faced god, and should be practised and researched as one set of pathologies affecting the brain. He spent the night building up the courage to visit Sir Aubrey Lewis, to request a transfer to the Department of Neurology at King's College Hospital across the road. Instead of sleep and pleasant dreams, he rehearsed his knowledge of the history of his chosen profession from textbooks and notes he had written as a student.

The history of the diagnosis and management of mental illness over the 2,500 years from the days of Hippocrates to the mid-20th century has been inglorious, to say the least. Even before the "golden age" of Athens and the codification of disease of the ancient Greeks, there was evidence of the diagnosis of insanity and recommended treatment from the decoded hieroglyphics of medical papyruses unearthed in the Valley of the Kings. Furthermore, there was evidence of the treatment of "mania" in the days before writing from skulls dug up by archaeologists in many lands, which exhibited burr holes discovered in Stone Age burial mounds, suggesting that the first shamans drilled holes in the skull with flint tools, to let out the demons from their patients, whose bizarre behaviour could only be explained by a troubled "ghost in the machine". That phrase in its own way is used to emphasise the problems associated with Cartesian dualism, in which the mind is seen as a nonphysical entity (a "ghost") that somehow inhabits and interacts with a mechanical body (the "machine"). Although the behaviour provoking trephination of the skull would not have been recognised as epilepsy or another known brain disorders back then, primitive surgeons would use this technique for people who were behaving in an "abnormal" manner, to let out what were believed to be evil spirits. The ancient Greek philosopher Aristotle (in approximately 335 BCE) held the belief that the brain was simply a radiator, in which its purpose was to stop the body overheating, claiming that the heart was the more superior organ. However, in approximately 387 BCE Plato suggested that the brain was the seat of all mental processes, *the mind*, and therefore had a larger role than was previously believed. The first classification of mental disorders, proposed by Hippocrates, has been translated as mania, melancholy, phrenitis, insanity, disobedience, paranoia, panic, epilepsy, and hysteria.

According to Hippocrates, the diagnosis and treatment of mental and physical diseases is linked to the theory of balance between the four "humours": blood, phlegm, yellow bile, and black bile. Mental disease was considered as the consequence of an excess of "black bile" (*melancholia* in Latin). Interestingly enough, Hippocrates recommended "art therapy", which included music and drama, for the improvement of human behaviour.

In 170 BCE, the Roman physician Galen established a schematic that explained that human moods and sicknesses are caused by imbalances of the four Hippocratic "humours", as liquids held in the cerebral vesicles. Treatments for depression (*melancholia*) involved bleeding and cupping to reduce the pressure of an excess of "black bile". These concepts were dominant and persisted for more than 1000 years, used by generations of physicians up until the mid-19th century.

It wasn't until 1664 that Oxford physiologist Thomas Willis published a diagram of the first "brain atlas". This atlas located various functions of the brain in separate brain segments.

Ironically this closely coincided with the witch hunt in Salem, Massachusetts, when 19 innocent citizens were hanged for being possessed by the devil for what today might be described as mass hysteria.

In 1909, Brodmann described 52 cortical areas of the brain, based on their anatomical structure. These segments are known as Brodmann areas, to this day. Yet, before any neuroimaging techniques were invented, scientists were unable to discover much about the functions of these anatomical subdivisions. The only other method of examining brains was through post-mortem examinations. They would find people who displayed non-typical behaviours or functions, mostly due to injury, then wait until they had died to examine the location and extent of the damage.

A hugely popular method of early neuroimaging in 19th-century USA and Europe was phrenology. This concept was introduced by physician Franz Joseph Gall, who theorised that various faculties and personality were localised in the brain, and that these could be read by feeling the contours of the skull. Gall believed that the strongest traits were the largest, and so would appear as bulges. Some of the regions Gall identified through his methods used words such as "cautiousness", "friendship", "hope", "benevolence", and "destructiveness". Gall's methods lacked any scientific rigour, and he ignored any evidence that contradicted his ideas, long since being identified as a pseudoscience. Despite this, Gall's idea that brain functions were localised to certain areas of the brain was the very reason Mathew wished to switch from psychiatry to neurology or a hybrid "psycho-neurology".

The following morning, after a wretched night and three cups of strong coffee, Mathew put on his best suit and kissed his wife goodbye, looking more like a man on his way to a funeral rather than an ambitious young doctor on his way to a meeting to visit the clinical director of his hospital. On the dot of 09.00am, Mathew was invited into the grand office of Sir Aubrey, who greeted him with a smile and offered him another cup of strong coffee. He could hardly refuse but started worrying about the diuretic effect of an overdose of caffeine. He then noticed another elderly gentleman sitting in the penumbra of the morning sun through a gap in the curtains on the south side of the Holy of Holies. He found it sinister not to be introduced and started to wonder if the stranger was the harbinger of his dismissal from the institute for some misdemeanour. To add to his concern the stranger had a grey beard and was smoking a cigar like the ghost of Sigmund Freud. Sir Aubrey broke the silence. "Well, Dr Barnet, what is so important that you need to see me so early in the day? Are you ill? You look white as a ghost."

Mathew pulled himself together and decided the meeting was a failure before it was started, so he thought there was nothing to lose by taking control. "Professor Lewis, if you'll forgive me, I was waiting to be introduced to that distinguished gentleman sitting in the shadows before starting with my agenda that I had hoped might be kept private between the two of us."

Sir Aubrey responded with a chuckle and turned to the stranger. "You see what I mean, Manfred? This young man won't tolerance nonsense and has a mind of his own." He then turned back to Mathew. "I apologise for our little game, I'm glad to say you passed the first test of character invented by my guest. Dr Mathew Barnet, please meet my old friend Professor Manfred Coldstream, professor of neurology at King's College London. I invited him to join us as we have a scheme that might be of interest to you having listened to your heresies at more than one seminar or grand rounds." Mathew felt he had been bowled a googly but then he had nothing to lose because his ideas would involve the chair of neurology at King's as much as the director of the Maudsley and the Institute of Psychiatry.

He then laid his cards on the table without further pause for thought. "I've only been qualified six years, sir, but ever since I was a first-year medical student I've been fascinated by the functions of the brain. I even stole a brain from the anatomy school to dissect at home, with disastrous consequences. I've also spent much of my spare time reading the history of psychiatry, psychotherapy, and neurology and have come to a radical conclusion that to my mind is self-evident. Yes, as you say, Sir Aubrey, I am a heretic, but here we are talking about clinical science, not some religious dogma like the Holy Communion. My 'heresy' is the false dichotomy between psychiatry and neurology. I cannot accept that mental health is in some way metaphysical, as Sigmund Freud would have us believe; for example, Korsakov's syndrome shares a common causality as tabes dorsalis infection with *Treponema pallidum*. One bug can explain insanity and loss of all sensation in the legs. With the greatest respect, I believe that psychiatrists should be taught neurophysiology and vice versa. This will encourage a revolution in research where in the end most psychiatric illnesses will be explained by organic damage, genetical, anatomical, cerebra-vascular, biochemical, or microbiological." Mathew ended his rant and Sir Aubrey ordered another jug of coffee.

In the silence that followed, the two professors went into a private conclave until Professor Coldstream broke the silence with two words that almost knocked Mathew off his perch. "We agree." He then continued with a tone of voice that suggested mutual respect between equals. "Dr Barnet – Mathew, if I may? You have pre-empted this meeting as Aubrey predicted. We will make a start in the new academic year this September. You will be appointed senior registrar in my department and exchange with the current incumbent, Dr Rajan Banerjee, who will replace you at the Maudsley. You two will be described as liaison officers between the two hospitals. You, Mathew, will be on call for patients with psychiatric symptoms in our surgical and medical wards, whilst Rajan will provide a neurological service on the east side of Denmark Hill. In addition, you will have access to my laboratory at King's College London on the Strand and an honorary appointment at the National Hospital for Neurology and Neurosurgery, Queen Square. Welcome aboard!"

Mathew could hardly wait to get home to pass on this good news to his wife. She in return passed on the good news that Peter Baring had passed his FRCS and accepted an appointment as a research fellow in the Department of Surgery at King's College Hospital. Peter and Fiona had also settled on the idea of buying a house in Dulwich Village.

Chapter 31

Mathew takes up Occam's razor

entia non sunt multiplicanda praeter necessitatem

Unlike all other medical specialities, in the 1960s there were no tests to confirm a diagnosis of mental disorders. Simple examples might include blood glucose levels in the diagnosis of diabetes or haemoglobin levels for iron deficiency anaemia. More complex examples might be the patient with iron deficiency anaemia and a change in bowel habit, or the patient with yellow skin, white stools, dark urine, and colicky pains in the right upper quadrant of the abdomen. The first example might show a cancer of the colon on a barium enema that was leaking blood in the stools, whilst the second example would disclose a raised level of bilirubin in the blood and X-rays, suggesting gall stones blocking the bile duct en route to the duodenum, whilst the pale stools illustrate the absence of bile in the faeces and increased levels of bile circulating in the blood accounts for the dark orange urine. Taking this last case as a good example, you have four symptoms but one unifying diagnosis. This illustrates the history and philosophy of the diagnostic method based on the teaching of a 14th-century monk, William of Occam. The principle of "Occam's razor" translates from the Latin: "Entities should not be multiplied beyond what is required". In other words, a patient with four groups of symptoms is likely to have a single causality. Thus, one could look upon the diagnosis of psychiatric illness as locked in the medieval era of medical history.

Instead of tests, psychiatrists relied on the handbook as

the gold standard of psychiatric diagnosis, the *Diagnostic and Statistical Manual of Mental Disorders of the American Psychiatric Disorders of the American Psychiatric Association* (DSM). The first manual was published in 1952 and the second edition in 1968. The latest edition, which appeared just in time for Mathew's new role as a "psycho-neurologist", described 182 diagnoses. To make matters worse, many British psychiatrists, particularly of the psychotherapy cult, denied the existence of clusters of cases adding up to a common diagnosis, and treated each case as a unique individual with his/her problems dependent on their childhood and dreams. This then implied that you couldn't learn from experience; everything that was needed to be known had already been described in Sigmund Freud's writings and therefore all psychoanalysts were disciples rather that students. Clearly it was time for Mathew to take out his Occam's razor and cut back the 182 symptomatic diagnoses from the DSM to a few meaningful neurological disorders with the potential for rational therapies. This decision was taken on 5 June 1967, but the wind was taken out of his sails on learning later that day that Israel had gone to war with all its neighbouring enemies. He rushed home to inform Minxy that he was needed in Israel and wanted to volunteer for the Israel Defence Forces (IDF). Her response was surprising. "I had the same idea, Mathew. At this time in the history of the Middle East, Mathew, there is an urgent need for art historians and psychiatrists. The war will be over in a week, and I've arranged a babysitter for a few days, but we must be back in time for the bar mitzvah of the Ginsbergs' boy." It took Mathew a moment or two before he picked up on his wife's deadpan irony, after which he slumped down in an armchair, holding his head in his hands.

As things turned out, Minxy's ironic prophecy of a one-week war turned out true but there was a need for a psychiatrist two years later when Mathew was invited to speak at a conference in Jerusalem on post-traumatic stress disorder (PTSD).

Three months after the Six Day War, Mathew started his new job at King's College Hospital. Once again early September coincided with the Jewish high holy days, but this time Mathew couldn't risk taking time off but salved his conscience by denying himself food and drink on Yom Kippur. After all, he was about to embark on the search for the neurological footprint of the "soul" with no Testament to guide him on his way. The structure and function of neurological anatomy had been mapped out beautifully in the 500 years between the codices of Leonardo da Vinci and the 27th edition of *Gray's Anatomy* he had inherited from his brother. But, apart from the cranial nerves that controlled touch, sight, hearing, and smell and the peripheral nerves that controlled muscular movements, little was understood. A catastrophic haemorrhage or blood clot in the left lobe of the brain could result in paralysis of one side of the body and if this extended anteriorly to "Broca's area" would result in loss of speech. A fractured spine that transected the spinal cord above the level of the first lumbar vertebra would result in paralysis of the legs and control of the bladder. In contrast to neuropathology, there were no clues for anatomy or function of the brain to explain psychopathology, for example why some patients think they are Napoleon, others are convinced that they are being spied upon by MI5, and all too often, other healthy adults take their own lives for no rational purpose. Mathew's self-set task was not so much to search for the "soul" but for the regions and functions of the brain that we might call "self" or personhood.

The attempts of imaging the living brain were primitive. There was the electroencephalogram (EEG), which involved using silver foil electrodes attached to the head by a rubber bandage. The electrical impulses that are being communicated in the brain got recorded in wave patterns on a role of paper. The different waves that were present in the typical functioning brain and those who may have had conditions such as epilepsy might be diagnostic. Despite this, a main limitation of EEGs is that they had poor spatial resolution, meaning they couldn't pinpoint exactly where in the brain the electrical dysfunctional activity was taking place. The only other neuroimaging method was cerebral angiography, which used X-rays to produce an image after the injection of a radio-opaque medium via a cerebral artery. The image was used to identify blockages or any other abnormalities in the blood vessels of the head and, in theory, being able to view blood vessels in the brain by X-rays would allow for more precise localisations of cerebral cancers. It was far too dangerous to be used as an experimental tool on a living human being.

In the end he decided to "map the brain" like ancient mariners, coastline by coastline, using brains from post-mortems of patients dying from any cause, who had demonstrated specific psychopathology in their lifetime. In these cases, normality as well as abnormality were of equal importance. At the suggestion of his wife, he wrote to her old friend, Oliver Sacks, now working in New York, who shared his views. The response came rapidly via airmail and was very enthusiastic and included some helpful suggestions to add to their joint research protocol. First, as a control group, they should examine as many brains as possible from those who died without any suggestion of mental illness. This was to detect what they called "incidentaloma". These might include random embryological variants, asymptomatic vascular aneurysms, or atherosclerosis of the major or minor cerebral arteries. Furthermore, biopsies from the major lobes of the cerebrum and cerebellum would allow them to build up a catalogue of microscopic variables. They then wrote a formal protocol to make it easy to collect and retrieve their data and to set up a triage to make sense of their observations, which included diffuse anatomical pathology, focal anatomical pathology, and no obvious anatomical pathology. Obvious examples in the first category would be dementia or Alzheimer's disease. Schizophrenia was difficult to pigeonhole and was also of interest because it ran in families, and one would assume that there was a genetic component in its aetiology. That for now would be in the third category. Anxiety and depressive illness would also be in the third group as they were most likely involving biochemical triggers from the endocrine system, for example the fight-or-flight response of the adrenal glands. The group with focal anatomical pathology would be those related to acute cerebrovascular events and tumours. Right from the beginning they realised that was too simple and left gaps for behavioural features, sexual orientation, aggression, alcoholism, and eating disorders. They then settled the problem simply by adding a fourth file, labelled "miscellaneous".

When the research protocol was complete, Mathew showed it to Sir Aubrey Lewis and Professor Coldstream. The two departmental heads were very enthusiastic and had just two suggestions to make. First, it would be appropriate to include Dr Rajan Banerjee as a research fellow who could act as the go-between between the Maudsley and King's College Hospital. As Mathew and Rajan were already good friends, this was no problem and the two chiefs reassured them that, as there would be more than enough material for two PhDs, they would not be competing. The other suggestion was to include a paragraph on informed consent from the patient or their next of kin, to allow post-mortem studies of the brain at the point of recruiting a patient to the study. This turned out to be a knotty problem both in legal and ethical grounds. The law was quite clear and was summarised in this paragraph.

There is no property in a corpse and as a consequence any direction in a will as to the disposal of the corpse is not binding. A corpse is incapable of being the subject of property transactions or offences; for example, it cannot be bought or sold, stolen or criminally damaged, or seized by the deceased's creditors as security for his debts.

Effectively they were free to do whatever they liked with the corpse's brain without the patient allowing it in a living will. Furthermore, the next of kin did not own the corpse and could not act as an agent with the power of attorney. The ethical dilemma was how to approach with these morbid questions a patient who was already disturbed and, if the patient was suffering from dementia, any permission would be null and void. In that case, the next of kin might be consulted, but they might have a conflict of interest and a religious objection. For example, the Orthodox Jewish teaching was that the body must be buried intact and objected to autopsy. In the end they decided to rely on the goodwill of the patient or next of kin, who would be recruited after they had read a layperson's synopsis of the study that described how they would be contributing to future patients who might be cured or prevented from the mental illness that was ruining or shortening their lives. This "informed consent" document would then have to be approved by an independent body of ethicists to make sure the content was not alarmist and there was no hint of coercion.

As it turned out, most patients or their next of kin were happy to be recruited into the study and looked upon it as an act of benevolence. Even the Jewish community, apart from the ultra-Orthodox, were supportive as they interpreted the research as an activity that might prolong the lives of future generations.

★ ★ ★

Within six months of starting the project they agreed that building a model of the functions of the brain was more like a three-dimensional jigsaw of the globe than mapping the shores of a newly discovered island. The third dimension were the neurotransmitters, dopamine, and serotonin, which sent messages from one zone of the brain to another. Furthermore, they soon realised that they were not alone in the search for the links of neuropathology to psychological disease. They appeared to be part of the phenomenon of *multiple discovery*.

Multiple discovery, also known as simultaneous invention, is the hypothesis that most scientific discoveries and inventions are made independently and simultaneously by multiple scientists. In other words, it had become the *zeitgeist* of a new era that reflected the dissatisfaction and scepticism of the previous era, dominated by the teachings of Freud and psychoanalysis.

Within the next three years the psychopathology of three types of dementia were defined. Alzheimer's disease, microvascular dementia in the elderly, and Korsakoff's syndrome were linked to alcoholism and tertiary syphilis. Biopsies of the brain at autopsy following the death of a patient with Alzheimer's disease showed plaques of amorphous material intertwined within the networks of neurones, whereas in older patients the aetiology was more obvious as the grey matter was punctuated with microscopic infarcts, suggesting multiple embolisms of blood clots in the cranial arterioles. Korsakoff's syndrome remained a mystery, because the slow loss of cognitive functions was accompanied by amnesia, confabulation, and loss of personhood. The centre of the brain that carried the sense of self-identity, or "soul", was like a search for the Holy Grail.

Chapter 32

Peter's story continued
Shifting the paradigms
1966–1970

With the support of his mentor, Mr Alex McKenzie, Peter Baring was granted a Cancer Research Campaign (CRC) research fellowship in the academic department of Professor Angus Stewart, at King's College London. McKenzie and Stewart were both part of the "Scottish Mafia" who had invaded the England in the 1950s, taking up senior academic or full-time consultant appointments as a consequence of the establishment of the NHS in 1948.

Peter was glad to get away from the malign influence of Morgan Duffield and Fiona was thrilled to be moving to the big city, although Dulwich felt more like a village than a tentacle of the behemoth that was swallowing up the south-east of England's green and pleasant land. Whilst Mathew was like most of the knights of the Round Table, failing in his quest for the Holy Grail, Peter entered the gates of King's College like a different class of knight errant, determined to track down and slay two dragons. In memory of his mother-in-law, he was determined to continue the work of Sir Geoffrey Keynes to annihilate the dogma of the radical mastectomy and secondly to rid the land of the bogus beliefs of the homeopathic brotherhood. What Peter never anticipated were the many "green knights" with conflicts of interests, who would put obstacles in his way.

His loyal wife, Fifi, was proud of her gallant husband but was delighted to learn that his 12-month scholarship did not involve any clinical responsibilities so he could spend the hours 9.00am to 5.00pm in the laboratories and library of the college on weekdays and spend all weekends at home.

To slay the second dragon, designated by the name *homeopathy*, was easy and could be achieved in his spare time but in doing so he would make enemies in the highest echelon of society.

To slay the first dragon, designated by the name *mastectomy*, would involve serious scientific research that involved the two steps, hypothesis generation and experimentation. He had just struggled through Karl Popper's *Conjectures and Refutations* on the advice of a close friend who worked in the Department of the History and Philosophy of Science at the London School of Economics (LSE) and discovered that he was probably the only one in the Department of Surgery who truly understood the meaning of science as a philosophy. He therefore planned to write a preface for his doctoral thesis explaining the scientific structure of his dissertation. He would start with the history of treatments for breast cancer and the hypothetical models of the disease that warranted the treatment leading up to the current era and the justification of the radical mastectomy. He would then describe the outlying clinical observations that challenged the contemporary paradigm. This would be followed by a section of the generation of a revolutionary conceptual model that had greater explanatory power. The final section would be both animal and human experimentation that would either support or refute his hypothesis. The animal experiments were easy and involved slaying hundreds of mice rather than just two dragons. The human experiments comparing two treatment regimens ran up against the barrier of *moral philosophy*, the "green knight" that would block the route of our knight errant, who was then linked in mortal battle that would last many years. The outcome of that joust will be described in the next chapter but for now Peter's preface might be of interest to the lay reader.

* * *

The expression "Natural History" has two meanings. Historically it has come to mean the systematic study of all natural objects, hence the famous collection of dinosaur skeletons, trilobite fossils and Darwin's specimens from the Galapagos Islands in the Natural History Museum, South Kensington, London.

Another meaning to this expression used as a medical term, is the behaviour of a disease in the absence of treatment or in other words left to nature.

In the modern world we accept the concept of the self-limiting nature of many mild ailments and can reassure our patients that their bad cold will get better within a week. With more serious conditions that are life threatening or could lead to chronic dysfunction we treat in order to favourably influence this natural history and rely on the history books to tell us what would have happened in the absence of treatment but with careful observation alone. Unfortunately, in the days before active treatment of serious disease, careful and systematic observation, were exceptional and this applies to carcinoma of the breast. Another relevant issue here is that we don't always see in a dispassionate way the objective reality of that which we observe but more likely a distortion, refracted through the prism of our personal prejudices. Observations that reinforce our prejudices are embraced and those that challenge our beliefs are ignored or rationalized away.

Surprisingly, the first evidence for the study of untreated breast cancer came about during a weekend away in Paris with our friends Dr and Mrs Barnet. Mrs Barnet has a MA in the history of art and wanted my medical opinion about a popular painting in the Louvre.

The Louvre houses a large and beguiling masterpiece by Rembrandt, "Bathsheba at her toilet". Completed in 1655, the painting shows a naked Bathsheba looking wistfully into the middle distance left, whilst holding a letter in her right hand. Her attendant bathes her feet in a pool and the background is dark and ambiguous. Perhaps she has just learnt of her husband's death in battle because of King's David's treachery, leaving her free to join the long list of the royal concubines. Mrs Barnet drew my attention to the dimple in the upper outer quadrant of Bathsheba's left breast. I had to agree with her, the model for this painting has the classical stigma of breast cancer. I encouraged her to research the history of the painting and its model. Her work on this ultimately appeared in print. In short, the model was Hendrekje Stoffels who doubled up as mistress and housekeeper for Rembrandt. She was in her thirties when the picture was completed and died eight years later. Her mode of dying was characteristic of breast cancer with secondaries to the liver. There is no record of her being treated, but in any case, treatment in those days was a futile hocus pocus based on the doctrines of Aristotle and Galen, yet she lived eight years after the clinically obvious disease, unknowingly portrayed in the painting, became apparent.

More recently a woman booked into my professor's clinic at Kings College Hospital, as an "old patient" yet his secretary had no record of her. It transpired that Professor Stewart had seen her on only one occasion and that was eight years previously. She was 49 at the time but was now 57. He had diagnosed multi-focal carcinoma of the left breast at biopsy and recommended a mastectomy. She firmly but politely declined his advice and as she put it, placed herself in the hands of Jesus and the prayers of her evangelical community. Not believing in the power of prayer to heal. He confessed to surprise at seeing her alive and called me over to witness the consultation. The only complaint to which she confessed was swelling of the left arm. He asked her to disrobe in the examination room bracing himself for the worst. Both breasts were now replaced by hard nodules of cancer and both axillae (arm pits) were full of the disease causing massive lymphoedema (swelling due to the accumulation of tissue fluid) of the arms, yet there was no evidence of distant metastases. Not wishing to push his luck too far by asking for another biopsy, he suggested that

Jesus now needed a little help from modern medicine as prayer alone would no longer hold the cancer in check. He suggested to attend the radiotherapy department to shrink the tumours and perhaps help the swelling of her arm. She politely accepted his advice and promised to return in one month to check on progress. Needless to say, she failed to keep that appointment in the radiotherapy unit. In Rembrandt's day that might not have been such a bad idea, but in the modern world, I would judge it irresponsible behaviour. One must not laugh at such profound faith, but I know that much of the suffering she can expect before she dies, could have been avoided. Two anecdotes don't make a thesis so just how typical were these examples?

Whilst searching for a publication in the library at the medical school on the history of medicine a more important one literally fell in my lap, (a process us scholars describe as library gremlins at play). This happened to be a treatise on breast cancer by one Dr Gross of Philadelphia published in 1880. Gross' treatise provides a clear insight into the status of the disease in the era immediately before the period when the developments in anaesthesia and antisepsis allowed surgeons to attempt a radical cure of breast cancer. He describes a series of 616 cases, most of whom had skin infiltration on presentation which had ulcerated through in 25% of the patients. About two thirds had extensive involvement of axillary nodes (glands in the armpit). Accepting that the meagre benefits of surgery seldom outweighed the risks in those days, he judged it ethical to follow the natural course of 97 cases that received nothing other than "constitutional support".

He describes how skin ulcers appeared an average 20 months after a tumour is first detected, with growth into the chest wall itself after a further two months and direct invasion of the other breast if the patient lived on average three years after the lump first appeared. A quarter of all these untreated cases went on to develop obvious secondaries in vital organs within a year and another quarter after three years. In the end only one in twenty survived more than 5 years.

I then went on to find the original reference of my search published in the Lancet by Dr Julian Bloom earlier this year. His data came from the records of 250 women dying of breast cancer in the Middlesex Hospital Cancer ward between 1905 and 1933. It should be noted that almost all of them presented with neglected disease many already with secondaries in vital organs. The survival rates from the "alleged onset" of symptoms were 5% at 5 years with only two alive at 15 years. The reasons for withholding treatment are also worthy of note: most of them were too old or infirm to withstand treatment and 20% refused treatment.

Although of historical interest I can't really believe that these studies help to provide a baseline against which to judge the curative effect of modern treatment.

From the popularization of the classical radical mastectomy at the very end of the 19thC to this day almost all patients with breast cancer, of a technically operable stage were treated with modifications of the radical mastectomy. Before considering this matter it's worth revisiting the conceptual model that allowed the radical operation to reign supreme for 75 years.

In about 1840, Dr Rudolph Virchow of Berlin, the founding father of the discipline of pathology, described a revolutionary model of the disease building on the development of microscopy and post-mortem examinations of the cadavers of breast cancer victims. He suggested that the disease started as a single focus within the breast, expanding with time and then migrating along lymphatic channels to the lymph glands in the axilla. These glands were said to act as a first line of defence filtering out the cancer cells. Once these filters became saturated the glands themselves acted as a nidus for tertiary spread to a second and then third line of defence like the curtain walls around a medieval citadel. Ultimately when all defences were exhausted the disease spread along tissue planes to the skeleton and vital organs.

The therapeutic consequences of this belief had to await the development of anaesthesia and antisepsis in the 1880s but were seized upon by Halsted in about 1895. William S Halsted of the Johns Hopkins Hospital, Baltimore was a very interesting man and a great surgical pioneer. He was a dapper gentleman who sent his shirts to London for laundering! In later life he became an opium addict but is best remembered for his pioneering work in postgraduate surgical education. He incidentally invented the surgeon's rubber glove although this was not in the name of antisepsis but in the name of love. He fell in love with his beautiful scrub nurse who then developed allergic dermatitis on her hands in response to the carbolic acid used for antisepsis at the time. The rubber gloves where to protect her hands whilst she continued to assist him.

Armed with the teachings of Virchow, the developments in anaesthesia and antisepsis and prodigious surgical skills, it seemed inevitable that his patients would be cured by radical operations that cut away all the breast, the overlying skin, the underlying muscles and as many lymph node groups compatible with the patient's survival.

So convincing were his arguments and so charismatic their chief proponent, the Halsted operation was adopted as default therapy all round the world.

At this long perspective we are entitled to ask to what extent did the radical operation add to the curability of the disease and what can we learn about the nature of the beast by its behaviour following such mutilating surgery?

William Halsted operated at a time when the triumph of mechanistic principles was at its peak when the common man had begun enjoying the fruits of the Industrial Revolution. Naturally, Halsted's 'complete operation' was based on mechanistic concepts about the nature of cancer.

His surgical expertise was remarkable, and for the first time, breast cancer seemed curable with recurrence rates of only 10% at 3 years, very low compared to the other series at that time. Unfortunately, only about a quarter of patients, treated by Halsted survived 10 years. The natural reaction to this failure was not to question the belief system, but to attempt even more radical treatment. Internal mammary lymph nodes under the sternum (breastbone) receive about 25% of the lymphatic drainage from the breast were not removed in Halsted's 'complete operation' but

*were included in the super radical operations that were fashionable
in the 1940-1960 era. Thus, even when the tumour seemed to
have been completely 'removed with its roots', the patients still
developed distant metastases and succumbed: about half of all
patients eventually dying of the disease over 10 years and with no
evidence of "cure".*

*Putting this all together it could be argued that the outcome of
treatment by surgery alone was pre-determined by the biology of
tumour versus any natural resistance. Indirect evidence of success
or failure of this battle could be deduced by the status of the glands
at surgery. Negative (uninvolved) nodes might suggest an intact
natural defence whilst positive (involved) nodes, representing
an exhausted system that has allowed the cancer cells to maraud
unchecked around the body. The therapeutic consequences of this
conceptual transformation could be summed up as follows. (A)
The extent of radical surgery might control the disease on the chest
wall but have no effect survival, the horse (cancer) having bolted
before the stable door (radical surgery) was slammed shut. (B)
If the outcome of treatment was pre-determined by the extent of
microscopic (occult) secondaries present at the time of diagnosis,
then the only chance of cure would be a systemic therapy targeting
these putative sites of disease, for patients with even localized
tumours.*

★ ★ ★

Having refuted the contemporary conceptual model of breast
cancer and its therapeutic consequence of radical mastectomy,
it was clear what the therapeutic consequences of his revised
conjecture were. He had made the case to continue the work
of Sir Geoffrey Keynes by developing a revised technique of
breast conserving surgery. Keynes used radium needles that
were no longer used in clinical practice, so he had to seek
the support of someone from the Radiotherapy Department
to help with his ambitious programme. The combination of
minimal surgery for the lump and external beam for the breast

and armpit would in theory prevent local recurrence but, as far as systemic therapy was concerned, he would have to wait to see whether chemotherapy being developed for lymphoma might one day be available for treating breast cancer in a way that might pre-empt the growth of metastases.

Chapter 33

Trials and tribulations

Dr Judith Archer, director of the Department of Radiotherapy, was a charming and attractive woman in her mid-40s. Her husband sat in the House of Lords, but she never used her title. She was very popular, and, behind her back, her friends and colleagues called her Lady Judy. She warmly greeted the tall, handsome young surgeon who knocked on her door on a Monday morning for a prearranged coffee break. Peter Baring found himself blushing at the warmness of her welcome. He rapidly found out that Lady Judy shared and indeed pre-empted his ambitions to develop a breast preserving technique for early breast cancer, defined as Stage I. The stage of the breast cancer was an arbitrary run of Roman numerals that reflected prognosis. Stage I was a tumour of 2.00cm or less, with no evidence of spread to the armpit. Stage II was a tumour 2.00–5.00cm, Stage III involved swollen lymph glands in the armpit, whilst Stage IV presented with distant metastases. Peter learnt that "lumpectomy" followed by radiotherapy to the breast and axilla was quite common in Paris and was being tested in Milan and Pittsburgh, Pennsylvania. That made her life easier as other radiotherapists and radiophysicists had developed a regimen that controlled the disease without burning the skin. This involved 22 visits of the patients to the department for external beams of their new cobalt-60 device, with 2.2 rads a visit. If you included a prior visit for planning, that involved the patient visiting the hospital every day, apart from Sunday, over a month. Clearly this would only be an option for patients with easy access to the hospital by public transport or private car. On learning that, Peter realised how naive he was thinking treatment would be one blast of X-rays but didn't reveal the depths of his ignorance. Somewhat chastened but still enthusiastic, he agreed to try to get permission from his boss, Professor Angus Stewart. Professor Stewart shared his enthusiasm but drew his attention to the newly established ethics committee governing clinical research at King's. It's worth noting that this was 20 years since the Nuremberg Code of 1947 following the trials of the Nazi doctors and their human experimentation. Fortunately, the ethics committee approved of the study, assuming the patient signed her permission. However, their permission allowed a trial of 20 cases with a three-year follow-up before accepting the treatment for all comers. Having set up the study, all went smoothly but he would have to wait until 1970 to complete his doctoral thesis. These years were not to be wasted as he was recruited to the surgical registrar rotation to complete his training once his fellowship ended.

★ ★ ★

He started his advanced surgical training in the academic department led by the professor and senior lecturer (consultant) Mr Colin Howe, a graduate of Guy's, who somewhat patronised young Mr Baring yet at the same time was a brilliant teacher of surgical techniques. As far as his wife, Fifi, was concerned, his *salad days* were over, and he was back covering surgical emergencies two nights a week and one weekend in three.

Although Peter wanted to end up as a "general surgeon", the rotation year on year would allow him to experience some of the other specialities, which included cardiothoracic surgery and urology. It seems to be an oxymoron to describe general surgery as a speciality when it embraces the treatment of skin cancers, the thyroid gland, the breast, the oesophagus, the upper gastro-intestinal organs including the liver and biliary system, the large bowel, and the anal canal, which would include piles and abscesses, hernias, and varicose veins. In the USA, they call this basket of procedures "hand surgery", meaning "anything I can get my hands on". But in the UK, with a 500-year history since the days that King Henry VIII gave the royal charter to the Company of Barber-Surgeons, this is how things evolved. In addition, the "general surgeons" were always on call for the wheat and chaff that was blown into the hospital Accident and Emergency (A&E) department. The academic department of surgery backed on to Coldharbour Lane, known affectionately as the "front line". It took you straight into the heart of Brixton and that was not a good place to be in the twilight of any day of the week but especially Friday night. The cultural and historic reason for this is of great interest.

In 1948 an old cruise ship, the *Windrush*, anchored at the London docks and over 1,000 men from the Caribbean disembarked. They arrived at the expense of the Labour government, invited to fill the jobs that would rebuild the nation after the Second World War.

These jobs included the production of steel, coal, iron, and food, as well as roles in running public transport and staffing the NHS. They arrived with great optimism, most of them unemployed at home, believing that the streets of London were paved with gold. They were disappointed to find the streets of London full of debris and burnt-out houses following the Blitz. Their disappointment turned to dismay when they faced, head on, the rampant racism amongst the working class of the poorest parts of the city. "Taking our jobs and raping our women" was the inhospitable theme of the meme they had to tolerate.

"No dogs or blacks" said the cards in the windows of guest houses. At least they had paid employment at the bottom of the scale of jobs the white men wouldn't want anyway, and somehow earnt just enough to live on and bring over their families. Naturally they lived in the poorest boroughs of the metropolis, where rents were the lowest and Brixton became one of the epicentres of the West Indians. In the long term, the contribution of these migrants saved the NHS, which had its gestation near the time that the *Windrush* docked.

The next generation of young men found themselves unvalued and unemployed, took to the streets, organised themselves in gangs, dealt in drugs, and rioted in the hot summers of the 1960s. Most of the wounded that found their way to the A&E at King's were the result of black-on-black assaults on young adults. Two examples of the carnage fell into the hands of Mr Peter Baring FRCS, which he would never forget. One was a gunshot wound and the other was a stab wound.

The first was a six-foot muscular young man who obviously lifted weights in his spare time.

The entry wound was obvious, and a quick X-ray showed the bullet deep in the musculature on the right side of the spine adjacent to the 12th thoracic vertebra. Once the patient was asleep, he was intubated and turned onto his left side. Peter put a probe deep into the track of the bullet and then started cutting through the hypertrophied muscles with an incision running parallel to the spine. First, he cut through the latissimus dorsi, but that wasn't deep enough.

He then cut through the serratus posterior and still the bullet was not found. At this point Peter lost his way and asked for the mobile X-ray machine. That was wheeled in, and the X-ray showed there was a bullet somewhere, but Peter thought he done enough damage already. Furthermore, he remembered that bullets are sterile, and it was only the clothing sucked in by the foreign body that was infectious. As the track had been surgically cleaned on the way in, and he knew that many survivors from the war walked around with bullets and shrapnel embedded in their muscles, he repaired the wound, started him on antibiotics, and arranged for him to be re-X-rayed the next day. The patient recovered rapidly and had to be handcuffed to the bed by the police, as a witness to a murder. The new X-ray again showed the bullet, but it seemed to have migrated to the level of the third lumbar vertebra. The following morning the bullet was defecated, embedded in his stools! He had, by a fluke, avoided peritonitis as the residual kinetic energy of the missile, after passing through the muscles and entering the retroperitoneal surface of the ascending colon, had been absorbed by a mighty stool.

The other case was so dramatic as to impact on his future career.

Another young gangster had been stabbed through the gap between the 10th and 11th ribs on the right side of the chest. He was gushing out blood and rushed to the theatre. Peter and the theatre staff bypassed the ritual of hand wash, cap, and gowning, pulled on their latex gloves and the moment the anaesthetist injected his intravenous hypnotic induction agent had taken its effect Peter rolled the patient onto his side and made a long incision along the skin and muscles of the intercostal space. He assumed that the bleeding was from the dome of the liver but on cutting deeper he was alarmed to find that the bleeding was coming from above the diaphragm. He had no experience of intra-thorax surgery, so he screamed at a nurse to find a thoracic surgeon.

He ploughed on, with the pages of his textbooks studied for his FRCS flicking through his memory. Once he had cut through the pleura, the lower lobe of the right lung bulged out.

By this time, he was joined by a medical student who was given a large flat retractor to pull back the lung. The charge nurse of the theatre passed a fearsome-looking device to the scrub nurse. She unwrapped it and passed it to Peter, who rapidly deduced it was a ratcheted rib spreader. He opened the cavity until all was revealed. The bleeding was coming from the right ventricle of the heart. Keeping his cool, he asked the scrub nurse to mount a large, curved needle carrying strong catgut suture and hand him the longest pair of forceps on the tray. Gripping the needle in the forceps with his arms in the chest wall almost up to his elbows, he was able to suture the 1.0cm hole in the heart muscle with one blanket stitch.

The bleeding stopped, and the blood from the transfusion lab arrived at the same time.

Time stood still. The anaesthetist concentrated on what anaesthetists do and the pool of blood in the thoracic cavity was sucked out. The suture held and the vital signs returned to normal. At that point the voice of authority broke the silence. "Well done, old boy. Nurse, get me a couple of large rubber drains, whilst I scrub up and show Mr Baring how to close the chest." That of course was Professor Gilbert Manning, OBE, FCRS, MS, MD, head of the Department of Cardio-Vascular Surgery. Peter felt giddy and was embarrassed at the applause from all those present.

Chapter 34

A pig and a poke

Having spent enough time practising general surgery, he was a shoo-in as the new registrar in the Department of Cardiothoracic Surgery. The head of the department, Professor Gilbert Manning, was one of those professors who went by the collective pronoun "an absence". He was too important and too busy to fulfil his putative duties in his own home. He was chairman of this and president of that. No international conference on the subject of cardiothoracic surgery was complete without a keynote lecture from this famous pioneer. In fact, it was a miracle that he happened to be passing through the department to change his carousel of slides on his way from Paris to San Francisco, when the call went out for a qualified expert in cardiothoracic surgery, to come to the help of Mr Baring. In practice, the department was led by his senior lecturer, Mr Patrick Carpenter, FRCSC. Those letters stood for Fellow of the Royal College of Surgery Canada. This left Peter as the only junior medical officer on the team, playing the combined role of registrar, senior registrar, and junior lecturer. Mr Carpenter ("Call me Pat") was mad. Deceptively charming but bonkers. His ambitions to rule the world of open-heart surgery were not helped by the memory of a sieve, the judgement of Neville Chamberlain, and the ego of the emperor Nero.

The year 1967 saw the first successful human heart transplant anywhere in the world. That patient, Louis Washkansky, 53, was terminally ill with heart failure. His surgeon at Groote Schuur Hospital in Cape Town, South

Africa, was Christiaan Barnard. Pat was determined to be the second man to transplant a heart whilst his boss was on a trip to San Francisco, but first he was going to practise on a pig. That left Peter in a predicament. He recognised that he was living through a decisive moment of his life, seeing the outcome of the next few weeks parallel his two selves in future lives. To see those near-misses and almost-weres and what-ifs reminded him of Laurence Olivier acting in the role of *Hamlet*: "Would the pig die or would the pig live?" Or perhaps Brutus plotting the assassination of Julius Caesar: "There is a tide in the affairs of men. Which, taken at the flood, leads on to fortune." On further consideration, he wasn't contemplating suicide or regicide. He wasn't even considering murdering the pig, although it had crossed his mind. No, it was a true sliding pivotal moment; if the pig survived the first attempt, he would become famous, part of the team to carry out the first heart transplant in the UK, but, if the pig died, his life would return to normal, just another surgical consultant in the NHS. With those thoughts you could see the *folie a deux* emerging when mixing with a mad man. He worked five and a half days a week and one in two weekends on call. Thursday afternoon was supposed to be time for study and reflection and a pint or two at the Swan in the evening. Unfortunately, Pat, "one of the masters of the universe", demanded his assistance with the pig. His mortality rate for open-heart surgery in humans was about 50%, giving Peter a 50/50 chance of getting home on his half day.

The pig was a "miniature" from a research farm in the country. It might be small in the piggery world but if it could stand on his rear trotters, it would be as tall as Peter. The pig was heavy and difficult to position and wouldn't help itself, until the third member of the team, a consultant anaesthetist, equally deluded, injected a porcine dose of sedative about twice that needed for a man. As the operation had to be carried out under general anaesthetic, the pig had to be intubated before it could be linked up to the ventilator. The distance from the pig's snout to the trachea is about twice that of a human experimental animal. So, a special laryngoscope had to be built to order. Peter had to hold the jaws of the pig open whilst it struggled and squealed as the sedation wore off as the tracheal tube was shoved past the animal's vocal cords. That shut him up. They then had to find a large vein and artery to hitch up the patient (sorry, experimental animal) to the extracorporeal circulatory system that would keep the pig alive whilst he had his heart removed like a sacrificial virgin on the top of the pyramid at Chichen Itza. Unlike the sacrificial virgin, the sacrificial pig had his heart reunited with its tubes and vessels. That was the tricky part. Assuming that was completed before the total exsanguination of the pig, they then had to kick-start the heart to pulsate and pump the blood by itself. That was achieved by using a defibrillator, which almost never works on humans despite the successes you may have seen on TV, yet surprisingly almost always worked on the pig. Yet this shouldn't be surprising as the pig's heart was in perfect shape before it was removed, whereas in real life the fat man on the floor of the restaurant has most of his coronary arteries furred up. So, in fact, the experimental pig was not a fair model for the first experimental humanoid.

The whole procedure lasted about four hours and, if the pig survived the op, he would be lifted onto a gurney to be wheeled into the intensive care ward, which discreetly kept a space in the corner for the "patient" to be carefully monitored all night. A folding bed was available for the doctor, who monitored the pig, sleeping side by side. That meant that Peter had to measure pulse, blood pressure, respiratory rate, oxygen saturation, and blood loss through the rubber tubes draining the thoracic cavity.

On that evening of the first attempt, Peter drifted off to sleep whilst philosophising about predeterminism, having been up the previous night dealing with surgical emergencies. He woke with a start at 11.30. It was now or never. Was the pig alive or was he dead? At that point, he noticed the line of teats on either side of the abdomen, so he had to reframe the question. Was the sow alive or was she dead? He immediately phoned his wife, Fifi, who was sick with worry for his non-appearance that evening. The conversation went like this. "Darling, do you want to know the good news or the bad news first?"

"The good news first, please."

"I'm coming home and aiming to be a consultant surgeon."

"And the bad news?"

"The pig died."

Chapter 35

Annus mirabilis
1970

After the debacle of the pig, Mr Carpenter returned to Canada and Peter returned to the surgical circuit, spending a year in urology. He liked the well organised undramatic pattern of work. With the use of the cystoscope to view the bladder and the intravenous pyelogram (IVP) to see what was going on in the kidney and ureters, surgical procedures were planned in advanced. Within six months he was skilled in both retropubic and trans-urethral prostatectomy for benign prostatic hypertrophy (BPH) for the elderly gentlemen who had to get up to pee three times a night. Surgery for prostatic cancer was way up above his pay grade. In contrast, removing a kidney (nephrectomy) was a piece of cake compared with surgery for lung cancer. Once that attachment was over it was time to complete his PhD.

By then his 20 cases of "lumpectomy" and radiotherapy had reached a three-year follow-up without any sign of a local recurrence. Professor Stewart, his supervisor, said he should forget about his animal experiments for now, as he had enough material to complete his doctoral thesis. This was well received, and he was very proud to wear a red gown, hood, and the tam, a floppy medieval bonnet, at the degree ceremony in the Albert Hall. His parents and wife, Fiona, were in the audience for the event. By this time Fifi was looking radiant, showing the signs of a seven-month gravid mother to be. Following on from this, Professor Angus Stewart summoned Peter to his office to make him an offer. He had just learnt that his senior lecturer, Mr Colin Howe, had been successful in his application for the chair of surgery at Bristol University, and he would like Peter to apply for that vacancy. A senior lecturer/consultant surgeon at the age of 35 was quite exceptional. However, there was one caveat: he was to abandon his campaign against homeopathy because rumours had come his attention that some very important members of the aristocracy resented his attacks on homeopathy. After all, there was a royal homeopathic physician who was director of the Royal Homeopathic Hospital, in Great Ormond Street, Queen Square, just next door to the National Hospital for Neurology and Neurosurgery. Peter was quick to accept this proviso because, if it was good enough for the queen and the prince of Wales, why should he care, as the humble lower classes had never even heard of this bogus nonsensical alternative to scientific medicine. Furthermore, he rationalised, as there are no active ingredients in these potions, they would be harmless. Two months later he celebrated his promotion at the same time as the christening of his baby daughter, in St Barnabas' Church, Dulwich Village.

This was the last time that the four friends, Dylan, Alastair, Mathew, and Peter, accompanied by their wives and children, gathered, 10 years after graduation.

Epilogue

2023

On 1st March 1984 the National Coal Board announced that it planned to close 20 coal mines, with the loss of 20,000 jobs. The year-long strike that followed changed the political, economic, and social history of Wales forever. Emlyn Williams, president of the NUM in South Wales, delivered this declaration of war with Margaret Thatcher's government.

> *The miners in South Wales are saying, we are not accepting the dereliction of our mining valleys, we are not allowing our children to go immediately from school into the dole queue, it is time we fought!*

The Prime Minister replied,

> *We had to fight the enemy without in the Falklands, but we always have to be aware of the enemy within, which is much more difficult to fight and more dangerous to liberty.*

The miners lost that war and Dylan Baddams committed suicide, irrationally blaming himself for publishing the toxic effects of coal mining, contributing to this outcome. Bronwen and two children were left to live on social security handouts, helped a bit by her occasional vocal engagement as a soloist in a choral oratorio.

★ ★ ★

Alastair Bannerman married his sweetheart, Janet O'Connor, and enjoyed a long and fulfilling career. He was awarded the MBE for services to the NHS in 1985. He had three children, one of whom studied medicine and joined him as a partner when he was 60 in the same year. He continued working full time until he was 70 but enjoyed covering surgeries when his staff was on holiday until he was nearly 80. By this time, he had a granddaughter following in the family tradition studying medicine at Glasgow University. In April 2020, at the hight of the pandemic, he insisted on volunteering to work in the respiratory unit at old Glasgow University Hospital as they were desperate for staff, as doctors and nurses were dropping like flies. His wife, children, and grandchildren begged and bullied him not to be so stupid. So, instead, he volunteered for the old cottage hospital in Campbeltown, which had now grown into a full-size regional hospital with a relatively light burden of Covid-19 infections but already had staff working 12-hour shifts. He argued that, having lived so long in the area and had treated thousands of locals with coughs and colds, he would be immune to any virus floating in the sweet air of the Mull of Kintyre. Three weeks later he developed a cough and a sore throat. He ended up intubated and on a respirator in the ICU and sadly died two weeks after that. His passing drew hundreds to the old church, with pipers leading his coffin to his final resting place overlooking the waters to the Isle of Islay. A memorial service took place in the town hall on Main Street a few months later, with speeches from the mayor and the president of the Royal College of Medicine in Edinburgh. In his will was a bequest for an annual scholarship for poor children to attend the medical school in Glasgow, to take a year off for an intercalated BSc. Janet was heartbroken as their love was like an everlasting fire and she gave up the will to live in the same year.

★ ★ ★

Mathew Barnet had a brilliant career, the right man at the right time in the history of psychiatry and neurology. He ended up with a personal professorship at the Institute of Neurology in Queen Square. He came close to finding to Holy Grail of the "soul" with his work on the nature of personhood. He had to wait a long time, until powerful computers were developed, before he could describe the complex network between the frontal lobe and the amygdala, which controlled personality, behaviour, emotions, the regulation of autonomic and endocrine functions, decision-making, and adaptations of instinctive and motivational behaviours, and activation of the fight-or-flight response. At the age of 65, close to the date of his official retirement, he learnt he was to share the Nobel Prize in Physiology or Medicine, shared with two colleagues, one from Harvard and one from the Karolinska Institute. Following that, he had many invitations from round the world for professorships to continue his work. He decided to take the offer from the Weizmann Institute in Israel because two of his children had already made *aliyah*. With the prize money together with a considerable sum from Minxy's inheritance, he was able to by a charming, terraced villa on the hillside of *Yamin Moishe*, in Jerusalem, overlooking the Kidron valley, where the setting sun illuminates the golden walls of the Old City. In 2015, Jeremy Corbyn was elected leader of the Labour Party, following which anti-Semitism in the UK became normalised. Two years later, Mathew and Minxy decided to follow their two children, who now had children of their own. They sold their house in Dulwich and started the process of taking up citizenship in Israel. At the age of 80 it was noticed that he was starting to become demented when one of his grandsons came to visit whilst wearing his army fatigues and carrying his Uzi combat rifle. He didn't recognise the boy and thought he was to be about arrested.

He died peacefully at the age of 83, just after his second bar mitzvah, sitting up in bed facing in the direction of the Western Wall of the Temple Mount.

★ ★ ★

Peter Baring was appointed to the chair at King's when Angus Stewart retired in 1980. He was to be an exemplar to other professors by working full time for the university and the NHS.

He was the first to recognise the importance of evidence-based medicine (EBM) by raising the funds to establish a clinical trials unit in the UK. He was also the first to recognise the importance of quality of life and symptom control in clinical trials and employed clinical psychologists to develop psychometric instruments to measure these subjective outcomes.

He was considered a feminist almost before the word appeared in the printed media. He encouraged young women to train as surgeons despite the systemic misogyny in the speciality. He even mentored two bright and ambitious female surgeons to be appointed as professors, one in Birmingham and the other in Perth, Australia.

He was one of the first consultant surgeons to specialise in cancer and was a founder member and ultimately president of the British Association of Surgical Oncology (BASO).

Later in his career he specialised in breast cancer, popularising breast conserving surgery and recognising that chemotherapy or hormone therapy, started just after surgery and radiotherapy was completed and delivered for a year or so, could prolong life. In the longer term this was reflected by a 50% reduction of breast cancer mortality in the UK.

When he was close to retirement from his clinical work at the age of 65, he was elected president of the Royal College of Surgery (PRCS) and with that he gained his knighthood.

He served the college well and when Tony Blair was appointed prime minister in 1997, he asked Sir Peter Baring to come up with a plan to improve the outcomes of cancer treatment in the NHS. When his three-year office as PRCS came to an end, Tony Blair invited him to take the Labour whip in the House of Lords. He chose the title Lord Baring of Southwark and bought Fifi a diamond tiara now that she was to be known as Lady Fiona.

In the spring of 2023, they celebrated their platinum wedding of 70 years together and were delighted to receive an invitation to tea from King Charles III.

Over tea and cucumber sandwiches, His Majesty cross-questioned him on the good old days in the NHS in the 1960s. Peter captivated HM with his tail of the pig's heart and the disappearing bullet. The last words from His Majesty as Lord and Lady Baring were leaving his presence were "You should write a book about your experiences as a young surgeon, Lord Baring."

"A great idea, sir, I think I will. *I think I will*," he replied.

End notes and acknowledgements

The idea for this book followed a conversation with my son, Richard, who shares my love of fine malt whisky. We were enjoying quality time together around in a cosy hotel in Campbeltown after a busy day visiting the distilleries. I was recounting some of my anecdotes from the early days working as a surgeon in the NHS. He interrupted me and said, "Dad, you should write a book of those olden days in medicine." To me it was all like yesterday for him it was like nearly 70 years ago! Yes, I turned 86 in May this year (2023). On further consideration, I thought this was a good idea and at least something to occupy my spare time, having long retired from my clinical responsibilities and 12 months since retiring from my last committee. This book was completed just under a year from that conversation.

This is not an autobiography but more like the observations of a living witness. Although much of the story is about surgery in the 1960s, I'm certainly nothing like the hero, Peter Baring, I certainly didn't go to a public school and am five feet, seven inches, not six feet, tall. I'm more like Mathew Barnet, although I never worked in a department of psychology or neurology.

All the characters, apart from Oliver Sacks, Sir Geoffrey Keynes, Sir Aubrey Julian Lewis and Professor Archie Cochrane, are fictional, yet built up like jigsaws from the characteristics of some of the best and the worst colleagues I've encountered.

I learnt quite a bit about general practice doing locums for my oldest brother, Geoffrey, and as an academic was cognisant of epidemiology. I qualified from the University of Birmingham Medical School in 1960, trained as a surgeon at King's College Hospital in London, and worked as senior lecturer in the Welsh National School of Medicine in Cardiff, during which time I did weekly clinics at the Caerphilly District Miners' Hospital. I think I can claim to be one of the first to link gastric carcinoma to coal mining (Craven JL, Baum M, West RR. Variations in gastric cancer incidence in South Wales. *Clin Oncol* 1979; 5:341–51). From there I was appointed professor of surgery at King's College Hospital and Peter Baring's stories about the bullet in the back, the stab wound in the heart, and the porcine heart transplant, are true amongst many of my adventures whilst training as a surgeon.

I had little experience of psychiatry in the 1960s but I thank two old friends, Professor Harry Zeitlin and Dr Howard Herschon, who worked at the Maudsley and Bethlem in those dark days, for describing their experiences. I also acknowledge Oliver Sacks's delightful book *The Man Who Mistook His Wife for a Hat* (Picador, London, 2011) for providing some anecdotes and insights from the 1960s and *DSM, the History of Psychiatry's Bible* by Alan Horwitz (Johns Hopkins University Press, Baltimore, 2021) for making sense of the chaos in the nomenclature of mental illness.

One of the joys of writing a novel is the research into esoteric subjects beyond your experience. Here I give an accolade to Jeremy Paxman and his book *Black Gold. The History of How Coal Made Britain* (William Collins, London, 2021). It was a pleasure to read and provided all the factual knowledge I required to write the chapters about Dylan Baddams and his coal mining family. Finally, I acknowledge Judy, my long-suffering wife, who tolerated all my absences when on call as a young surgeon, as well as my absences as an old professor travelling round the world giving lectures in the far-flung countries of the developed world.